Burning Twigs

Charles Tabb

Cover design by Ebooklaunch.com.

DEDICATION

For Dennis, Laura, Alex, and Cameron. The wonder of love belongs to you, too.

ACKNOWLEDGEMENTS

This book would not exist without the following people, who have helped me in ways both minor and major, but all help is appreciated. To my editor, Kristine, and Sue, Chuck, Trisha, Dee, and Elin, my beta readers, thank you for always coming through with your valuable insight. Your work improves my books in a hundred ways. To Harry, Joe, "Gator" Jack, Paul, and Larry, my friends and fellow authors, thank you for being my friends and keeping me on task by always asking how my latest book is coming, thereby keeping my brain focused on what needs to be done. You always help me do my best.

"Everything has beauty, but not everyone sees it."

--Confucius

"Although the world is full of suffering, it is also full of the overcoming of it."

--Helen Keller

"God, grant me the serenity to accept the things I cannot change, the courage to change the things I can, and the wisdom to know the difference."

--Reinhold Niebuhr
The Serenity Prayer

Other books by Charles Tabb

The Twigs Series

Floating Twigs

Finding Twigs

Gathering Twigs

Saving Twigs

The Detective Pantera Series

Hell is Empty

The Purger

The Whirligig of Time

Like an Untimely Frost

Stand-alone books

Canaries' Song

Stories I Told Myself: from Humor to Horror

1

Amber Hanson heard the dog barking, rousing her from her sleep and making her wonder what was going on. Her first thought was that they didn't have a dog, so why did this one sound so close? Then the quality of the noise helped her realize the dog was outside. Someone must have been walking a dog. No, not that. It had to be after midnight. The barking dog must have escaped its home or yard to wander the night away.

She sat up to go to her bedroom window to shout at the dog to shut up when she realized that another sound was growing louder. A crackling, popping sound invaded her thoughts. The acrid odor of burning wood filled her head as recognition pushed the racket the dog was making into the background and the reality swarmed her.

Something was burning, and from the sounds of it, the fire had begun to rage. With dawning terror, she realized the worst: the thing burning was the small house she rented for herself and her son, Paul, who was only fourteen. Their home had become a deathtrap.

Rushing to the door that led to the hallway, she put her hand on the doorknob but yanked it back as blisters formed on her palm from the searing metal. She needed to get to Paul and get him out before fire made that impossible. She looked toward the window and took her first steps to reach it.

In his room, Paul heard the bark of the dog, too, and was aware the house was burning. He had seen fire safety videos at school and knew he needed to get outside, that rushing into the hallway could mean his death.

As he gripped the window to raise it and his mother was taking her third step to escape the inferno, an explosion rocked the house. Paul vaguely felt himself being propelled through the night air, his pajamas on fire. Still barely conscious, he managed to roll on the ground enough to put the flames out. Pain consumed him. He remembered wondering beneath the fog of the pain if his mother had escaped the house before the explosion.

Then darkness took him.

Moments after Paul passed out from the shock and pain of the explosion and the burns it caused, one of their neighbors, Santiago Martinez, awoke from the thunder of the blast. The darkness to the west of Santiago's house had turned a bright orange as flames stretched toward the sky.

Lifting the receiver of his phone, he dialed 9-1-1. The operator answered. "9-1-1. What's your emergency?"

Santiago, too panicked to remember to speak English, said, "*Hay un incendio en la casa de los Hanson!*"

"What?" the operator said. "I don't speak Spanish! Do you speak English?"

"Sorry!" Santiago answered. "The Hanson house on Driftwood Drive. It's on fire! There was an explosion! It woke me up!"

"Do you know the address?"

"They are my neighbors! I guess it's 417 Driftwood. But they can just come to this area. The flames are shooting up into the air! They'll see it!"

"Hold on," the 9-1-1 operator said. He took steps to notify the fire department, the hospital, and the police.

When he was back with Santiago, he asked, "What is your name, sir?"

"Santiago. Santiago Martinez." Santiago suddenly had the clarity of thought to be thankful he and his family were legal residents of Denton, Florida. The authorities would surely check.

After Santiago answered a few more questions, the 9-1-1 operator ended the call, telling him someone from the police would be around to speak to him.

Santiago's wife, Maria, had awakened by that time. She now stood looking with worry at the flames performing their beautiful, yet frightening, dance into the sky above the Hanson house.

"*Dios mío*," she said, crossing herself.

"*Sí*," Santiago said, and put his arm around her while they each prayed in silence for the mother and her young son who lived in the house that by morning would be nothing but a charred mass of rubble.

Fire trucks roared up to the house and stopped, the men jumping out and hurrying to douse the

3

flames, more to prevent the fire from spreading to the trees in the area than to save the structure, which already seemed beyond hope. The nearest hydrant was not far from the house, and soon the home and nearby property were being drenched in cool water.

As they were completing the first steps to putting the fire out, they discovered the bodies of Amber and Paul Hanson. Two ambulances arrived just as they found them, and medics jumped out of the vehicles within a second of coming to a stop.

The area became awash with the swirl of red lights that spun lazily atop the emergency vehicles. As two patrol cars arrived, their blue lights joined the odd ballet. The lights, along with the flames, highlighted the smoke that hung in the air as each group of first responders did their work to save what they could.

When the first pair of medics arrived at the body of Amber Hanson, they found she had succumbed to the flames and super-heated air that had filled the house. Her body was charred in places, her eyes, intact, stood open to stare at the scene dully. As the swirl of lights danced over her features, the dead eyes haunted what had once been the lawn where her son had played.

"This one's alive!" one of the medics shouted as he and his partner hunched over the burnt body of Paul Hanson. The other medics left the corpse of the boy's mother and ran to help out in whatever way they could.

"Go see if there are any more!" Ed Taylor, the medic who had found Paul, said, and the other medics hurried off.

Finding no other bodies, they returned several minutes later. Ed and his partner, Sandy Roslan, had IVs inserted into the child's arm and had begun a drip of saline. While Ed injected needed medicines into the drip, Sandy turned her attention to cutting away Paul's clothing, which stuck in places to the charred skin. She felt bad that this boy would have to go through the excruciating process of healing from the second and third degree burns that covered most of his body.

The flames began to recede from the sky, and soon the fire was out. Investigators would take over the scene the following morning, piecing together the clues as to its source and the manner in which the fire moved throughout the home. An explosion had been reported, meaning it was likely a gas line had severed. They would find that, too.

As dawn broke, the men of the Denton Fire Department began to pack up their equipment. A pall hung over them, and nobody spoke while they went about their duties. The coroner had arrived and taken away the body of Amber Hanson, and Paul Hanson had been taken to Wharton Medical Center in the larger, nearby town of Wharton.

The sun rose into the sky as it always did, an emblem of nature's detachment from the woes of the universe.

2

When he finally drifted into consciousness, Paul was aware of only one thing: he was in severe pain. He'd never experienced pain like this before, not even when he broke his leg when he fell off the roof of their house in Opelika, Alabama, where they'd lived before his mother divorced his father months ago. He'd not seen or heard from his father since the move to Denton.

Glancing around and fighting back the pain-induced tears, he saw he was in a hospital room. For a moment, he wondered what had happened to land him here. Where was his mother?

He wondered how long he'd been there. Hours? Days? More?

As his mind sought the answers, he slowly remembered. A fire. The smell of burning wood. The sound. The terror and fear. He seemed to recall flying through the air, and then nothing. With dawning horror, he realized what was causing the pain. He'd been burned, and probably badly since this didn't feel like any sunburn he'd ever had.

As he lay remembering the events, a near panic seized him. Was his mother alive? As he became more aware of his surroundings, he realized his face was covered in bandages. Only one eye, his nostrils, and his mouth were open to the air. A tube ran to his nose, and he knew it was probably for oxygen.

He did his best to see more of the room, but he

was unable to move his head more than an inch or two. If this was a hospital, wouldn't there be a call button somewhere?

He tried to call out, but all he could manage was a whispering squawk that did not sound like him at all. His voice sounded airy and weak.

As he struggled to keep himself from plunging into panic, the sudden memory of why he had gone flying through the air slammed him. Suddenly, his memory of the events were sharp and detailed, as if he were watching a slow-motion movie of his perspective of the world at that moment.

The explosion. He'd been trying to open his window and had managed to raise it halfway when he felt himself being propelled like a large bullet through the window that seemed to shatter even before his body could reach it. He had thought to roll on the ground and put out the flames that had already done their damage. It had been almost like instinct, and he supposed it had been. The instinct of survival.

Now, he wondered if he shouldn't have just let the flames take him. The pain now was excruciating and relentless, as if the flames were still there, consuming him.

Oddly, some areas of his body did not feel the pain, and he thought those areas might have escaped the harm done. Some of those painless areas were on his face.

So why was his face covered in bandages?

Minutes passed as he lay there, staving off the terror that wanted to consume him like new flames.

Finally, the door to his room opened. Paul could

not see who it was until the person stood beside the bed. It was a nurse. She went about the business of changing the plastic bag that dangled from a hook on the small wheeled cart used for such things. Later, he would find out they were called IV stands. She did not seem to notice he was awake.

When he grunted, she looked down at him. Her eyes widened in surprise. "Oh! You're awake!" she said, smiling at him. Paul wondered if what he saw in her smile held a hint of pity. He hoped not.

She moved out of his sight as she said, "Let me tell them to contact your doctor. He wanted to know the moment you came around."

The sound of the door opening was followed by silence as she left the room. Moments later, she was back. "Dr. King will be here soon. Can you talk?"

Paul whispered more than spoke. "A little."

"Okay, dear. That's fine. Just relax until the doctor gets here."

"Where's my mother?" he managed.

She looked at him for the briefest of seconds before answering. "The doctor will fill you in on everything," she said, but Paul could see in her eyes she knew the answer but didn't want to say.

Fear squeezed his heart. Either his mother was at least as bad off as he was, or she was dead. He knew she hadn't come through this unharmed. Otherwise, she would have been at his bedside when he awoke to this living nightmare of pain and loss.

If she died, what would happen to him? His father was the definition of the absent parent. Would he be forced to return to Opelika to live with him? He had considered running away recently, but now the fact he might truly be alone in the world hit him. If he was forced to live with his father, he would definitely run away. He couldn't take that.

Closing his eyes, he prayed to the God he'd barely taken the time to know. He prayed that his mother would be alive, and he wouldn't have to go live with his father. As he prayed, he couldn't help feeling that his mind was talking to nobody but himself. Or if God did exist, then God would surely ignore him just as Paul had ignored any thought that any kind of God was out there. Then he remembered something he'd heard about prayer, that sometimes God's answer was *no*. He stopped praying, certain the outcome of this horror would be anything but good for him.

He did his best not to think about his mother and the pain that consumed him, both physical and emotional. He felt the tears begin to soak the bandages that covered his face.

The ten minutes that drifted between being told the doctor was coming and his arrival felt more like an hour. On the one hand, Paul wanted him there to tell him how badly he was hurt, but on the other, he dreaded seeing him. He would have the news about his mother, which was likely worse than any diagnosis he could give Paul about his condition.

Finally, the door opened, and a man wearing a doctor's white coat entered the room. Paul took him in at a glance as he bent over the bed to peer into Paul's eyes. The nurse from earlier stood behind him, peering at Paul over the man's shoulder.

"Welcome back to the land of the living," the

doctor said, smiling at Jack in an effort to reassure him.

Dr. King didn't seem very tall, under six feet, though Paul thought he'd have to be able to sit up to really tell. He was stocky but not fat, with short, reddish-blonde hair and piercing blue eyes. His look was serious, despite his attempt at a joke.

"I'm Dr. King," he said. "Dr. Dennis King. Nurse Dana tells me you can talk okay. Is that right?"

"Yes," Paul whisper-squawked.

"Excellent. Can you tell me your name?"

"Don't you know it?"

Dr. King smiled. "Yes, I just want to test your cognitive function. How well your brain is working."

"Oh. I'm Paul."

"Last name?"

"Hanson."

"How old are you?"

"Fourteen."

"What town do you live in?"

"Denton."

"Can you count backwards from twenty?"

Paul began to count down until he reached fourteen, and the doctor stopped him there.

"Okay, that's good. I doubted there was a problem, but I needed to make sure. Are you in pain?"

"Yes."

"Okay. You have second and third degree burns. The third degree burns aren't painful because the fire destroyed the nerves there, but the second degree burns can be very painful. We will give you some medicine to help with that, but not too much. We don't want you leaving here hooked on anything, and the drugs are powerful."

"I've been burned?"

"Yes. You have first, second, and third degree burns over most of your body. I'm not going to lie to you. Getting better is going to be difficult." He paused. "And very painful."

Paul finally found the courage and asked the question. "Where's my mom? Is she going to be okay?"

Paul could tell that the doctor could see the fear in his eyes. Dr. King set his jaw for a moment and said, "I'm afraid not, Paul. She died in the fire."

Sobs began to wrack his devastated body. He lay helplessly crying in the hospital room. The emotional pain matched the pain from the burns. The nurse reached out and held his right hand, which was one of the only areas of his body not blistered from the flames that had taken his mother and left him scarred for life in more ways than one.

Paul sobbed until he could sob no more and lapsed into silent weeping. The nurse dabbed his eyes and did her best to smile down at him. He could see tears in her own eyes as well.

The doctor left with the nurse, who returned with a syringe. She attached the syringe onto the luer lock of the tubing that led into his arm and said, "This is a painkiller. It will probably make you sleep, but at least you won't be out for three days like before."

"I was out three days?"

"Yes. We only removed the breathing tube yesterday once the doctor felt you could breathe on your own. We had to wake you, but I doubt you remember. You were mostly out of it." She disposed of the syringe and turned toward him, leaning over to look into his eyes. "I can tell you're a strong one, Paul. You'll get through this." Her smile reminded him of his mother's, and his tears came again.

She shushed him, pulled a chair next to the bed, and sat down, holding his hand while he cried himself to sleep, which didn't take long, thanks to the drugs he'd been given.

As he drifted into sleep, his last thought was of his mother, making him wonder what would happen to him now that she was gone.

3

Joe Sissler had worked in northern Florida for over twenty years investigating fires, and the fire at the home of Amber Hanson and her son, Paul, had been one of the easiest he'd worked. The cause was clearly arson.

The fire had been set by pouring an accelerant onto the sofa and surrounding floor in the living room of the small house. The burn patterns he found there were obvious enough they created a textbook case of arson.

One side of the house was mostly charred rubble, typical of what would be found after a fully destructive house fire, but the back half had exploded. Joe had determined that the explosion had been caused by a can of gasoline that had been left in the house. Joe found a charred can of charcoal lighter fluid in the rubble. He suspected that had been used as the accelerant since pouring gasoline on the sofa and floor before lighting the fire could produce an instant explosion. The remains of the gas can lay among the smoldering ruins of the house.

As Joe and his team gathered evidence, he wondered what would cause someone to do something like this. He also considered that this could be the first of a string of arsons in the area. He prayed that would not be the case. Then again, if it wasn't a serial arsonist—someone who found a thrill in setting fires—it meant someone likely intended to kill Ms. Hanson and her son. Again, the thought occurred to him—why?

The investigative team would gather the evidence, and Joe would submit everything with his conclusions in a report that detailed what he discovered regarding the fire's cause and any contributing factors.

Taking a swig from his thermos of coffee, Joe shook his head at the senselessness of such a crime.

Three days later, Joe, carrying a bag that contained several items sealed in evidence bags, entered the office of Detective Bob Ebert of the Denton Police Department. Bob looked up from some paperwork on his desk when Joe entered. When Bob saw Joe's face, his own smile at seeing his friend faded.

"You don't have good news for me, do you?"

"Afraid not," Joe said.

"Please don't tell me the Hanson fire was arson."

"As clear-cut a case as I've ever seen. There was no attempt at all to even disguise what happened, though that wouldn't work anyway."

Bob nodded at the bag. "I take it that's for me?"

"Yeah. A charred lighter fluid can and the pieces of an exploded gas can." Joe placed the bag on Bob's desk gently and reached into his back pocket, withdrawing an envelope. "And pictures of the crime scene." He lay the envelope on the desk beside the sealed evidence.

"Clear-cut, huh?"

"Yep. Why they did it, I can't say, but it's definitely arson."

Bob shook his head in dismay. "And murder, along with attempted murder."

"The kid's gonna live?"

"Yeah. Burned, but alive. Recovery will be bad."

"Where's his dad?"

"We asked the deceased's friends. They tell me she moved here from Opelika after a divorce. Apparently, her ex was a deadbeat."

Bob removed a chain-of-evidence form from his desk and filled out the initial details before handing it to Joe for him to sign that he had collected the evidence, placed the items in sealed evidence bags, and delivered them to Bob on the date and time indicated.

When that was done, the two men were silent for a moment before Bob said, "Well, I guess I should start moving on this. You got anything else?"

"Just my wishes for good luck."

"Thanks. I'm gonna need it."

After Joe left his office, Bob completed paperwork to get the evidence tested and printed. When he'd finished, he hand-delivered the evidence bags to the lab, having the tech there sign the chain-of-custody form.

"How long will it be before I have something?" Bob asked.

"We can have prints done later today, though identifying them may take as long as a week."

"Thanks. Could you let me know if something comes up in AFIS?" Bob asked, referring to the

Automated Fingerprint Identification System. It would be up to a fingerprint analyst to match the prints, but the AFIS database could make that much simpler and eliminate a lot of people.

"Sure."

That afternoon, Bob received a call from the lab tech. When he answered, the tech said, "I don't know what this is about, but we raised some prints, and they look like they're from a kid."

"A kid? You sure?"

"Yeah. Either that or an adult with very small hands. And I do mean very small. I'm going with the odds here, since adults with hands this small are uncommon."

"Could it be a woman's?"

"You mean like a regular adult woman?"

"Yeah."

"Nope. Too small again."

"How clear are they?"

"Pretty clear. If you can find the person who left these prints, it'll be a cinch matching them up.

Bob hung up the phone, wondering if maybe some kid in Denton had decided to start burning down houses.

He'd have to talk to Paul Hanson to see if he had any enemies.

Picking up the phone, he called the hospital and spoke to one of the nurses in the unit where Paul was being treated and was informed he'd become conscious again earlier that day.

"Can I speak to him?" Bob asked.

"I'm sorry, Detective. That might be a few days.

He's on some powerful pain meds. You'll have to talk to Dr. King, his doctor."

Bob was given a number where he could reach Dr. King and called him. He was connected to his answering service and left a message. The doctor would call him when he could.

When Dr. King called back, Bob asked him if he could speak to Paul Hanson.

"He's mostly out of it right now. He's on some heavy medication that makes him groggy. Can it wait a few days?"

"I guess it could, but I'd prefer sooner. You see, the house fire was no accident. I need to find out if he or his mother had any enemies."

"How long will this take?"

"Five minutes, tops."

After a moment, Dr. King said, "Come by tomorrow morning around nine. He should be able to answer a few questions."

As Bob scribbled a note to himself, he said, "Thank you. See you then, Doctor."

At nine sharp the next morning, Bob strode up to the nurses' station on the floor where Paul was and identified himself, adding, "I have an appointment to see Paul Hanson for about five minutes."

The nurse, whose name tag read *Brian Long, RN*, said, "Yes, Detective Ebert. Dr. King said you'd be here." He escorted Bob to a room, knocked, and entered with Bob following.

"How are you feeling today, Paul?" Brian asked.

"The same." Paul's voice sounded hoarse, and Bob wondered if the fire may have caused damage to his vocal chords.

Brian continued, "This is Detective Ebert with the Denton Police Department. He has a few questions for you." Brian excused himself and left them alone.

Bob couldn't see Paul's expression beyond his eyes, but they looked frightened and wary.

"Paul, I'm sorry about what happened to you and your mother. Have they talked to you about her?"

"Yes," Paul whispered.

"We have found something disturbing about the fire, Paul. Apparently, it wasn't an accident. Someone set fire to your house on purpose, even leaving a can of gasoline inside, probably near the doors to your mother's bedroom and yours." He paused, allowing that news to sink in. "I was wondering if you knew anyone who might do something like that."

"On purpose? Someone set the fire on purpose?" Paul asked, his whispers sounding both sad and frightened.

"I'm afraid so."

"Are you sure?"

"The fire investigator says it's a textbook case of arson. No doubts."

Bob watched the tears build and spill over, wetting the bandages nearest his eyes. "I'm sorry you have to deal with that on top of everything else."

Paul was silent beyond the quiet weeping for a moment before he said, "Who would do something like that?"

"That's what I was hoping you could help me

with. Do you know anyone who had a grudge against you or your mother?" Bob didn't mention that the fingerprints were those of a child. He didn't want Paul focusing only on kids his age. It could have been an adult using his or her son or daughter to carry the cans of fuel. As awful as that sounded, he'd seen such things before. One famous example was The Beltway Sniper attacks in 2002, when a man and his son turned out to be the killers.

Paul said nothing for a moment, and Bob repeated his question.

"No," Paul said. Bob wished he could see Paul's face to help him determine if he might be holding something back, but it was what it was. Bob didn't think that was the case.

"Paul, if you think of something you feel might help me, no matter how small you think it might be, let me know. I'll leave my number at the nurses' station."

"Okay," Paul said.

When Bob left his card at the nurses' station, the nurse told him that Paul would be transferred to Shands Burn Center at the University of Florida when he was able to travel in a few days.

"Could you pack my card with his stuff?" Bob asked.

The nurse promised him they would do that and Bob left. He had a mountain of work to do to find out who killed Paul's mother and left Paul scarred for life.

As he drove back to the station, he thought about Paul and what would happen to him. He would become a ward of the state if they couldn't find

Paul's father. He hated that the boy would likely end up in foster care. Depending on the circumstances of Paul's placement, it could be either a terrible experience or one that was at least tolerable.

A thought struck him, and he made a mental note to call Jack Turner, someone he'd known since childhood.

4

On his way to the school to see if he could speak to some of Paul's friends, Bob used Siri to find the number to Shelton and Turner, Attorneys-at-law. Chuck Shelton had retired years ago, but Jack had kept the firm's name since it had become one of the top firms in northern Florida, and name recognition was important for business. As the phone rang, Bob hoped Jack would be amenable to his idea.

"Shelton and Turner," the receptionist answered.

"This is Detective Bob Ebert. Is Jack available?"

"Hold on, Detective. I'll see." After he was put on hold for a minute, the young woman was back. "He's with someone right now. Can he call you back?"

"Yes, please. It's not urgent, but it is important." He left his cell number and clicked off.

Arriving at the school, he went into the office and asked to see the principal. He was directed to her office after a call was placed to ensure she was not somewhere else in the building.

When he entered, Carolyn Miller rose and extended her hand, which he shook.

"Detective Ebert. How may I help you?"

"I'm here to see if I could talk to some of Paul Hanson's friends."

"Yes, of course. It's terrible what happened." She sat and asked, "Do you know what's going to happen with him?"

"I'm not sure right now, but I do need to ask some questions of his friends to see if they can help in the investigation."

"Investigation? Is there a problem?"

"Actually, yes, there is. The fire was intentionally set."

Her mouth dropped open. "Oh, my Lord!"

"I just want to see if Paul may have told a friend something that might help. The more I can learn about his life and his mother, the more I will have to help my investigation."

"Let me call one of his teachers. She should know who his friends were. You won't be accusing them of anything, will you? If so, I need to have one of their parents present."

"No. If it comes to that, we can stop the interview and call their parents, but I seriously doubt it will be more than asking about Paul."

"Okay," Ms. Miller said and dialed a number.

When a woman answered, Ms. Miller said, "Ms. Eden, someone is here who needs to speak with Paul Hanson's friends. Could you give me the names of his best friends?"

"Certainly, but he really only had two friends."

"Okay, that's fine. What are their names?"

After writing down the two names and hanging up, she opened a page on her computer. She searched the names and called their current teachers, asking that they be sent to the office.

Ms. Miller turned to Bob. "Is there anything we can do here to help Paul? It's awful he's lost his mother so suddenly. How bad are his injuries?"

"Pretty bad, I'm afraid. They will be sending him to Shands Burn Center at the University of Florida. He'll probably be gone from school for some time."

"They'll have a teacher working with him to keep him up-to-speed in his studies," Ms. Miller said. "At least he won't fall far behind."

Bob nodded, thinking his education was important, but not as important as his physical, mental, and emotional healing at this point.

Ms. Miller must have read his mind. "Not that it matters much right now. He'll need more than good schooling." She shook her head. "That's where a mother would come in handy."

"So you have no information about his father?"

"No. I assume there was an ugly divorce. When this happened, I took the time to look over Paul's records from his previous school in Opelika. Two parents were mentioned, but then a divorce decree was issued giving the mother sole custody."

"Do you have the father's name?"

"It's in the records. I can get it for you."

"Thank you."

At that moment, a call came from the front office telling Ms. Miller Paul's friends were there.

"Send one back and keep the other there for now," Ms. Miller said and hung up. Moments later, a timid knock sounded. Ms. Miller called out for the boy to come in.

A chubby boy with dark hair and glasses entered and sat. He looked frightened. His fright seemed to grow when he saw a man he didn't know was there as well.

Ms. Miller said, "You're Randall, am I right?"

"Yes, ma'am."

"Randall, you're not in any trouble here. This is Detective Ebert with the police department, and he's investigating the fire that destroyed your friend Paul's house."

"Okay." Randall looked confused, as if wondering how he could help with something like that.

"Randall, mostly I want to know about Paul. What he liked to do, and anything he might have said that could indicate his mother, or even he himself, had any enemies."

Randall shook his head, seeming to consider. "He never said anything like that. I mean, we have enemies, but they mostly leave us alone."

"Mostly?"

"Yeah. You know. They just don't like us, but it's not like they are, like, real enemies. Why?"

"Nothing much, really. Just needing to find out about Paul's life. Did he mention his father much?"

"He didn't like his dad, but they never saw each other."

"Did he say why he didn't like him?"

Randall shrugged. "No, just that he wasn't a good dad."

"What was his relationship with his mother like?"

Randall shrugged again. "You know. Just like most kids. They got along okay, but she sometimes made him mad."

"Anything recent?"

Randall shrugged, but Bob could see he was not telling something.

"I really need to know these things, or I wouldn't ask," Bob said. "You see, it will come out in the papers tomorrow anyway, so I can tell you that the fire wasn't an accident. Someone set it."

This news clearly stunned Randall. "You mean like arson?"

"That's exactly what I mean."

Randall's gaze wandered around the floor near his feet as if an answer might be there. "Who would do something like that?"

"That's what I'm trying to find out."

"I mean, Paul had a big fight with his mom because she wouldn't let him go camping with me and Les, but that's all. It's not like he would burn his house down over it."

Bob nodded. It was very likely true that Paul wouldn't do that, but he'd known of kids who would take some drastic measures in the past.

"Do you think any of his enemies at school might do something like that?"

"I don't think so. I mean the fire happened in the middle of the night, didn't it? People die in fires like that."

Bob changed the subject. "What kind of friend was Paul?"

Randall shrugged again. "He was a good friend. People picked on him because he looked like a younger kid. He's kinda small. Looks more like a ten-year-old than fourteen. But he's funny, you know. Likes to joke around. That kinda thing."

"Does he have a temper?"

"Not more than any other kid, I guess. Though he did say he'd kill his dad if he could." Randall looked at Bob. "But not his mom!" he said.

"Why did he say he'd kill his dad if he could?"

Again, he shrugged. "I don't know. He just didn't like him."

"Is there anything else you can tell?"

"Not really. He's just a regular guy, you know?"

"Yeah," Bob said.

Randall was dismissed back to class, and Les, Paul's other friend, came in. With Les, there were no shrugs, just straight answers. Bob didn't find anything else out about Paul, though Les offered his opinions about Paul's anger at his mother and his hatred of his father.

"Paul was real angry at his mom. I mean, she wouldn't let him do anything. We just wanted to go camping out in the woods on a Saturday night, but she wouldn't let him. Randall and me are scouts, so it's not like we don't know what we're doing when we camp, but she acted like we were wanting to take him to Siberia or something."

When asked about Paul's relationship with his dad, Les said, "I got the feeling his dad got—you know—funny with Paul." Les glanced over at Ms. Miller and blushed. "I mean he never said anything, but I figured that had to be it. I mean, who wants to kill his own dad like that. When he talked about him, he—I don't know—kind of changed. I've never known anyone who hated someone that much."

Bob asked, "And he never told you why he hated his dad so much?"

"No. That's kind of why I think—" He glanced at Ms. Miller before continuing. "Well, why I think what I do."

When the interviews were finished, Bob rose and thanked Ms. Miller for letting him talk to the students, though he didn't have much to go on. The dad was out of the picture, and the only thing he had was that Paul was extremely angry with his mom because he saw her as preventing him from having the fun many boys his age enjoyed without much question.

As he drove back to the station, a call came from Jack Turner.

"Jack, thank you for returning my call."

"What do you need?" Jack asked, obviously puzzled by the call.

"Can I stop by your office later today? I just need about ten minutes of your time. I have something I want to discuss."

"What? Did you get arrested and need an attorney?" Jack asked, chuckling.

"Nothing like that," Bob answered and laughed. "I just need to see if you're willing to help out on something."

"Let me check my calendar," A moment later, Jack said, "If you want to meet when you're off-duty, maybe we could meet somewhere for a beer after hours."

"That sounds fine."

"How about six o'clock at Perry's?"

"Six at Perry's is fine," Bob answered. "I'll see you then."

5

Bob was late arriving at Perry's Restaurant. When he entered the bar area, he saw Jack at a table for two, nursing a beer. Bob sat across from him.

"Detective Ebert!" Jack said with mock enthusiasm. "Glad you could make it."

"Sorry. I was leaving when Captain Coghill called me into his office to discuss a case."

"It happens. How's the good Captain Brian Coghill doing?"

"He's fine."

A server came by to get Bob's order. After telling her his choice of beer, he turned to Jack.

"I have a case you might be interested in?"

"Wait a minute. I have to write this down. The cops are seeking defense counsel for a criminal?"

"Not at all. I have a kid who was burned in a fire. He lost his mother in the fire and his father is out of the picture."

"Is the father dead? In prison? Missing?"

"No."

"Then call it what it is, Huggy," Jack said, using Bob's childhood nickname. "He's not 'out of the picture.' He's a deadbeat dad. Willing to have the fun making the kid but lacking the responsibility to raise him."

"Okay. His father is one of the millions of deadbeat dads in this country. In any case, it leaves the kid without a parental figure. I don't want to see him get in the system and be placed with a family only interested in the support money they get from the state for taking him in."

Jack figured out instantly where this was going. "You want me and Jenny to take him in, am I right?"

"That's right. He seems like a good kid from what I can gather, though I'm going to have to clear him as a suspect."

"Suspect?"

"Yeah. The fire was arson. Someone is guilty of murder and attempted murder."

"The culprit could claim he didn't know there were people inside."

"Jack, it was the middle of the night, and her car was parked outside the house."

"Doesn't prove anything. If the person who started the fire didn't know there were people inside, it's arson and second-degree manslaughter."

"Jack, quit thinking like a defense attorney."

"I'll quit doing that when you stop thinking like a detective."

The server set Bob's beer down, and he took a swallow. "Okay, point taken. So how about it? Can you take the kid in?"

Jack would have asked Bob why he didn't take the boy in, but Bob was a widower and didn't have time for raising an adolescent.

"I'll have to discuss it with Jenny," Jack said.

"That's a foregone conclusion. But what do you think she'll say?"

"She'll start doing her best to talk me into it."

Bob looked at Jack, sipped his beer, and said, "It's too bad you two couldn't have kids. You'd have been a great father."

Jack shrugged. "It is what it is."

"Yeah, but you would have."

"Is this your effort to talk me into taking in your suspect?"

"He's not a suspect. Just a person of interest. I have to exonerate him is all. Strike him off the list of possible perps."

"You didn't answer my question."

Bob smiled. "Nope. I didn't, but it's a true statement." He sipped his beer. "You'll talk to Jenny?"

"Yeah. What's the kid's name?"

"Paul Hanson. He's fourteen, but small for his age. He could pass for eleven easy." Bob sipped his beer again. "That's what makes this tough. There were prints on the gas can that were small enough to be from a kid his size. I checked out the one hand that isn't bandaged when I visited him. He has small hands, narrow fingers."

"Maybe the gas can belonged to the mom."

"Maybe. Still, it raises questions that have to be dealt with."

Jack nodded. "I understand. Just don't make a decision on the perp if the boy's prints match the ones on the can. There are a thousand explanations."

"Tell you what, Jack. I won't tell you how to defend people in court, and you won't tell me how to conduct an investigation."

Jack chuckled.

"What?" Bob asked.

"It just occurred to me that our relationship has been adversarial since sixth grade. I grew up to be a defense attorney; you grew up to be a cop."

Bob raised his glass to toast. "To adversarial relationships. They keep life interesting, at least."

Jack smiled and clinked his glass to Bob's. "So, how badly was young Paul burned?"

"Pretty bad. The doctor told me he has second and third degree burns over much of his body. Paul doesn't know how bad it was, actually. The doctor told me they had to remove his left eye. He'll be fitted for a prosthetic one. He'll be badly scarred, especially his face, chest, and arms. It's not that bad below the waist. They're moving him to the Shands Burn Center at UF in the next few days," Bob said.

"Any idea how long he'll be there?"

"Nope. You'd have to ask the doctor."

"Who's his doctor?"

"Dr. Dennis King."

"If we decide to do this, I'll talk to him."

"You'll do it."

"Probably. I'll just tell the judge in family court that my wife and I are willing to take Paul in and give him a home for now."

"Okay. Approval should be easy since everyone there knows you two," Bob said. "Keep me posted."

With that, he downed his beer and stood. Jack stood and they shook hands.

"See you around, counselor," Bob said.

"I'm sure you will." Jack smiled at his old nemesis, finished his beer, and went home.

When he arrived, Jenny was already home. He

could smell their dinner in the oven.

"Mmmm," Jack said. "Roast chicken?"

"Yes. I hope it's good. I ran out of basil and used about half of what I usually do."

"I'm sure it will be delicious," Jack said and leaned against the counter. "I have a question, and I'm unsure of my own answer to it."

She pecked him on the lips and said, "Welcome home. Now, what's your question?"

"How would you feel about taking in a fourteen-year-old boy who has been badly burned recently in a fire?"

Jenny's face showed her concern. "Do you mean Paul Hanson?"

"You know about him?"

"Yes. Leanne was talking about him today. She said his mother was killed in the fire."

"I really have to do more to keep up with what's happening in town," Jack said.

"What made you start thinking of taking him in?"

"Actually, Bob Ebert asked me to."

"Huggy Bob?"

"Yeah, Huggy. He's investigating the fire."

"It's arson?"

"Apparently. He says he has to eliminate Paul as a suspect."

"That's ridiculous! Why would a kid set fire to his own house in the middle of the night?"

"Don't get upset. He said it more as a formality to remove him from the list of people of interest."

"Did he mention any other people of interest?"

"No, and he wouldn't. He only mentioned Paul

because he asked us to take him in, and I guess he wants us to go in fully aware of everything going on with him."

"That is such a shame. What do you think we should do?"

"I was hoping you could answer that. As I said, I'm unsure of my own answer. I want to help the boy out, but I have a wife and career to consider, not to mention his rehab will take time and commitment on our part."

"I'm willing if you are," Jenny said.

"You're not going to try to talk me into it?"

"Only if you say no," she said as she poured them both a glass of wine. They went to sit in the living room.

"Why do you want to do this?"

"Jack, you know I love children but couldn't have any. That's one reason we started Bridge Over Troubled Water. I need someone to mother. It's in my genes."

"Yes, it can get old being mothered by my wife. So there's that. You'll have someone else."

She slapped him playfully on the shoulder. "I don't mother you!"

"Actually, you do, but it's okay. It's one way you show you love me, but it would be nice if we had someone else to receive some of that."

"Are you really okay with bringing him in?" she asked.

"I guess. It gives me a chance to do for another young person what Hank did for me."

"Then it's settled."

"He's going to be fragile, emotionally."

"I'm a clinical psychologist specializing in adolescent psychology, especially for troubled teens. I think we can handle it."

Jack raised his glass and clinked it to Jenny's. "I'll call Bob after supper. Speaking of which, when will it be ready?"

"In about fifteen minutes. You can call Bob while we wait."

"Afraid I'll change my mind?"

"You know me too well, Jack Turner."

"I could say the same to you."

She rose and returned to the kitchen as Jack looked up Bob's home number and went to their house phone.

"We'll do it," Jack said when Bob answered.

6

The next day, Jack placed a call to Child Welfare Services to set up the foster care. He and Jenny knew most of the employees there, and he was told their application would be easily approved, which he had expected. He also phoned the hospital in Wharton to see if he could visit Paul to let him know of the arrangements that had been made. After speaking to several people there, arrangements were made for him to come in that afternoon to see him.

Arriving at the hospital, Jack went to the pediatric ward where Paul was housed and stepped up to the counter at the nurses' station. He was very familiar with this part of the hospital. He smiled remembering the children he'd visited there when he was thirteen and had more or less been forced to visit the first time by Mrs. Dawson, the woman he came to know and love as a surrogate mother to him.

"Hi, I'm Jack Turner. I'm here to see Paul Hanson. Is he awake enough to see me?" he said to one of the nurses behind the counter.

She looked up and smiled at him. "Yes, Mr. Turner. We were told to expect you." She rose and came around the counter. "Just follow me," she said and strode down the hallway, entering a room Jack realized he had visited before.

"Paul, you have a visitor," she said.

Jack approached the bed. As he did, he wondered what kind of monster could set a fire that would do such damage to anyone, especially a child.

"Hi," Paul said, his voice mostly a whisper.

"Hello. I'm Jack Turner. I have what I hope is good news."

"What?"

Jack knew that Paul was aware he was basically an orphan now. He had almost certainly wondered what would become of him. "My wife and I are going to be your foster parents until your father can be located."

"Don't want father."

Jack paused before asking, "Why not?"

"Just don't."

"I suppose that will be taken into account if they find him," Jack said. "In the meantime, you will come live with us when you're finished with your initial recovery."

"But I don't know you."

"That's true, and we don't know you either, but we're very happy to have you come live with us."

Jack could see the wariness in his eyes. Jack smiled, doing his best to reassure Paul. "Don't worry. We're very nice people. I'm an attorney in Denton, and my wife is a psychologist."

Paul's one eye blinked several times again. "You're a lawyer?"

"Yes."

It took a moment for Paul to respond again. "Are you wanting to sue someone about this?"

"Well, first I'm a criminal defense attorney, so litigation isn't part of what I do. Second, my wife and I have no motive for taking you in beyond wanting to help you. We're kind of famous in Denton for that kind of thing. You see, we run this organization called Bridge Over Troubled Water for teens to talk out their problems."

"And you want me to talk about my problems?"

"If that's what you want to do, then certainly, but that will be totally up to you. I'm just letting you know we are used to being around people your age and enjoy helping them. I want you to feel comfortable with this arrangement."

"Do I have a choice?"

Jack sighed. "We always have a choice, but you wouldn't want to take the only other option available to you, which is living in a group home for kids whose parents can't care for them or have died. You'd be much happier living with my wife and me. We have a very nice home and we even have a dog who loves kids."

Paul's eyes seemed to brighten at that news. "A dog?"

"Yes, and he loves to play fetch and be petted as though he owns the world." Jack smiled at Paul, hoping this would help convince him to accept his situation and become their temporary son willingly rather than forcibly.

When Paul didn't reply, Jack asked, "So, you willing to give us a chance?"

"I don't like taking charity."

Jack flashed back to his own childhood and his strong desire not to be the recipient of the state's charity. "I understand that. This isn't charity. It's a loving couple wanting to share our lives with you."

"Okay," Paul said, his voice echoing his reluctance tinged with hopeful apprehension.

"You know, I've actually visited someone in this room before," Jack said, feeling that a story about his childhood would help ease the movement to acceptance and friendship.

"Oh?"

"Yes. You see, my parents were alcoholics. They weren't abusive, just neglectful. I ended up meeting some adults who took me under their wings, so to speak. One of them, Mrs. Mary Jane Dawson, brought me here to see some kids who were worse off than I was. It helped me realize that while my situation was far less than ideal, I had it pretty good compared to some."

He looked at Paul, who was listening, waiting for the story of how he came to visit someone in this same room.

"Anyway, when she brought me here, I visited a kid just a little younger than I was in this room. His name was Toby. We used to play checkers."

"Was he good at checkers?"

"Yes. Though he was three years younger than I was, he usually beat me more often than I beat him on my visits."

"Visits? Like more than one?"

"Yes. I ended up coming out here again to visit him. He was nice."

Paul raised his bandaged arms a few inches and let them fall back down. "I can't very well do that." His tone suggested he was making a joke.

Jack smiled. "You'll be able to sooner than you think."

Paul seemed to look around the room as if searching for something. "I guess a lot of kids have died in this room."

"Maybe," Jack said, "but I wouldn't dwell on it. It's just a room. You won't be dying here. That I can guarantee."

"Did you visit any other kids here?"

"As a matter of fact, I did. Actually, I count one of the girls I met as my first girlfriend."

"Really?"

"Yes. Her name was Suzanne. She was my age, but because of her illness, she looked much younger."

"What was wrong with her?"

"She had an illness of the immune system. Her body didn't fight off diseases well."

"So you dated her?"

"Well, date is a bit strong. I only saw her twice, but I learned a lot from her."

"Like what?" It was the question Jack hoped Paul would ask.

"She taught me that we need to say what's on our minds, especially if it's something nice about someone."

"Did you tell her you love her?"

Jack thought back. "Not in so many words, but then we'd barely met, and we were only thirteen."

"I'm just a year older than that."

"Yes, I know."

"Did you love her?"

"I guess as much as a thirteen-year-old boy can in such a short time. I also learned that we can love someone quickly, but it doesn't have to be a lifetime kind of love, just a way of caring."

Paul lay in silence before changing the subject. "They're taking me to another hospital soon."

"Yes, I know. The Shands Burn Center in Gainesville."

"Will you come visit me there?"

"I'll see what I can do."

"Yeah, I guess you're kind of busy with your work."

Jack heard the disappointment and vowed to himself he would visit Paul as often as he could. He knew actions convinced others you cared, not words or money or anything else. He'd learned from Hank and Mrs. Dawson that time was the most valuable gift someone could give another.

Jack made sure Paul was looking at him when he said, "I promise I will visit you at Shands. More than once, in fact. I'll even bring my wife, Jenny. She's really looking forward to having you live with us."

"Is she nice?"

Jack smiled. "Nicer than I am, even."

Paul looked lost in thought for a moment, then asked, "What should I call you?"

"Jack is fine. You can call my wife Jenny."

"Okay."

They chatted for a few more minutes until the nurse came to shoo Jack out.

As Jack left the hospital, he thought about how well their first meeting went. He hoped Paul felt the same. He couldn't wait to tell Jenny about it.

7

A week later as Bob drove to the hospital in Wharton, he considered what he had to do there. He didn't think Paul had anything to do with burning his house down and killing his mother, but there was enough evidence he couldn't ignore the possibility.

He knew Paul would be leaving in the next few days for the Shands Burn Center, and he needed to take care of this before he left. Because Paul would be leaving town soon, he had taken the effort to have a warrant signed to require Paul to provide his fingerprints in case Paul refused. It was a small matter that would take only a few minutes. He had a live-scan device with him to record Paul's fingerprints electronically.

As expected, the application for Jack and Jenny to become Paul's foster parents had been expedited, and they were now Paul's temporary guardians. Bob had spoken to Jack about getting Paul's prints, and Jack had not argued.

"Even if they're his, that doesn't mean he's guilty," Jack had said.

"Spoken like a true defense attorney," Bob answered before getting Jack's permission to print Paul, despite the warrant.

"I don't need to be there," Jack said. "It's fine with me."

Bob agreed that the prints would not be enough to charge Paul if they did match the prints from the cans, but if they didn't match, it would allow Bob to cross Paul off the list of potential suspects. If they did, more investigation of Paul would be necessary.

Bob found Paul staring at the TV suspended from the ceiling. A cartoon with stilted movements by the characters, one that Bob was unfamiliar with, was playing. Bob found himself wondering how many kids today had ever seen an animated feature that was drawn frame-by-frame by highly skilled artists, like the old Warner Brothers cartoons, or even the older Disney films.

Paul turned to look at him when he entered. "Hi." His voice seemed to be improving. It was stronger now.

"Hi, Paul. You feeling okay today?"

"Still hurts," he answered. "And it's still kinda hard to breathe. They say my lungs were damaged."

"Yes, I suppose it's going to be a while before you feel okay again."

"Yeah." Paul turned back to the TV. He must have thought Bob was just stopping by to see if he was feeling any better.

"Paul?"

He faced Bob again. "Yeah?"

"I'm afraid I have to get your fingerprints."

"Why?"

"I have to eliminate you as a suspect in the arson."

"What?" Paul's response suggested Bob had just said he needed to help Paul float above his bed.

"Yes, I need to get your fingerprints. We found

some on what remained of the gas can that was left in your house, possibly by whoever started the fire. I need to make sure they're not yours." Bob didn't mention the can of charcoal lighter fluid.

"They probably are if it's our gas can. I had to mow the yard."

"When was the last time you filled the mower with gas?"

Paul thought for a moment. "About a month ago. Fingerprints don't last that long, do they?"

"Yes. In fact, they can last for years. Getting prints from an arson can be tricky because fire destroys surfaces sometimes, but because the metal didn't melt, we were able to get some prints."

"Oh." Paul thought for a moment and said, "Are you arresting me?"

"No, of course not. I just have to rule you out as the last person to touch that gas can."

"Were there other fingerprints on the can?"

"Not that we could raise from the surface."

"Then if the only fingerprints on the gas can are mine, you have to think I did it."

"Not necessarily, but we can cross that bridge when we get to it. First, let's see if we can eliminate you as a suspect."

Paul's hands were damaged from the fire, but not so much that Bob couldn't get a good print, especially of Paul's right thumb, which was the best print they were able to get from the gas can and the charcoal lighter fluid container, which had not been damaged since it had been found outside the home. It was fully intact.

Bob took the fingerprint scanner out of its small case and scanned Paul's fingers to capture his fingerprints electronically. He made sure the right thumb's image was clear before packing the scanner away again. He chatted with Paul about sports as he did his work, wanting to put the boy at ease.

After leaving the hospital, Bob drove to his office and downloaded the images. Then he looked at the images of the prints they had raised from the can and lighter fluid. He felt his heart sink as he realized that the right thumb prints looked identical. He was no fingerprint expert, but even he could see they looked very much the same. He had to be sure of his suspicions and forwarded the scanned and lifted fingerprints to their experts. He requested the work be expedited.

Around two hours later, he received the information he'd been sure he already knew. The prints matched.

Bob thought about this. The prints on the gas can could be explained. Paul had used the can to gas up the lawn mower.

But what about the can of charcoal lighter fluid? Paul's right thumb print was there as well. There were no charcoal grills on the property. He would have to ask Paul about that. While he needed to solve the case, the possibility that Paul was the arsonist made his stomach churn. Was it possible this kid who didn't look capable of swatting a dog's rump be the murderer of his own mother?

Bob could easily imagine a kid Paul's age miscalculating the speed a fire would spread and being too late getting out of his bedroom window. Further investigation had shown the gas can had sat on the floor between his bedroom door and his mother's. The charring pattern of the floorboards showed a fiery explosion had occurred on one side of the boards.

He didn't understand the processes involved in drawing those conclusions, but he knew that Joe Sissler did. Joe was convinced from his investigation that the gas can had been purposely placed at that exact spot in the hallway.

This was murder, and Bob prayed it wasn't matricide.

Taking out his phone, he called Jack. After he answered, Bob said, "I thought I would catch you up on some things. Just don't tell Captain Coghill we talked," Bob joked. "I might be the only person on the force who likes a defense attorney."

"He'll never hear it from me."

"Actually, as Paul's guardian, you need to know that the prints on the gas and charcoal lighter fluid cans came back as a match for Paul."

"Do you think Paul did this?"

"At the moment, I'm not sure what to think. But the prints being on the cans doesn't exactly exonerate him."

"Bob, this kid looks and behaves like he

wouldn't swat a fly."

"I've heard Ted Bundy was the same way as a kid. Even as an adult."

"I don't know. Paul seems genuine."

"And Bundy didn't? It was his charm that got all those women to go with him."

"He just doesn't strike me as another Ted Bundy."

"Me either, but I'm just letting you know. In fact, if I did think he was like Bundy, I wouldn't have called you to give you a heads up in the first place. I just figured you would want to know."

"You mean in case he needs a defense attorney?"

"That's not a stretch at this point, but it's also not a certainty."

"Okay, I appreciate the heads up, Bob, but I think if you go after him on this, you'll be barking up the wrong tree while the real killer runs loose. Besides, I could tear up the whole prints angle in about five minutes in court."

"Jack, I'm not saying he's a suspect. He's still nothing more than a person of interest at this point. I am letting you know that I will need to do some more investigation of Paul. I did find out he was angry at his mom."

"Kids get angry at their moms all the time. It doesn't mean they kill them."

"Jack, I'm just letting you know that I can't drop it until I find solid evidence he didn't do it."

"I understand. If there's anything I can do to help, let me know."

"Will do," Bob said, and they ended the call.

Jack called Jenny to let her know about Bob's call. She expressed concern that Bob was continuing to look into Paul as a possible suspect.

"Who else does he have to investigate? It is odd that only Paul's prints were found on the gas and charcoal lighter fluid cans."

"Jack, you're the one who told me you seriously doubted he would do anything like that. You're not going to suspect him now, too, are you?"

"No, of course not. I'm just stating the obvious reason that Bob is looking into Paul as a suspect, or at least a person of interest."

Their call was tense, but by the time Jenny arrived home, her feelings had calmed some.

8

After Bob left his room, Paul lay there and considered his life. The explosion had severed his life in two. He would always have the before and the after. The before wasn't great. He'd been happy when his father and mother divorced, but his life in Denton wasn't exactly the best either, just better.

His mother had refused to let him do much of anything that didn't involve helping out around the house. He had friends, but only in school. When they wanted to get together after school or on weekends, she would always have something he needed to do instead.

His mother had worked at the local elementary school as a teacher's aide. He knew it didn't pay much, and his father never sent them anything, partly because his mother had refused to tell him where they were now. Paul didn't blame her for that. He didn't want his father to know either, but she could have at least made him put money in an account with branches everywhere so she could get to it to help out.

Then again, that could possibly lead to his father finding them, and he knew his mother wouldn't want that to happen. She was afraid of him, and Paul didn't blame her for that, either. Paul himself had been one of his father's punching bags, though his father had been careful not to cause any bruises that were visible when Paul was dressed.

He had flunked gym in sixth grade because he refused to dress out for P.E. many days so people wouldn't see the bruises. This happened so often that Mr. Harris, his P.E. coach who had a sadistic sense of humor, had taken to calling him the bench warmer, but when he said it, he would say it like a name, as in, "Hey, Bench Warmer! At least gather up the basketballs and put them away!" It was humiliating, and he could tell the coach enjoyed doing it.

When they had moved to Denton, he had not been aware that his mom had a friend who lived there. It was one of the girls she hung out with as a teenager. For some reason he didn't know, that relationship had soured. His mom hadn't explained it. She just stopped getting together with her friend as suddenly as she'd moved them to Denton. His mom had an associate's degree in education from a community college in Alabama. She wanted to be a teacher when she was younger. She had planned to get her degree and a teaching certificate, but she had married his dad, and his father didn't want her getting the degree. Now Paul realized it was because his dad felt dumb around her and didn't want her getting an education.

He was thinking more about his past than his future, and he had to force himself to look at what the rest of his life would be like. Part of the reason he avoided thinking of that was he might end up in prison. He hadn't started the fire, but he knew innocence wasn't a guarantee. He'd heard about plenty of people spending years in prison for crimes they never committed.

His future wasn't rosy, even if he didn't go to prison. He had once dreamed of being the romantic ideal for girls, but now he would be shunned by them. What girl would want to date a guy covered with scars and with only one eye?

The answer was none. He would be spending his life alone. He might as well get used to the idea.

Part of him wished he had died in the fire. Then he wouldn't be without a mother. She was a good person despite never letting him do anything fun. And now, he would be working to heal his body for months, if not years. They'd talked to him about physical therapy as well as psychological counseling, so his mind wasn't all that healthy either.

He was suddenly aware he was crying, and he wondered when that had begun. He didn't know how long he had been thinking of his miserable life, but the tears could have started at any point.

One of his eyes was covered with bandages because it was no longer there. He closed the other one and cried himself to sleep.

When he woke, a woman was sitting in the chair beside the bed, reading a book. He'd never seen her before and he wondered who she was and why she was sitting in his room.

He considered trying to go back to sleep but was curious about her.

"Hey," he said. "Who are you?"

She looked up from her book and smiled. The

smile was genuine, pleasant, and warm. "Hi, Paul! I'm Jenny Turner. My husband, Jack, talked to you about coming to stay with us when you're better."

He felt himself smile despite his mood. She seemed nice, like her husband. He prayed they weren't just faking it to get his trust.

"Hi," he said. "I'm Paul Hanson."

She giggled. "Yes, I know."

He could tell she wasn't making fun of him for introducing himself like that when she obviously would know who he was. She was just amused by it. The cruel streak that had been in Mr. Harris wasn't part of who she was. He could tell she already liked him, despite what he would look like when the scars were all that were left of his face and body.

"Jack and I are going to come visit you every weekend at Shands Burn Center," she said. "If one of us can't make it, and that would probably be Jack, the other one will. Jack's work might make it impossible for him to come sometimes, but I will."

"That's nice," he said, then added, "Why would you do that? It's a long way."

She smiled at him again. "Because we want to. We feel you need to have someone who cares about you visit you there."

That made him think. They cared about him?

"You don't even know me."

"Sometimes, you don't need to know someone to care about them. You just need to know how to love for no reason."

Paul didn't understand this. He had never considered that there were people in the world who could love someone without knowing them, and knowing them well.

He said nothing because he could think of nothing to say in response. He sensed she could tell he didn't understand her feelings, but she didn't say anything about that. Instead, she asked what subjects he took in school besides the required ones.

When he told her he took art, she asked what he liked about it.

"I don't know, really," he said. "It's just—I don't know—something I enjoy doing." This thought brought fears he wouldn't be able to draw anymore, so he added, "At least, I did."

"You will again, I'm sure."

"What if my muscles don't want to do what I tell them to do?"

"You'll figure it out," she said. "We always figure out how to do something that's important to us." She told him about a man who had painted pictures while holding the brush in his teeth because he was paralyzed from the neck down.

"But he must have been, you know, abnormal. That's not something other people do."

"He wasn't abnormal, Paul, just determined not to let his handicap stop him from doing what he loved."

Then she gently placed a warm hand on the bandages covering his forehead, as if being careful not to apply too much pressure in case it was painful. "Do you like the feeling of creating something beautiful from nothing? Is that part of why you like art?" she asked.

"I guess so," he said, and felt she was close to

the truth, which he had never really thought about before.

"I'll be sure to get you some art supplies. Maybe you can have a few of them at Shands. I'm sure they'll be fine with that. In fact, they might even have supplies there for people to use for their rehab."

"Thanks."

"Do you like dogs?"

"Yes, but my mom would never let me have one."

"Well, we have a dog. His name is Darrow. He's a black labrador mix that we got from the pound. He likes to play and he's very protective."

"That's a weird name for a dog."

"It's after Clarence Darrow, a famous lawyer."

"Oh. Does he bite?"

"Nope. At least he never has before, and he's old enough he would have by now. By protective, I mean he has this routine where he does things to make sure we're safe at night."

"Like what?"

"At night, he sleeps inside. We have a bed for him, but he doesn't sleep in it. I've watched him, and every night, he will lie down in our bedroom for a little while. Then he gets up and leaves our room. I have followed him and he goes into every room in the house and sniffs around to make sure nobody is in there that shouldn't be. Then he goes to our front door and lies on the floor with half his body against the door and the other half against the wall so anyone coming in will have to push him out of the way."

"Wow!" Paul said. "You taught him to do that?"

"That's the amazing thing. We never taught him that at all. He just does it. See? Protective."

"He sounds like a great dog."

"He is. I'm sure he'll love having you around. Sometimes, Jack and I are too tired to play with him as much as he'd like. Having you around will help. Are you interested in playing with him?"

"Yeah," he said before correcting himself. "I mean, yes, ma'am."

She smiled down at him again, and he could see she was thinking about something, but she wouldn't say what. Her look suggested she was concerned.

"I'm going to be okay, aren't I?" he asked, wondering if she'd been told something he hadn't.

"Yes, of course you are. It's just—well—your treatment and rehab are going to be painful and difficult. I was just thinking how much you have that you have to accomplish, but I'm absolutely certain you will get there. I have no doubt at all. It's just going to be a tough row to hoe."

He changed the subject. "Are you and Mr. Turner approved to have me come live with you? I know it's not something you do without someone saying you can."

"You're right. We have been approved to be your foster parents. They were able to decide quickly because we know a lot of people here in Denton from our work, and we're even known for helping out teens with a group we started called Bridge Over Troubled Water. It's a group for teens who want to talk out their problems with other teens and Jack and me. The people at Social Services know us, and it was mostly a case of completing the paperwork."

"Your husband mentioned Bridge Over Troubled Water. He said it was where kids talk about their problems."

"Yes. Think of it like an Alcoholics Anonymous for teens, but not because of any addiction issues. It's more like teen problems anonymous. They come every week, and we talk about what's bothering them and ways to handle dealing with that."

"Do you want me to join?" Paul felt he would have a world of problems to talk about.

"Certainly. We were going to ask you if you wanted to, but we don't want to force you. If attending isn't voluntary, it doesn't do much good. We learned that the hard way."

"What happened?"

She paused a moment and said, "I'll tell you all that later. Suffice it to say, we learned our lesson and don't force anyone to attend anymore."

"Is what happened too depressing?" he asked.

She laughed. "Yes! You have me figured out already."

They continued talking for nearly an hour more about everything from school to what life would be like when he came to their house to live. When she casually asked if he had a girlfriend, he got quiet for a moment.

"No. Probably never will."

When he saw that his answer upset her, he regretted not giving her a better response.

"Paul, I wouldn't count anything out if I were

you. Never accept limitations on life. Never. They are bindings you form and tie yourself, and they rarely actually exist beyond your own mind."

He was struck by her reply.

"Okay," he said.

They said their goodbyes, and she promised again that they would visit him at Shands.

"Will you stop by here tomorrow?" he asked.

She grinned. "Well, I could, but you're being taken to Shands in the morning. We'll see you there Saturday."

He had one final question. "Who's going to pay for my treatment there? Or my hospital bill here?"

"You're a ward of the state, so they will handle all that. You don't have to worry about that at all.

She left him there with his thoughts. He barely knew her, but he was beginning to understand her comment about being able to love people he barely knew.

The next morning, they loaded him into a vehicle and drove him to Shands Burn Center, which was part of Shands Medical Center in Gainesville.

Paul had learned the extent of his burns. Second and third degree burns covered over 60% of his body. The third degree burns were the ones that were the worst but weren't painful because the nerves had been destroyed.

It would be a long time before Paul felt no physical pain. The emotional pain would last much longer.

9

On Saturday, Jack and Jenny flew to Gainesville. Jack had canceled a meeting to be able to go because he felt that first weekend would be the most important one to visit. Paul would be lonely and in need of some company to help him adjust.

Jack had purchased a Mooney Bravo M20M and had paid for Tom Gordon, his childhood nemesis who had become his investigator and friend, to get a pilot's license. Tom had been flying now for nearly five years and had managed to get his instrument rating. Jack insisted he fly for at least an hour every weekend to keep himself in practice.

Tom flew a fairly direct route, flying over Perry Foley Airport in Perry, Florida, before turning toward Gainesville to the east-southeast. They had a good tailwind and touched down in Gainesville about an hour after taking off from Denton.

After picking up the pre-arranged rental car, they set off for Shands Medical Center, which housed the Shands Burn Center.

Upon arriving, they were directed to the burn center and Paul's room.

"Hey!" Paul said when they came in. "I didn't expect you this weekend!"

Jack said, "We promised to visit every weekend we can, and we were able to this weekend. I'm sure at least one of us will visit you every weekend."

Paul noticed Tom. "Who are you?"

"I'm Tom Gordon. I work for Jack."

"Doing what?"

Tom chuckled. "Mostly, whatever needs doing, but I'm chiefly his investigator. It's nice to meet you, Paul."

"Nice to meet you." Paul smiled behind the bandages but then grew serious as he spoke to Jack and Jenny. "They won't let me see myself in a mirror when they change the bandages. I want to see what I look like."

"I'm sure they will soon," Jenny said. "It's just they need to make sure you're ready. There will be scarring, and your face will look different to you."

"I just want to see."

Jack said, "I'm sure you do, but they'll let you see yourself when they feel you're ready." Changing the subject, he said, "Do you like flying in a plane?"

"I never have."

"Would you like to?"

"Sure."

"Great. I own a plane, you know. It's how we got here today."

"Really? How big is it?"

"It seats four. I figure Jenny and I will have our pilot take us all up for a flight around Denton and Wharton to let you see the sights from a few thousand feet up."

"Wow, you must be rich or something."

Jack smiled at him and shrugged. "Or something."

"Does it go fast?"

"It has a cruising speed of around 200 knots. That's about 230 miles per hour."

"Wow!"

Jenny said, "Maybe we'll come fly you back to Denton when they release you from here."

"That would be awesome!"

They visited for a couple of hours before they had to leave. After they were on the way to the airport again, Jenny said, "I think our visit did him a lot of good."

"I agree. Did me some good, too," Jack added.

Jenny smiled. "Yeah, me too."

Back in Denton, Bob was doing his best to clear Paul of suspicion, but it wasn't working out that way. He had stopped by the remains of the house and was poking around in the charred debris. He wasn't sure what he was looking for, but he felt he would know it if he saw it.

As he was searching, a woman stopped by to chat.

"Investigatin' the fire?" she asked.

"Yes."

"I'm Dora Willings. I live down the road a piece," she said, pointing down the street. "You ask me, that boy did it."

Bob was bent over, looking at the sofa, which Joe Sissler had said was where the fire was started. Hearing this, he straightened and looked the woman in the eye. "Why would you say that?"

He's friends with my boy, Tucker. They don't play together much because Paul's mom wouldn't let him play with a lot of the kids in Denton. Don't know why, though. Must be snooty or something. I don't know her well enough to say. Anyway – yesterday, Tucker told me Paul was aimin' to run away before the fire. Said Paul didn't like his mom or something. Said he'd be better off without her."

"Paul said that?"

"Yeah. Least that's what my boy says."

"Is he home?"

"Tucker? Yeah. He's watchin' cartoons. You need to see him?"

"If you don't mind."

"No problem. Come on." She turned and headed toward her home.

When they entered the small house, Tucker, a boy about Paul's age, was sitting in front of a large-screen television. A cartoon Bob didn't recognize was playing. Bob looked around at the worn furniture that seemed out of place with the nice TV.

"Tucker, this is the detective lookin' into the fire at your friend Paul's house. He has some questions."

"In a minute," Tucker said.

His mother picked up the remote and turned off the TV. "Not in a minute. Right now."

Tucker heaved a sigh and looked at Bob. "What do you want to know?"

"Your mom said you think Paul may have started the fire."

"Yeah."

"Why do you think that?"

Tucker shrugged. "He just didn't want to be here, I guess. Felt she was in the way."

"In the way of what?"

Another shrug. "Just livin', I guess. He told me she left his daddy up in Opelika. He was glad of that, but he said he'd rather be on his own."

"And you think he'd set fire to his house and kill his mom to do that?"

"I don't know. He wasn't happy and he thought he'd be happy without her. That's about all I know."

"Did he ever mention harming his mother before?"

Tucker seemed to consider the question before he answered. "Nah. It's just when the fire happened and I heard it was on purpose, I just figured Paul did it. It was like 'oh, someone started the fire, musta been Paul.' That kind of thing."

Bob looked at Ms. Willings. "How well do you know Paul?"

"Not at all really. I just know he and Tucker hung out some, but not that much really. Like I said, Paul's mama wouldn't let him do much, even play with kids here."

Tucker interrupted. "So, can I get back to my show?"

Ms. Willings tossed him the remote. "Knock yourself out," she said.

When Bob had returned to his car, he phoned Joe. When he answered, Bob asked, "I have a question about that can of charcoal lighter fluid you found at the Hansons."

"What?"

"If my memory is correct, it was nearly full, wasn't it?"

"Yeah. It was almost completely full. Why?"

"I need to find out when and where it was purchased, and if Paul purchased it."

Are you thinking the boy did it?"

Bob felt his stomach turn at his answer. "Yeah. It's starting to look that way."

10

The following Monday when Paul was finally allowed to see himself in a mirror, he wanted to do anything but look at himself afterwards. The bandages were being permanently removed, except the one over his missing eye, so they had no other choice than to let him look. A nurse stood by as he stared into the handheld mirror he was given. He'd had several surgeries to graft new skin onto his face, and what he saw made him think of the old Frankenstein movies or the more modern *Elephant Man*. He recalled the story of the real person named Joseph Merrick. It was a sad story in the movie, with only a few good things happening to the man with inner beauty in an ugly shell of a body.

What he saw in the mirror was unrecognizable. Beyond the surgeries, they had been treating him for his wounds, and the flesh looked raw, the skin swollen and shiny. Scars would cover his face once he was finished with the indignity of suffering the pain of treatments that would not make him even close to good-looking. He'd never considered himself to be particularly handsome, but he had looked better than this. Much better.

Looking into the mirror, he said, "I'll never look like myself again."

"Sure you will," the nurse offered.

"No," he said, looking at her through the blur of

his tears as he tossed the hated mirror onto the bed. "It's just as well. That guy's gone forever anyway."

"Oh, honey. You're still you on the inside."

"You don't understand. People are mean. Nobody will want to be around me now. The other kids will make fun of me. Call me names like 'Elephant Man' or 'Frankenstein.' The only ones who will want to be around me are the ones who love making fun of me." Self-pity welled in him like fire in a sealed volcano. "Or the ones who want to look good by comparison."

"This will be a really big adjustment," the nurse said. "I know it's hard, but there will be plenty of people who won't care what you look like. Besides, some of the scars will diminish over time."

Paul pointed at the burnt tissue that had once been his nose. "Will this one heal? Am I going to grow another nose?"

He suddenly regretted everything he'd ever done, as if he had committed some crime against the world that had led to this.

That afternoon, a doctor he'd not met before came in to talk to him. Paul was sitting in a chair when the doctor entered and smiled down at him. Adjusting his glasses, the man said, "My name is Dr. William Keller. I'm a clinical psychologist. I'm here to help you deal with the changes in your life. They tell me you didn't react well to how you look when your bandages were removed, and I understand that, but your psyche has been injured as well as your body, and it will take time and treatment to get both to heal."

Jenny had mentioned that she was a clinical psychologist, and Paul now wondered if that had not been an accident. Perhaps the state had asked Jack and Jenny to take him in to allow Jenny to work with him as a patient.

"Tell me how this happened to you," Dr. Keller asked.

"I got burned in a house fire."

"How did it happen?"

"They say someone started it."

"Do they know who?"

"No. At least they haven't told me if they do."

"I heard you lost your mother in the fire."

Paul wondered at this. If he knew this much, why was he asking about it?

Paul turned his one good eye to his lap. "Yeah." He looked at his burnt fingers, already beginning to scar, and said, "If you know my mom died in the fire, why are you asking about it? You already know this stuff."

Dr. Keller smiled. "It's something we doctors do to get people to talk about what's bothering them."

"Well, I don't want to talk about it."

"I understand that. It's painful. But I have to tell you that talking about it will help ease the pain."

"How?"

"It puts the events in perspective. As you talk about them, you're better able to deal with the loss and the results." He didn't have to say what the results were that he meant.

Paul shrugged, dismissing the topic.

"Tell you what, why don't you just tell me about yourself. What grade are you in?"

"Seventh."

"How do you like it?"

"It's okay, I guess. The kids are kinda mean, though."

"Have you been bullied there?"

Paul shrugged. "Not yet."

"Do you have any pets?"

"No, but the people I'm going to live with when I get back to Denton have a dog."

They talked more about his future staying with the Turners. As they talked, Paul began to feel better, though not totally okay by any means. It was just that he realized that living with the Turners was the only thing he was looking forward to. They had actually flown in their own plane to visit him. Paul didn't know how much planes cost, but he knew it was a lot, so they weren't poor like his mom. Plus, talking about playing with their dog sounded fun. That was something about dogs and other animals. They didn't care what you look like. It was as if dogs could look under the skin to see what people really were.

"Is it okay if I discuss what we've talked about with Dr. Turner? It's important that she know how things are going with you. If you ever tell me something you don't want me to talk with her about, just say so, and it will remain private."

Paul considered the request and said, "Okay."

When Dr. Keller left the room, he sat in the small office he shared with two other psychologists to make some notes about his first visit with Paul.

He had noted that Paul had perked up when

talking about moving in with the Turners. That would help with his treatment. Keller would only be seeing Paul until he left Shands. He knew Dr. Jenny Turner from an annual convention on psychology and behavior that he attended. She was well-known for her work with adolescents. Paul had been surprised when told Dr. Turner was sort of famous among psychologists and that her book, *My Successes and Failures in Treating Teens: A Memoir of Case Studies*, was well-regarded.

He placed a call to Dr. Turner, finding her phone number in Paul's file as a guardian. He wanted to keep her abreast of Paul's treatment and issues. Even if she didn't treat him, it was best that she be informed. Paul would be living with her and her husband, and she could at least be made aware of anything that could affect Paul's psychological recovery that he might uncover.

When she answered, Dr. Keller filled her in on what had happened in his first meeting with Paul, promising to keep her abreast of any developments. She thanked him, and they disconnected the call, leaving Dr. Keller considering how to approach Paul the next time and Jenny thinking of the psychological difficulties Paul would face.

In his room, Paul considered the visit he'd just had with Dr. Keller. He wasn't sure he wanted to continue talking with him, but he seemed like he just wanted to help. Still, it was painful to talk about his life right now.

He could not sit for long because of the pain from surgeries and the healing process, but lying down could be just as bad. The truth was that just being awake hurt.

When two nurses stepped in to give him his pills and apply an ointment to his burns, he wanted to jump out the window.

The male nurse helped him to the bed and watched him swallow his meds with some water. He left the room for about a half hour and when he returned, he began to apply the ointment. The salve had to be applied over most of Paul's body, including his buttocks where they had removed flesh to do their best to reconstruct his face. He was always embarrassed when that area was exposed during these procedures. He endured the humiliation, doing his best to remind himself that the nurse probably saw bare backsides all the time, and at least it was a male nurse.

When the nurse finally left the room, Paul wore a grimace of pain long after they were gone.

11

Paul lived his life with each day being the same: wake up, breakfast, therapy, lunch, therapy, therapy, therapy, supper, sleep. The only good parts were the meals and sleep. That was the case until one morning when he woke from a dream he'd had that was both pleasant and disturbing.

The pleasant part was what he'd been doing early in the dream. He'd been playing baseball for the team he'd played for in Opelika before his mother moved them to Denton. He had hit a walk-off home run in the dream, something he'd never done in reality, and his teammates had swarmed him. Apparently, they had won the Little League World Series in the dream because of his home run.

Then the dream had veered the way dreams do. Suddenly, his father was among the boys congratulating him. In the dream, that part seemed normal, though his father had never come to any of his games.

His father had told him they needed to leave, and he'd grabbed his gear. The next second, they were in a car, and his father had turned to him and said, "If you'd done that in yesterday's game, you wouldn't have had to play today. You could have done it a game earlier and avoided all the drama of having to win the final game of the series."

This had been more like his father than the one

who never came to a game. No matter what Paul did, it was never good enough.

"But we won!" dream-Paul had said.

The next thing Paul knew in the dream, his father had pulled the car to the side of the road and started lighting cigarettes and burning Paul on his arm. In the dream, Paul had screamed, but he'd done nothing to get away from his father, only sat there to, as his father said, "take your medicine."

That had been a favorite saying of his dad when Paul or Paul's mother had been forced to suffer anything, whether or not it was something his father did to one of them. Any pain suffered was lumped into a category his father called "medicine."

He'd awakened in a cold sweat, the image of his father burning him with a lit cigarette still fresh in his mind. He wondered if he blamed his father somehow for what had happened.

He would talk about the dream to Dr. Keller when he saw him later that day. Dr. Keller came by for at least a few minutes to check on him every Monday, Wednesday, and Friday. Today was Monday. On Mondays Dr. Keller would spend a half hour with Paul, talking about his life and what plans Paul had for when he returned to Denton, especially how he would handle the kids who made fun of his scars. Paul knew that would happen, as did Dr. Keller. They both agreed that people, especially kids Paul's age, could be cruel.

"Sometimes young kids are as cruel as they are because they don't realize the damage they do," Dr. Keller had said.

As he lay there, Paul replayed the dream in his

mind several times to make sure he would remember as many details as he could to share with Dr. Keller, though the memory was uncomfortable.

Around mid-morning, Dr. Keller came in. "How goes it, Paul?" he asked as he pulled up a chair and sat, smiling at Paul as if the whole world was in a happy state.

"I had a bad dream."

"Oh? Do you remember it?"

"Yeah. It was about my father." Paul had mentioned his father before, and Dr. Keller knew their relationship had never been good.

"Tell me what you remember."

After Paul related what had happened, Dr. Keller stopped tapping on his laptop, where he was taking notes, and asked, "Do you think the dream means anything?"

"I don't know. I was hoping you could tell me."

Dr. Keller smiled. "Actually, what a dream means is up to the person who dreamed it. Tell me your thoughts about the dream, what it means to you or what it makes you believe it means."

Paul thought a moment, prompting Dr. Keller to ask, "What was the first thing you thought when you first wondered what it meant?"

"I wondered if I blamed my father for what happened."

"Okay, so the dream upset you quite a bit?"

"Yeah, it did."

"How do you think your father might be responsible for what happened to you? Do you think he started the fire?"

"No. He doesn't know where we live." Paul

thought about that and added, "At least, he didn't know where we lived."

"Why do you think that was your first thought when considering the dream's meaning to you?"

"I don't know. I guess because in the dream he was burning me with a lit cigarette."

"What are some things you do blame your father for?"

Paul considered this. In a tone that suggested he wasn't sure if this had anything to do with the dream, he said, "I blame him for my mom deciding to move. If we hadn't moved, we wouldn't have been in that house or even in Denton. Do you think that might be it?"

"What do you think?"

"I guess it could be."

"Then you might have your answer to the meaning of the dream. You blame your father for being in Denton where you were burned. Your brain used that to manufacture the events in the dream. At least, that sounds like what it might be. Then again, sometimes a dream means nothing at all, but we try to give them meaning."

Paul sighed. "Dreams are weird."

"They certainly can be." Dr. Keller said and returned to his laptop for a moment.

After typing for a minute, he said, "So, let's change the subject. What are you going to say to someone who makes fun of your scars?"

The conversation continued for the remainder of the thirty-minute session. Finally, Dr. Keller stood and said, "Well, I—."

"Have other patients to see today," Paul finished,

interrupting him. It was the same line Dr. Keller used every time the session was ending.

Dr. Keller smiled. "I guess I'm predictable about that."

"Yeah," Paul said, smiling. He felt the skin pull against the scar tissue when he did, reminding him that his smile would never be the same as it was before the fire.

"One last thing. Did the Turners visit you Saturday?"

"Yeah. I think they're really nice to come visit me like that every weekend."

"They care about you. As we agreed, I've spoken to Dr. Turner about your case since you'll be living with her and her husband. She's really looking forward to having you there."

"She's nice."

Dr. Keller smiled. "She's more than nice. I think you'll enjoy being with them."

"Mr. Turner says he's going to take me up in their plane." Paul could feel the skin pulling against the scars again.

"I bet that's going to be fun," Dr. Keller said. "I hope you're not afraid of flying."

"Afraid? No way!"

"Well, you have fun with that."

When a nurse stopped by to check on him later, Paul asked, "How long will it be before I get to leave here?" He had been either in the ICU in Wharton or here for months.

"I'm sure it won't be too long. You can ask your doctor when you see him."

More weeks passed. The only good thing that happened were the visits by Dr. Keller and the Turners. One weekend, Mr. Turner wasn't able to make it, but Ms. Turner came. She explained that Mr. Turner had something come up and he needed to work that weekend.

Paul supposed that was what life was like. Sometimes, your time didn't belong to you.

Finally, Dr. Kellerman, the lead doctor treating his burns, came in one morning, smiled at Paul, and said, "So, you ready to get out of this place?"

For a moment, Paul couldn't believe what the man said and thought he'd misheard it, or maybe the doctor was suggesting going into town for a hamburger or something.

He stared at the doctor for a moment and said, "You mean, like go home?"

"That's precisely what I mean. Today's your last day. We've notified your guardians, and they're flying in tomorrow to take you back to Denton."

Paul was shocked at the sudden tears that burned and slid down his cheeks. He was scared of going back to Denton, but he was also thrilled by it.

Later that day, despite it being a Thursday, Dr. Keller stopped by to say goodbye. Paul hugged him and thanked him for everything, and Dr. Keller stayed for about five minutes.

Smiling down at Paul, he said, "Well, I have" and paused.

"Other patients to see," Paul finished, smiling.

When Dr. Keller left, Paul was alone with his thoughts. They were good thoughts for the most part. He felt prepared for the return to as normal a life as he could hope for.

Unfortunately, the normalcy didn't last long.

12

Jack and Jenny were all smiles as they entered the hospital room for the last time. Paul returned their smiles as best he could and gathered what few belongings he had.

Before leaving, he glanced in the mirror at the face that was becoming more familiar with each day. Scars were evident over most of the image that gazed back at him, but the doctors had done their best to help his appearance. He would be dealing with physical therapy for a long time, and he would get a prosthetic eye, but at least he was alive.

"Did y'all come here in the plane?" he asked the Turners as they waited for the elevator.

"Yep," Jack said. "And you get to sit in the co-pilot's seat."

"Really?"

"Really."

When they arrived at the building that served private pilots, Tom was waiting for them.

"Are you ready to help me fly?" he asked Paul as they moved out to where the plane was parked.

Paul grinned. "I don't know how to fly a plane."

"Then I suppose this will be your first lesson."

"Sure," Paul said, though he thought Tom was joking.

Paul sat in awe as the plane picked up speed and rose from the runway, defying gravity as it soared up from the ground. A floating sensation took over the moment they were airborne. "Cool!" he said as he watched the ground sink below them.

When they reached cruising altitude, Tom looked at Paul. "You ready to take the controls?"

"You mean you were serious?"

"Of course."

"But what do I do?"

"Three things. Steer where I tell you to steer, don't push on the yoke—that's what the steering wheel in a plane is called—and keep your feet off of the pedals."

"What do the pedals do?" He wondered if maybe they would stop the plane midflight or something, the way brakes in a car would.

"They control the rudder. Not knowing what you're doing could cause a real problem."

"Is it hard to steer?"

"No," Tom said and laughed. "It's easy. Now, landing is another story. That takes a lot of practice. But up here, you have a lot of room. No planes right beside you the way it is when driving a car. Now, put your hands on the yoke and hold it firmly, but not too tightly. You don't want your muscles to wear out or cramp."

Jack and Jenny watched from the rear seats as Paul took the yoke in his hands. Tom released his grip, and Paul was flying the plane.

When Tom noticed that Paul was spending too much time looking at the instrument panel, he said, "Look at what's outside the plane, not what's in it. Nothing in here can hurt you, but there's plenty out there that can."

Paul followed the advice and watched the world slipping by beneath them.

You want to look mostly at what's in front of you, but you also want to glance to each side every ten seconds or so."

"What am I looking for?"

"Anything that might come into your flight path. A flock of birds, though you won't see any up this high, or another plane, which you certainly could see."

After a moment, Tom said, "Okay, just glance at the digital compass." He reached out and pointed at it.

Paul looked at it. "Okay, what about it?"

"What is your heading?"

"It said 282."

"Good, that means you're heading just north of due west, which is 270. We're going to turn a bit farther to the north, to a heading of 295 degrees. You ready?"

"Yeah."

"When I say, I want you to turn the yoke just a little bit to your right. But only a little bit. You don't want to turn hard. That could cause the plane to roll."

"Okay," Paul said.

"As you turn, glance at the compass. Don't stare at it. When you see it hit around 290, turn the yoke back to level."

"Okay, when do I turn?"

"You can do it now."

Paul gently turned the yoke to his right, and the plane tilted, banking in that direction. When he glanced at the compass, it was already past 290. It was passing 296. By the time the plane stopped turning to the north, their heading was 302. "Oops," he said after he had leveled the yoke.

"That's okay. You did fine for a beginner," Tom said. "Just nudge the yoke a little bit to your left, but only for about two seconds."

"Now?"

"Yes, now."

Paul did this, and the plane leveled out at 294. "I'm not at 295," Paul said.

"That's fine. You've just made your first instrument turn. Good job!"

Jack spoke up. "Having fun, Paul?"

"Yeah!"

After a few minutes, Tom took the controls. He executed a few maneuvers to show what the plane could do, and Paul was fascinated.

His fascination grew when Tom was bringing the plane in for a landing at the airport in Denton. He listened as Tom communicated with the tower. When he was done, he said, "The wind is from the east, so we have to go around and land into the wind."

Flying past the airport, Tom turned the plane perpendicular to the line of the runway before turning to line the plane up with the end of it.

Paul watched in wonder as the end of the runway passed beneath the plane before they settled gently down to the ground.

After they taxied to the hangar where Jack paid for a space to house the plane out of the weather, they climbed out.

When they arrived at the home where he would be living for at least the time being, Paul felt his jaw drop. He'd never seen such a beautiful house. It seemed far too large for only two people.

"This is your house?" he asked Jack as they entered the driveway.

"Well, now it's your house as well."

Jack and Jenny took Paul to his bedroom to allow him to settle in and smiled at his response to seeing it. "This is huge!"

After he had put his things away, Paul came downstairs to find Jack and Jenny had gone outside into their back yard. It faced the Gulf of Mexico, and a light breeze wafted across the small lawn.

When Paul opened the sliding glass doors that led outside, a large dog bounded to him, sniffing Paul and offering his head for scratching. Jack tossed a tennis ball, and the dog ran after it, a look of sheer glee on his face.

When the dog returned to Jack with the ball, Jack pointed at Paul and said, "Give." The dog immediately ran over to Paul and dropped the ball at his feet before smiling up at him.

"Wow! He's a smart dog."

Jenny laughed. "Sometimes too smart for his own good."

"And his name's Darrow?"

"Yes."

Paul bent down and nuzzled him. "Hi, Darrow!" Darrow bent down and touched the ball with his nose. Paul laughed. "Okay, boy!"

Jack and Jenny watched as Paul played with the

dog, tossing the ball and rubbing Darrow's head, face, and back. They were both obviously in love with each other.

"You hungry?" Jack asked.

"Yeah. What are we having for lunch?"

"I figured we would go out for lunch. You know, celebrate your first day with us. But only if you feel up to it."

"Cool!" Paul said. He looked tired but excited to eat out.

Jack drove to Crabby's Shack, a small place that overlooked the harbor.

As they entered, a few heads turned to look at them and Paul could feel the stares of people who hadn't expected someone covered in burn scars to eat with them today.

As they sat at their table, Paul did his best to ignore the stares. After a few minutes, most of the people had turned to their food and were ignoring him, but not all of them. One table nearby was occupied by a family with two kids. The younger one, a girl, looked to be around seven. She was staring at him with what could only be described as a look of horror and distaste. Her nose wrinkled at the sight of him, as if he smelled bad.

He glanced at Jack and Jenny, and he could tell they were noticing the stares as well. Jenny leaned over to him and whispered, "People, especially children, aren't used to seeing someone who was burned badly. I know it will be hard, but you have to learn that some people will stare at you and you need to ignore them for their ignorance and rudeness. Some people just lack the ability to see below the surface of others. Children are more curious than anything."

As she said this, the young girl at the nearby table said, "What happened to him?" She was speaking to her mother.

The woman glanced over at Paul, blushed, and leaned over to her daughter, speaking too low to be heard. The young girl gave Paul a final look and turned back to her food.

Paul ordered and ate his food, but he didn't enjoy any of it. He wondered for perhaps the thousandth time what kind of reaction he would get when he returned to school.

He was fairly certain it wouldn't be a good one.

13

Months before Paul's release from Shands, Detective Bob Ebert had continued his investigation into the arson at the Hanson home. He'd heard that Paul was back in Denton, and this prompted him to look over his notes he'd gathered while looking into the arson. Paul had become his prime suspect, his only suspect since nobody else had shown up as a possibility, and he was waiting for Paul's return to continue with the investigation. He needed to ask him some questions before proceeding further.

He considered what he'd discovered before he had paused his work until Paul's return. After talking to Tucker Willings, Paul's neighbor, Bob began trying to find out if Paul had purchased a can of charcoal lighter fluid. He started with the convenience store nearest Paul's home. After showing his badge, he held out a photo of Paul taken from his school's yearbook.

"No, I don't recognize him, but I only work weekdays while my kids are in school, so I don't see many kids in here. You could stop by to ask the other clerks. Gretchen and Zach work early evenings and weekends, mostly. They might have seen him."

Bob indicated the camera aimed at the cash register area. "Do you have footage I can look at to see if he was here?"

"Yes, but you'd have to talk to the manager about that."

"If the other employees can't help me, I might have to do that."

"Like I said, you'd have to get with the manager."

"Sure. Thanks for your help."

Bob stopped in that evening and met Gretchen, who took one look at the picture and said, "Yeah, I've seen that kid in here. Lots of times. He usually buys a soda and a candy bar, but sometimes other things."

"Do you remember if he ever bought charcoal lighter fluid?"

Gretchen looked surprised. "Yeah, he did! I figured he was getting it to cook on a grill. I remember asking him if he needed charcoal, but he said no."

There was no grill at the home, and they'd also found no charcoal at the scene. This alone made Bob curious. Why would a kid Paul's age be buying charcoal lighter fluid if his family had no charcoal? To set his house on fire? That seemed the obvious choice until another explanation surfaced, but Bob could not imagine what that explanation could be.

That was one of the things he wanted to ask Paul, but Paul had been sent to Shands Burn Center by that time. He had asked his captain if he could go speak with Paul, but the captain had said Paul wasn't going anywhere, so Bob had bided his time.

He checked notes he had on another interview with one of Paul's school friends. He'd also interviewed his teachers. While the teachers were more careful about what they said about Paul, the friend, Leon, was very open about Paul's anger at his mother and his desire to run away.

One note from that interview struck him. Leon had said, "Paul wanted to run off but was afraid his mom would find him and bring him home. Paul felt like he should be able to make his own decisions."

Bob considered how independent a fourteen-year-old would have to feel to consider running away and believing he was capable of being self-sufficient. He supposed that on many occasions Paul had been left to his own devices for food and other necessities as he grew up. If he had made his own decisions in life for a lot of his childhood, he would think he was capable of being on his own.

Still, Bob's instinct told him Paul was a good kid and incapable of setting fire to the home where he lived. Besides, setting a fire was not a sure way to kill someone unless that person had been rendered unconscious before starting the fire, not to mention Paul would have set the fire and left the house.

Either that, or Paul wanted to kill both himself and his mother, but that didn't seem plausible either.

Then again, Paul was still a kid and may not have been thinking straight when he set the fire. He may have assumed he could get some clothes before the fire got out of control. Or maybe he didn't think of that until after the fire was lit, and he returned to his bedroom to hastily pack a few things and the explosion happened. It was possible that he went to the room, gathered a few things, and found he could no longer get out through the door and was trying to go through the small window in his bedroom when the explosion happened.

This theory of what happened held a lot of suppositions, but it was the only thing he could come up with, based on the evidence he had so far.

Now, Paul had returned to Denton and was available to speak to, and Bob could try to clear up some of these issues.

Bob called Jack's office and waited while being connected to him. When Jack answered, Bob said, "Jack, Bob Ebert. I need to talk to Paul about a few things. Can you arrange that?"

"Yes. What do you need to ask him?"

"Just a few items that need to be cleared up. When can I talk to him?"

After a moment, Jack said, "This is his first day back at school, and I'd prefer not to do it today, but then again, I'm not sure tomorrow would be any better, so we might as well get it over with. How does this afternoon sound? I can meet you with him somewhere, or you can drop by the house."

"What time?"

"How does 5:30 sound?"

Bob smiled. "Sounds fine to me. I'll see you at your house at 5:30."

After disconnecting the call, Bob made some notes about what he wanted to ask Paul. The main points were the can of charcoal lighter fluid, his relationship with his mother and reports he wanted to run away, and the precise details as to what happened the night of the fire.

The case was mostly circumstantial, but he'd seen circumstantial cases when the evidence implicated someone enough to make an arrest. He just didn't like arresting a person Paul's age without more to go on.

Bob realized he was hoping Paul would have good answers to his questions. Doing poorly with the interview would only raise Bob's suspicions to near certainty.

He'd prefer finding out that a mentally disturbed bum had decided to set a house on fire.

Bob arrived at the Turner home at 5:30 and rang the doorbell. Jack opened the door seconds later.

When Bob entered the family room where Paul sat, he was taken aback by the sight. Scars covered his face, and a patch lay over where his eye once had been. His ears were malformed from scar tissue as well. Bob imagined how his schoolmates had reacted, which may have been the reason for Paul's sad mood. This would have been his first day back in school after his lengthy stay at Shands.

Bob smiled at Paul and offered his hand to shake. Paul seemed to take it reluctantly without looking into Bob's eyes, one of the surest signs that someone was feeling guilty before questions were asked.

Or maybe his reaction was just an extension of how he'd been treated by his classmates. Bob wasn't sure which, so he began with a question to help him figure out if that were the case.

"I understand this was your first day back in school after the fire. How'd it go?"

Paul shrugged, and Bob glanced at Jack, who more or less mimicked Paul's shrug.

"Come on, you can tell me. Did your schoolmates react badly to your scars?"

Paul picked at a piece of lint on his pants and shrugged again. "Yeah."

"I know it doesn't seem like it now, but they'll get used to it. Soon, you'll just be the same kid they knew when you left."

"I guess."

Bob chalked up Paul's reluctance to look him in the eye as a result of his day and moved on.

"Paul, I have a few questions I want to ask you about the fire and a few other things I've discovered while you've been away. Can you answer them for me?"

Paul shrugged. "I guess."

"Tell me again what happened the night of the fire. Begin with your last conversation with your mother." Bob had asked him this question before without requesting an earlier starting point. Basically, all he knew from that night was that Paul had figured out he couldn't leave through his bedroom door and had started to climb out the window when the explosion occurred.

Paul's reluctance to talk about that night was palpable, but it was necessary Bob get this added information.

Looking mostly at his lap and the floor, Paul said, "She was watching TV. Some program my mom liked. I was playing a game on her phone. Yahtzee. When the show ended, she said it was time for bed, so I told her I wanted to play a little longer. Of course, she said no."

"How did that make you feel?"

"Her saying no?"

"Yes. Were you angry?"

"Not really. It's what she always did. I knew when I asked she wouldn't let me."

"Were there a lot of things you wanted to do that she wouldn't let you do?"

"I guess."

"Like what?"

Jack watched this interchange and wondered where it was leading. He expected Paul to be possibly suspected in starting the fire and hoped this wasn't related to that.

"Like she wouldn't let me go camping with some friends. That kind of thing." Paul's voice took on a slight pleading quality. "All my friends were able to do stuff like that, but my mom always said no."

"And that made you angry?"

Paul must have suspected the true meaning of the question, so he said, "All kids get angry at their parents."

"Were you angry she left your dad? I understand she didn't want him to find out where you'd gone."

"Where did you hear that?"

"Around. I've talked to a lot of people since the fire. It's part of the investigation. So, how about it? Did that make you angry?"

"No. My dad was a—well, he was not a good person."

"So you didn't want to go live with him?"

"No."

"Have you tried to get in touch with him?"

"No. Why would I?"

"Just asking." Bob moved on, changing the line

89

of questioning. "Why would you buy a can of charcoal lighter fluid?"

At this point, Jack knew where this was headed and interrupted. "Bob, do you think Paul had anything to do with this fire? That's insane."

Bob looked up at Jack from where he sat in his chair. "Just trying to find some answers, Jack."

"How do you know he bought lighter fluid?"

"His prints were found on a can near the rubble of the house after the fire." He left out the part of talking to the clerk at the convenience store. He wanted to see if Paul would mention it first.

"That doesn't mean he bought it – or used it to start the fire."

Paul was now looking directly at Bob's face. "You think I started the fire?!"

"I'm not sure what to think. I'm just trying to figure out what happened. I do know that the fire was arson, and I am just searching for answers. Why would you buy a can of charcoal lighter fluid?"

"No more questions, Bob. I just assigned myself as Paul's attorney. He won't answer another question until I've talked to him. Let's reschedule this for another time."

"Okay, Jack. Could you bring him to the station tomorrow after school?"

"Will you be arresting him?"

"With the scant evidence I have now? Of course not."

"So you're waiting for him to incriminate himself before Mirandizing him, right?"

"It's not like that, Jack."

"Isn't it? I'll have him at your office tomorrow afternoon at four. He'll answer the questions I allow him to."

"Alright. Then I'll see you both tomorrow."

"Goodbye, Bob."

Bob left the Turner home. As his suspicions grew, he drove to his office to make notes of what little he'd learned from the too brief interview.

Or should I call it an interrogation? he thought.

14

After Bob had left, Jack sat down beside Paul. He thought for a moment about how to begin this conversation. He didn't want Paul believing he had done anything wrong.

"Paul, I think we need to talk about some things. Is that okay?"

"I guess."

"Detective Ebert seems to think you might have had something to do with the fire that burned down your house. He was going to ask about a can of charcoal lighter fluid. Did you buy one?"

Paul seemed to consider the answer before answering. "Yes, but I didn't use it to start the fire."

"Where did you buy it?"

"At the 7-11 near the house."

"Why did you buy it?"

Paul's head ducked. "I'd rather not say."

"I'm now officially your attorney. You can tell me anything about this, and I can't tell anyone what you said."

"Don't I have to pay you something first?"

"Not if it's pro bono. That means I'm working for free." He paused a moment. "Okay, let's make it official." Standing, Jack went to his study and returned with a form. He showed it to Paul. It was a contract for legal services.

Taking a pen, Jack filled out the important parts, Paul's name and address and checked a few boxes.

When he was done, he passed the contract to Paul. "Sign here," he said, handing the pen to Paul.

After some consideration, Paul signed the form making Jack his attorney.

"Okay. Now, whatever you say is confidential."

"Like with Jenny?"

"Yes." He gazed at Paul and asked, "So, why did you buy the charcoal lighter fluid?"

Taking a deep breath, Paul said, "I was planning to run away from home and needed something to help me build fires when I stopped for the night."

"Are you still planning to run away?"

"No. I like it here."

"Why did you want to run away before?"

"My mom. Well, she wasn't that nice a lot of the time."

"How so?"

"She—" He paused a moment. "Well, she would never let me do anything fun."

"Paul, a lot of mothers are like that. It's no reason to run away."

"It was more than that."

"I'm listening."

"I had to do everything. I had to clean the house, do the laundry, cook the meals. Everything."

"You cooked?"

"Well, mostly I heated things up in the microwave, like frozen dinners, but I knew how to cook stuff like Hamburger Helper. Simple stuff. Or I would heat up hot dogs. Nothing like a big meal or something, but we never had a big meal."

"Okay, I can understand that you didn't appreciate those things along with not being allowed to have fun with friends, but still, is that worth running away? You'd still be having to do all the cooking and cleaning, but you wouldn't have a microwave to make it easier. Were you planning to go back to Opelika to be with your dad?"

"No. He was worse than she was. He'd hit me a lot." He pulled up one pants leg and pointed where scars were covering his calf. "That's from the fire at the house, but before that, I had a scar from where my dad burned me with a cigarette."

Jack considered his own parents and was suddenly thankful they were not worse. His parents were self-absorbed alcoholics, but they were not abusive. Mostly, they were just neglectful, causing Jack to have to raise himself most of the time. Hank, the man who took him in when his parents died in a car wreck, had become the best father he could have hoped for. Jack promised himself that he would become a Hank to Paul, whose life so far had been miserable if what he said was true.

Paul's mother was mostly unresponsive to the needs of a kid his age. Friendships and being able to hang out with friends was important at his age, even crucial in his social development.

His father, though, had been cruel beyond measure.

"Okay, I understand and believe you would not have returned to your father, but what about the life with your mom? Couldn't you have tried talking to her? Getting her to understand your need to have friends and hang out with them sometimes?"

"No. She never listened. And she had started hitting me, too, like my dad had." Then more to himself than to Jack, he added, "At least she wasn't burning me with her cigarettes. Not yet, anyway."

Jack had a sudden understanding of Paul's life. He was feeling trapped, and a trapped animal will do anything to escape.

Of course, anything also included burning down a house.

"Look me in the eye, Paul." He waited until Paul was looking directly into his gaze. "Did you set the fire that burned down your house?"

Normally, attorneys didn't want to know the answer to the question regarding guilt or innocence when defending someone. Knowing could lead to ethical problems later. The most obvious of these was to know a client committed the crime for which he or she is accused and being forced by a trial's circumstances to put the client on the stand. Allowing a client to knowingly commit perjury was a serious breach of ethics.

Still, he felt he had to know in this case. Paul was more than a client. He was his foster child. If Paul admitted to the crime, Jack would do his best to get him help instead of jail time.

Keeping his gaze locked on Jack's, Paul said, "No. That's one thing I would never do."

Jack saw the tears welling in the boy's eyes. Reaching out, he pulled Paul into an embrace that lasted for nearly a minute.

He held Paul as the tears became sobs.

"Are they going to arrest me?" Paul asked, his face buried into Jack's shoulder.

"I don't know, but if they do, I'm here to help. They will need more to go on than a can of lighter fluid with your prints on it, especially with a viable explanation for that."

Jack hoped he sounded surer of himself than he felt. He knew Paul would likely be the only suspect, and the prints didn't help. He prayed they would find nothing else incriminating.

The next day, precisely at four o'clock, Jack and Paul entered the Denton police station and told the person at the desk they were there to see Detective Ebert. After a call to the detective, Jack and Paul went to the detective squad room and were met by Bob.

Rising, Bob extended his hand and shook hands with them both, saying, "I apologize if yesterday didn't go well. I'm just trying to find out what happened."

"I understand," Jack said. "I think you'll agree Paul had a legitimate reason for buying the charcoal lighter fluid, even if it wasn't a good one."

They followed Bob to an interrogation room and sat across a table from the detective. Bob began by asking, "So, Paul, why did you buy the charcoal lighter fluid?"

"I was planning to run away from home and needed something to help me start campfires."

Bob continued looking at Paul for a moment before continuing. "Did you have an argument with your mother about anything that night?"

"No."

"Were you angry at her for any reason?"

"I don't remember if I was. Maybe. It's not like I was never mad at my mom for anything."

Bob wasn't sure he believed Paul didn't remember. Tragedies often caused people to keep considering what had happened just prior to them in the belief they may have been able to prevent it. Still, he couldn't force him to change his answer.

"Why did you want to run away?"

"Just wanted to be on my own."

At this point, Jack leaned close to Paul and whispered, "You need to tell him everything, Paul."

Paul looked at Jack with surprise, glanced at Detective Ebert, and leaned close to Jack. "He might think I did it."

Jack said to Bob, "Give us a moment."

Bob stood up. "I needed to stretch my legs anyway. I'll be back in a minute." He closed the door behind him as he left.

When they were alone, Jack said, "Paul, if you don't tell him the truth and he finds out the truth later, it will be much worse. He's been looking into this for months. I'm sure he has spoken to some of your friends, and if they know something, they will have told him. It's best to be honest with him about your relationship with your mother. Besides, most kids don't get serious about running away unless they have a reason that seems good to them, at least."

"What if he suspects me?"

"Paul, he already does. Otherwise, he wouldn't be asking these questions."

"Then won't my answers make him suspect me more?"

"Lies will make him suspect you more than the truth would. You aren't guilty of arson, so tell him the truth. I wouldn't volunteer more than what he asks for, though. Believe me, he's asking questions about your relationship that he almost certainly already knows the answers to. Be honest. If the questions go where I don't want them to go, I'll stop the interview."

"Okay."

After a moment, Bob re-entered the interrogation room. "So, how about it?" he asked Paul, resuming his seat.

Paul told him about how miserable he had been living with his mother at the time of the fire and why he wanted to run away. When he was finished, he looked at Jack, who nodded approval.

Then Bob asked Paul to recount again what happened that night after he went to bed.

"I woke up to the sound of a dog barking. I could smell smoke and stuff, and figured out the house was on fire. I couldn't go out the door because of the fire, so I went to my window. I was opening it to crawl out when the explosion happened. The next thing I remember was being in the hospital."

Bob had watched Paul closely during this short monologue. It was short and to the point, with no real details other than the bare events that had happened. If he was lying, he hid it well. When being interrogated, most liars go into too many details, as if hoping that adding them would make their story more plausible. Paul barely mentioned any details.

Standing, Bob said, "Okay, that's all. I have to say I am totally flummoxed by this case. It was obviously arson, but I don't know who could have done it." Turning to Paul, he said, "How about you? Do you have any ideas or thoughts on who could have set your house on fire?"

"No, except maybe my dad. But he had no idea where we were. Still doesn't as far as I know."

"Why would your dad do it?" Bob asked, knowing the answer but seeing what Paul would say.

"He hates my mom." Pausing, he added, "And me, too, I guess."

"Would he be capable of doing something like that?"

"Yes. He was actually the first person I thought of when you told me it was arson, but it's impossible since my mom made sure he didn't know where we were. Anyway, I would think he would just show up at the house and kill us instead of setting the house on fire. I mean, if I'd woken up three minutes earlier, we'd probably both be alive."

Bob considered the truth of that statement. It was odd how things worked sometimes. Paul was right. Three minutes would have resulted in life for his mother and no injuries for Paul.

"What kind of steps did she take?"

"We left when he was on a fishing trip with his friends. We've never been here before, and she didn't let anyone know we were leaving, not even her own mom."

"Did you tell anyone?"

"I didn't know we were leaving until I got home from school. We were on the road before she told me. She didn't even tell me where we were going until we were in Montgomery."

"And you didn't contact any friends from your hometown?"

"No."

"And to your knowledge, your mother never told anyone where you were?"

"I know she didn't."

Bob considered this and wondered if the man had still somehow found his wife and son. It was worth looking into, at least.

"Didn't she tell her mother?"

"She doesn't talk to her mom. I've never met her and don't even know where she is."

"What about your dad's mom?"

"His folks are dead. He has a brother somewhere, but I don't know where. I've never met him either."

"What's your dad's name?"

Paul's eyes widened. "Are you going to tell him where I am?"

"Your mother has a restraining order?"

"That's what she said."

"And she got full custody of you in the divorce?"

"Yes, at least that's what she told me."

"Then I'll do my best to keep him from finding out, but there's no guarantee."

"Okay, his name is Howard."

"Thank you, Paul," Bob said. Bob shook hands once again with Jack and Paul as they left. He had a call to make to the Opelika PD.

15

As he drove home, Jack cast a few glances toward Paul as he stared silently out the window of the car. He'd seemed depressed since school had started, and this new situation would only add to his problems.

"Are you okay?" Jack asked, hoping to start the conversation he'd wanted to have for days.

Paul shrugged. "Yeah."

"You know Jenny and I are here to talk to as well as supply a dog to play with." He hoped the humor would help lighten the mood that hung heavy around them.

"I know."

"I can tell more is bothering you than what we just encountered with Detective Ebert."

"It's fine."

After a moment, Jack said, "I'd believe that if you weren't acting so sad and depressed."

Paul turned to him, and Jack could see the tears that threatened to roll down his cheeks.

"Mostly, it's school. Nobody likes me there."

"What about the friends you had before?"

"They don't want to be with me anymore."

"Have you asked them why?"

"I don't have to. It's because of how I look now. All the scars." He touched what remained of his right ear. "My whole head is just one big scar. I'm too ugly to want to hang around with."

"I know people can be judgmental about such things. Looks, especially to kids your age, are more important than they should be. Good looking people are often not very nice on the inside. Looks mean nothing."

"Tell that to the kids at school."

"Actually, I think they already know that, but they've been socially conditioned to mistreat people they consider physically less than the ideal."

"You mean ugly people, don't you?"

"You've heard the saying, 'beauty is in the eye of the beholder'?"

"That's easy for beautiful people to say."

"Well, the opposite is also true, so is the lack of beauty."

"What are you saying? How does that help me?"

"If you let people see the beauty of who you are on the inside, they will begin to see the beauty of who you actually are. You aren't the body you inhabit. You're the person who lives inside that body. It will take time for them to notice, but I think they will eventually. If you stop letting their opinions of your looks bother you, they will see that and possibly change their opinion of you."

"Name one person who sees who I am on the inside."

"I can name two easily. Jenny and me."

"Y'all don't count."

"Why not?"

"Because, you're like my parents now. Parents have to be that way with their kids."

"Tell you what. You remember Jenny and I talking about Bridge Over Troubled Water?"

"Yeah."

"I am fairly certain that if you come to a meeting, you'll find there are kids your age or close to it that don't care what you look like on the outside."

"I doubt that."

"Only one way to find out," Jack said, pulling into his driveway.

"And what if they react to me the way everyone else does?"

"We can cross that bridge when we get to it. In the meantime, our group can be your bridge over the troubled water of your life right now."

Paul began climbing out of the car. "Okay. I'll give it a try. It can't be any worse than school. But why can't I get a private tutor like I had at Shands? You guys seem to have enough money to hire one for me."

"That's true, but sooner or later you have to learn how to live in this world with other people and figure out how to make them accept you for who you are. That can't be done very well if you never interact with kids you age."

As they entered the house, Paul said, "Whatever." He went into his bedroom, leaving Jack alone to wonder how to get through to him.

He figured that the kids at BOTW were used to dealing with problems that had led them to join their group and would be more accepting of someone whose current problem was something he couldn't help. Yes, Paul had some other problems, not the least of which was that he was apparently being investigated for arson that had taken his mother's life. Paul, though, was much more worried about his social life, which was typical of teens his age. Jack had had only two real friends when he was Paul's age—Lee and Roger. Beyond that, his classmates had ignored or bullied him, and that list had included the person who grew up to be Detective Bob Ebert, or Huggy Bob as they had called him for his penchant for hugging the girls in their class.

Bob had grown up to be a good person, as had his chief tormenter from those days, his investigator Tom Gordon, who'd gone by Tommy back then.

It occurred to him that Paul might think that people remained basically who they were throughout their lives: good kids became good adults and bad kids became bad adults. The idea that people could change over their lifetime had probably not occurred to him yet. It was a typical belief among children and teenagers, as if lives were set in stone from the beginning.

He himself had changed drastically over his lifetime. Had he never met Hank and Mrs. Dawson—or even Bones, his first dog—he likely would have ended up much more like the young Tommy Gordon as an adult. He had definitely been headed down the wrong path back then.

Going to Paul's bedroom door, he knocked and waited to be invited in. When Paul said he could come in, he entered.

"I think we're not quite through with our conversation."

"Oh?" Jack could tell Paul wasn't happy about that.

"You remember Tom, the guy who flew the plane when we brought you back here?"

"Yes."

"What have I told you about him?"

"Only that he's your investigator and your pilot."

"Well, he's more than that. He's a friend, but he didn't used to be. In fact, when we were kids, he was my worst enemy, as well as the worst enemy of a lot of kids. A real bully."

"Really?"

"Yes, really. He actually tried to poison my dog once."

Paul stared with his one eye, obviously having difficulty squaring these two versions of Tom. "Why would he do that?"

"As I said, he was a bully back then. But he's changed. I would trust him with my life now."

"What made him change?"

"That's easy. Love. Love from me. Love from Jenny. Love from the woman he married and the children they had."

"You showed you loved him?"

"Mostly, I showed him he was worthy of love. He never felt worthy before. You see, a lot of people change a great deal over the course of their lives. We start down one path but find a better one. The same thing happened with me. My parents were alcoholics, but when I met my first dog and, because of that, a man named Hank Moreland, I ended up seeing that I had a better path to take. I wasn't on a good one before that."

"So I guess you're telling me that the kids at my school can change?"

"Yes."

"How?"

"It takes caring on your part and patience. Lots of patience."

"What kind of caring?"

"Caring about them, regardless of how they treat you now."

"What if they don't change?"

"That's where the patience comes in. I'm sure that once you show you are still the same kid they knew before, they will come around. People will actually forget what you used to look like. That will happen quickly."

Paul sighed. "How do I start?"

"Just be yourself, and when you see someone in need of something that you can provide, step up and provide it, even if they don't want you to at first. Your feelings will get hurt. That I can promise you. But in the end, you will feel better about yourself. You can start by coming to the BOTW meetings."

"Okay."

After Jack left his room, Paul lay there, thinking about what he'd said. He recognized that people might not react well to his attempts, but then they already didn't react well to his being in the same room with them.

He considered various ways he could help people and wasn't sure it would work, but he wanted to do it anyway. At least he would try.

He looked forward to the BOTW meeting. Maybe some of them would be his friend, even if nobody else would. They were his age, so they probably went to his school. He hoped they would accept him. Jack seemed to think they would, but Paul wasn't sure. The pressure from everyone else at school to ignore him or worse would be a big part of whether or not it would work.

That evening as they had supper, both Jenny and Jack noticed Paul seemed to feel better about himself.

They prayed that would last.

16

Bob Ebert found the number for the Opelika Police Department and placed a call. It was answered by someone at their switchboard, who took his information and told him he would receive a callback to the Denton PD phone number within a half hour. Bob knew that was more to verify they were talking to a real detective than anything else.

When the call came through from an Opelika PD detective about fifteen minutes later, Bob introduced himself and said, "I'm looking for information on someone who lives there. A fellow by the name of Howard Hanson."

"Do you have an address?"

"No. I just know he lives there."

"Why do you need him? Do we need to pick him up?"

"Actually, I'm not sure yet. His son was badly burned in a fire that was arson, and I just want to find out a few things about him."

"When did that happen?"

"Months ago."

"And his father doesn't know?"

"No."

"How old is the kid?"

"Fourteen. I'm told the mother divorced Mr. Hanson, who doesn't have visitation rights. The mother received full custody."

"Hang on a minute. Can I put you on hold?"

"If it's not too long."

"Okay, I'll be right back with you."

After two minutes, the detective he was speaking with came back on the line. "Sorry to make you hold. I wanted to do some searches. I found the divorce records on the clerk of court's information website for public records. She got sole custody of the kid, though he was ordered to pay some child support. I have no idea if he was paying it."

"That's doubtful," Bob said.

"I do know who he is, though. He's been a guest of our facility a few times."

"What for?"

"B and E, public intoxication, minor assault. Nothing major."

"B and E isn't that minor."

"According to what we have on file, it was related to intoxication. He broke into a store to sleep one off once. The owner was fine with Mr. Hanson paying for the repairs, so it didn't go to court."

"Have you had any other crimes he might have committed but you were unable to arrest him for?"

"Like?"

"Arson."

There was silence on the other end, and Bob waited, hoping the silence was because he'd guessed right.

"As a matter of fact, we had a problem with that about a year ago. Four fires, all arson."

"When did they stop?"

There was a silence while the detective checked some details on his computer. "About eleven months ago, nearly a year."

Bob checked his notes. That was about the time that Paul and his mother had left Opelika. "What kind of structures?"

"Two empty houses, a local bar, and the school."

This made Bob sit back and consider this information. It was entirely possible that Paul started the fires if the school was one target.

"Any reason to suspect Howard Hanson?"

"Not really. We always figured it was a student at the school."

"But why would a kid set fire to a bar?"

"Angry that their dad was a drunk who spent time there?"

Bob chewed his lower lip as he thought about this. It was certainly feasible. That the fires ended when Paul moved away was not helpful to the boy either.

"Do you know if Howard Hanson still lives in Opelika?"

"As far as I know. He's not been arrested in a while, though, so I can't say for sure. It's not like we keep tabs on him."

"Could you give me his last known address? I'd like to find him if I can."

The detective provided the address and asked, "What's this all about?"

"The arson here killed Howard Hanson's ex-wife and nearly killed his son."

After disconnecting the call with the Opelika detective, Bob began a search of information about both Howard Hanson and the address where he had lived, hoping to get some details on whether or not Hanson still lived there. He found that the house was owned by someone named Jess Morris, who also lived in Opelika. After searching for information on Morris, he discovered this person was a local realtor there. Apparently, Morris was the owner of several rentals in the area. His information included an email address and phone number.

Dialing the number, he was connected, and after a few rings, a woman answered. "Jess Morris Realty."

"May I speak to Mr. Morris?"

"He's with a client right now. May I ask what this concerns?"

"I'm a detective in Denton, Florida, and I need to speak to Mr. Morris about a house he owns there in Opelika. Mr. Morris is not in any trouble. I just need some information about a tenant."

"What kind of information? Maybe I could help. Mr. Morris might be a while."

After giving the woman the address, Bob said, "I need to know if Howard Hanson is still the tenant there, and if he isn't when he might have moved out."

"I don't know if I can tell you that. How do I know you're really a detective?"

"First of all, I'm not asking for confidential information. I just want to know if he's a tenant. I could just be someone at a bank who's looking into giving him a loan. Second, if you want, I can have the local cops come by and ask, if that's what you prefer."

"Oh, no. I don't think that's necessary. I just like to be sure about these things. Mr. Morris wouldn't want to find himself in court for giving out confidential information."

"Believe me, verifying if he still lives there is not confidential information."

Bob could hear the woman typing. Seconds passed and she said, "No. Mr. Hanson and his family moved out nearly a year ago."

"Did he leave a forwarding address?"

There was a slight pause before the woman said, "You're a detective?"

"Yes."

"I can assume you are looking for Mr. Hanson?"

"Yes, though I'm not saying he has committed any crimes. I just need to speak to him about something."

"Well, he committed one here. If you find him, tell him we need the $2,280 he owes us for damages to the house."

"He skipped out owing you money?"

"You could say that. There was only a $500 damage deposit. That wasn't enough to cover the damages."

"May I ask what damages occurred?"

The woman sounded as if she were reading from her screen. "Big holes in the walls like someone had punched holes in them, some kind of stains on the floors that required some of the flooring to be replaced, and some smoke damage in a bedroom."

"Smoke damage?"

"Yes, in one of the smaller bedrooms, so I would imagine it was the one his kid stayed in. The records say they had a son. Of course, they could have used it as some kind of storage, but it was the second largest bedroom, so I would imagine the kid stayed there."

After considering this for a second, Bob said, "Thank you. May I call back if I have any further questions?"

"Sure. Mr. Morris owns that house, and he was livid when he saw the condition they'd left the place in. I mean, it's not a real nice house or anything, but it had to be fixed up before he could rent it again."

"Thank you. If I find him, you'll hear from me."

"That would be great."

After disconnecting, Bob leaned back in his chair and thought about what he had learned.

Howard Hanson had moved out of the house in Opelika. Renting another house in the area would have made him easier to find, and he had to know Jess Morris would want him to pay for the damages. Bob figured he was no longer in the Opelika area, though, which was a problem.

And the smoke damage in what had likely been Paul's bedroom raised more red flags. Had Paul been playing with fire and accidentally caused damage to the house? It didn't seem likely that Howard Hanson had started a fire in his son's room. It was certainly possible, just improbable.

And the fact that someone set fire to the school suggested the firebug was a kid. Why would an adult set fire to a local school?

Finding Howard Hanson was going to prove more difficult than he'd expected. He didn't have the time to go to Opelika and ask around, and without any known associates to ask, he wasn't sure if such a trip could prove fruitful.

He would have to ask Paul about his father's most recent jobs. From there, Bob could contact his employers and find out if Hanson had any friends who might could help locate him.

Dialing Jack, he waited until the call was answered. When it was, Bob asked to speak to Paul.

"What do you need to talk to him about? He was pretty upset from your last conversation."

"I need to ask him some questions about his dad."

"Oh? Like what?"

"Where he worked for one thing. He's not living in the same house, probably not even in Opelika anymore, and I need to ask some of his former coworkers where he might have gone."

"Do you think he might have started the fire?" Jack asked.

"Right now, I don't know what to think." He did not mention what he'd found out that suggested Paul might be their arsonist.

"Okay, but keep the questions to just asking about his dad, okay?"

"No problem," Bob said.

Seconds later, Paul was on the line. "Hello?"

"Paul, this is Detective Ebert again. I'm sorry I have to call you, but I'm having some trouble locating your father. I was hoping you might be able to help with that."

"How can I do that? I don't know where he is."

"I was hoping you could tell me where he worked when you lived there."

"He didn't work. At least not like you think. He'd do odd jobs for people sometimes. My mom earned all the money. He would only go out and make some money if he wanted something she wouldn't buy."

"What kind of work did he do?"

"Little stuff. You know, like clean people's garages or mow their lawns. Stuff like that."

Bob was taken aback. "He never held down a real job where he would get a paycheck every week or two?"

"Not that I know of. I don't remember any job like that, anyway."

"What about friends. Do you know the names of any of his buddies?"

"No. Mom wouldn't let him bring his friends around. She told me she was scared of them. He'd mention a guy named Zack, but that's all I know."

"Did she say why she was afraid?"

"No, only that she didn't want them coming around the house."

Bob could imagine what the problem had been and considered his ideas to be correct. Most women who were afraid of their husband's friends had been the subject of unwanted attention.

"Okay, thanks, Paul. I'll see what I can find out."

"Okay," Paul said.

Bob thought of something else. "Oh, Paul?"

"Yes?"

"I don't suppose you know your dad's social security number, do you?"

"No. How would that help?"

"I could find out if he ever had a job in Opelika."

"Oh. I don't think he did, though. My mom always said he was too lazy to hold down any jobs."

115

"Okay, thank you again, Paul."

"Okay," Paul said, and they ended the call.

Bob wondered what his next move might be. He was at a dead end as far as finding Howard Hanson was concerned. And he may have just ended a phone call with someone who was an arsonist that had killed his own mother, whether or not killing her was intentional. If one fire got out of hand, it was easy to imagine another one doing the same.

Then again, with the gas can being left in the hallway of the house, as Joe Sissler had said it likely was, the killing appeared to be no accident. He would have to consider these details before moving on with the case.

He shut down his computer and left for home. As he drove, he wondered if he could get Jack to help find Howard Hanson. Perhaps the man could answer some questions about his son and the fires that occurred in Opelika before Paul left there, especially the fire in his son's bedroom.

17

On Monday, Paul went to school and prayed his attempts to be nice to others would be successful. He doubted it, but it was worth a try. Jack didn't seem to understand how much the other kids did their best to avoid being around him.

After going to the cafeteria where the kids would gather before the first bell, he found his usual seat at an otherwise empty table. As he sat there, looking around at the others gathered at various tables, he wondered what he could do to be nice to someone. It wasn't as if he could just stroll up and start a conversation. He would be ignored at best, but it was more likely that someone would offer a cruel response showing Paul's presence was unwelcome.

That's when he noticed a girl getting breakfast but having trouble with carrying it and a project that was evidently due that day.

Jumping up, he approached the girl warily as she struggled with her food, her backpack, and the small diorama.

"Can I help you carry something?" he asked.

The girl, whose name he didn't know, looked at him. She seemed to notice something behind Paul before looking back at him. "No. I got it," she said. She skirted past him and took a seat at a table with another girl.

As Paul turned to go back to his seat, he noticed that several boys at a nearby table were looking at him. They were in the direction of where the girl had looked before answering him. The boys were snickering among themselves, obviously responding to something one of the boys had said.

Paul did his best to ignore them as he returned to his table, but he couldn't ignore what one of the boys said as he passed by them. "Strike out with another attempt at a girlfriend, Scarface?"

They burst out laughing at what they considered to be the height of humor at his expense.

No, this was not going to be easy. Not at all.

As the day wore on, he continued searching for a way to be nice to someone, but that failed again. It wasn't as if kids his age were in search of help from another student, let alone one that had scars covering his face and an eyepatch over where his left eye had once been.

At lunch, he noticed a small group of boys nearby who were talking about getting together after school to play Dungeons and Dragons, which was a game he liked to play before the fire. These were not kids Paul associated with the "cool" guys. They were what many would call "nerds." They even looked the part. One boy had thick hornrims, and another was actually wearing a tie, something students at his school almost never did.

If any group of kids would be willing to accept him for what he was, it was this one.

He stepped warily over to their table, and spoke.

"Hi," he said. All four boys stopped their conversation and looked up at him as if wondering what a science experiment specimen might do next. Their look said it all: *why are you talking to us?*

"I overheard you talking about playing D and D."

"So?" Hornrims said.

"I'm pretty good at it," Paul said. "You mind if I join you?"

The four looked around at each other, silently asking which of them would reply. Finally, Hornrims answered, probably because he had been the only one to speak so far.

"You're Paul, right?"

"Yeah." He gave a small salute and attempted a smile in an effort to look like "just one of the guys" at school.

Hornrims pushed his glasses up onto the bridge of his nose automatically. "Look, we got nothing against you. It's just that there are some guys in school who—well—have made it known you're unwelcome in any group. They'll beat the snot out of any kid who's nice to you or lets you join their group of friends."

As the boy spoke, Paul noticed him cut his eyes to another table about forty feet away. Paul glanced that way and saw the boys who had made fun of him that morning. They were ignoring him for now, but the look on the faces of this group of boys he'd wanted to play D and D with told him everything.

They wouldn't mind being his friend, but they would suffer the consequences for months to come if they allowed him to join in.

Paul shrugged. "Okay. I understand." He left the four boys at their table and returned to his own.

No matter what he did, nobody would be his friend. He could save the life of the most popular kid in school, and he would still be ignored.

He decided to make one last effort by approaching Randall and Les, two boys who had been his friends before the fire—well, as much of a friend as his mother would allow, anyway. They had hung out together at school some at least.

"Hi, guys," Paul said as he approached. Both boys looked as though the worst possible thing had just happened as Randall glanced toward the table of the bullies, fear in his eyes.

"Okay, never mind," he said and returned to his table.

This would be his life as long as he remained in Denton. Heck, it might be his life even if he moved to California, for all the difference that would make. Every school he could attend would have its resident group of boys who would make sure Paul never had any friends. The weird part was how popular these boys were in every school. Both girls and boys flocked around them as if they were the kings of the school.

And in a way, they were. They told everyone who was approved and who wasn't. Get on the unapproved list, and your life was basically over.

Paul managed to get through the rest of the day and decided to walk home. He was supposed to ride the bus, but he didn't want to be around other kids. Besides, one of the ruling class boys rode his bus, and he would have something snarky to say to Paul when Paul climbed aboard and sat down. It had only been a few days since Paul had returned to school, and the comments were as reliable as the sunrise.

Paul wasn't in the mood for anything like that

today. He was never in the mood for it, but today was even worse. He considered he might punch the kid in the face if he said anything, and that would lead to being slaughtered by the kid.

That evening, Jack came into his bedroom when he got home from work. "So how'd it go?" Jack asked.

"Bad."

"Want to tell me about it?"

"Not really."

"I can't help if I don't know what's going on."

"You wouldn't be able to help anyway."

"Now, how do you know if you've not shared what happened today? I can tell it wasn't good. Were you bullied?"

Paul considered the question. Oddly the answer was yes and no. He'd been bullied indirectly by some boys whose behavior would not change just because someone told them to stop. He didn't want to talk about his day, but the fact that Jack and Jenny were always wanting to help made him decide to talk about it anyway.

"Not exactly," he answered.

"Then what exactly?"

Paul told him about approaching the boys about the game and what they had told him.

"So these boys who tell others what to do and not do are omniscient?"

"Huh?"

"Omniscient. It means all-knowing. In other words, I'm saying they can't possibly know everything that goes on. For instance, if you were to invite those boys over to our house, I seriously doubt those other boys would know unless one of the kids you invited told them, and I seriously doubt they would."

"I guess."

"Paul, you can't let bullies rule your life. At some point, you have to take a stand."

"I don't want them beating up other kids just because they were nice to me."

"I understand and agree. But still, you can't allow bullies to control your life. If these other boys come over for a party of sorts, maybe even a campout, that's up to them. If they would like to do that, they should if their parents give them permission."

"Maybe the parents don't want them hanging out with a guy other kids call 'Scarface.' Maybe they don't want their sons to be friends with me."

"I doubt that, but how do you know unless you try?"

"I guess I don't."

"Tell you what. Tomorrow, go up to those boys and ask them to come over to hang out for a little while this Saturday. Tell them not to tell anyone else. Let them know they need to be able to have whatever friends they want, as long as their parents don't object."

Paul considered this and figured Jack wasn't going to leave this alone until he said he would. He could decide tomorrow whether or not to go through with it.

"Okay."

"Believe me, Paul. There are plenty of kids out there who would be your friend. Some might not even care what the other kids say about you. Also, these bullies will lose interest in you in a few weeks at most. It's like the news. The most important events fade into the background faster than you'd think."

"Thanks."

"Don't mention it. Now, dinner will be in about twenty minutes. We'll see you in the dining room then."

"Okay."

At dinner, Jenny was filled in on the possibility of a small party of boys that Saturday.

"That sounds great!" she said. "Any idea how many?

Paul looked at her and said, "Anywhere from just me to me and four other guys."

She looked at him and smiled, but Paul could see the slight sadness in that smile, even with only one eye.

18

Paul was nervous when it came time for his first Bridge Over Troubled Water meeting. His experiences at school had made him wonder if he would ever have a friend again other than Jack and Jenny and their friends. Adults didn't mind his appearance much, but kids his age acted as if it might be contagious.

They either bullied him or ignored him since the fire. He didn't expect things to be much different at these meetings. He knew they wouldn't bully him, at least. With Jack and Jenny both there, the kids would know that bullying would not be tolerated.

But ignoring him would be easy.

They arrived thirty minutes early, and as he climbed out of the car, he hesitated before following Jack and Jenny into the building.

It was a small place with three rooms and two bathrooms. The first room was as wide as the building and took up its front half. The other two rooms each had a bathroom and were half the size of the front room. The front room had about twenty chairs, and each room had several tables. The chairs were on wheels to make moving them easy. The walls were covered in drawings and quotations that the kids there had added over the years. All of the quotations were positive in some way.

One caught Paul's eye: "You become who and

what you believe yourself to be." Paul wasn't so sure about that. He could believe himself to be handsome and popular, but that would never happen.

As they entered, Jack told Paul to have a look around while they set up for the meeting. There wasn't much to look at except the artwork of teens over the years, and the words they had scrawled on the walls.

Paul looked over at one section of the wall to his right as the entered the building and found it covered in signatures. He walked over to it and did his best to read some of the names there. It wasn't hard to figure out they were the signatures of previous attendees of the meetings. Jack's and Jenny's signatures were not there.

"Why don't you two sign this wall?" he asked.

Jack stopped helping Jenny put the chairs in place for the meeting and said, "Because the walls are only for the kids to write and draw on. It's their space, so we don't infringe on it."

"What if someone wrote something bad?"

"Then we'd talk to that person and have them paint over their words, but it's never happened before. We call the walls The Positive Space. Only positive words can go on it. We have kids sign the wall to show they are something positive, not negative, which too many of them feel when they first arrive."

"Do you want me to sign it?"

"Yes, but it's ceremonial, so you need to wait until we start the meeting."

"Oh, okay." Paul didn't want to be the center of

attention, but he figured Jack and Jenny had opened their home to him, so he would do it for them.

The first person to arrive was a girl a few years older than he was, maybe sixteen. He noticed she was with what was probably her mother.

She greeted Jack and Jenny when she entered, and the lady said, "I'll be back for her at eight."

"See you then, Ms. Garrison," Jack said.

Paul watched as the girl sauntered over to him, feeling his tongue get tied in knots as she approached and smiled at him. The smile was friendly, and Paul wondered if she was pretending to like him to please Jack and Jenny.

"Hi. You must be Paul," she said, surprising him.

"Yeah. How do you know my name?"

"Jack and Jenny have talked about you, telling us you were going to come live with them."

"Oh." He wanted to say more but his mind was blank.

"I'm sorry about your mom. That must be tough."

"Yeah." Again, nothing else would come to him to say. He must sound unbelievably boring.

"You don't need to be shy with me. I don't bite." She grinned at him, and it seemed genuine.

He finally thought of something to say, and he felt like kicking himself for not realizing it sooner. "What's your name?"

"Michelle. Glad to meet you, Paul."

"Glad to meet you," he replied and meant it. She really did seem like a nice person who didn't care a bit about the fact scars covered most of his face and he was still wearing the patch over his left eye. He was scheduled to get a prosthetic eye in a couple of months. He was surprised it would take that long, but Jack had told him such things take time.

"I'm also sorry you were burned in the fire. That must have been really painful."

"It was." For a moment, he couldn't believe he was talking to someone who wasn't put off by his appearance. She seemed not to notice that he was ugly. "After a while, though, it sort of becomes your life."

She nodded, seeming to consider his answer. "That's how it is with everything, I guess. People just fold their misery into their lives and go on."

Others had begun to arrive, and Paul noticed one boy his age that he'd seen around school. He was quiet, never drawing attention to himself. He did have a friend at school, though, but he didn't know that kid's name. He didn't know this guy's name either.

Glancing over to Jack, he saw that he was watching Paul's interaction with Michelle and smiling.

At that moment, Jenny called the meeting to order and everyone sauntered to one of the chairs that faced the center of the room and sat. Paul noticed that Michelle went to sit with a girl about Paul's age that she knew. He didn't want to intrude on Michelle's friendship with her friend, so he sat next to the kid from his school. He wished he could remember his name.

As they grew silent, Jenny smiled at Paul and said, "We have a new friend with us tonight. He's Paul Hanson. Jack and I spoke about how he has come to live with us, and he wants to be a part of BOTW."

"Hi, Paul," everyone said, more or less in unison.

"Hi." He looked around at the circle of faces and was surprised that not one of the kids seemed bothered by how he looked. Had Jack and Jenny warned them not to act that way? He would understand if they did, but he hoped not. A forced friendship is no friendship at all; it was a duty.

Jack spoke up. "Paul, please stand up."

He did, wondering what was going to happen next.

"Paul," Jack continued, "will you do your best to be kind to the others who come to the Bridge Over Troubled Water meetings and accept them for who they are and offer encouragement always and provide help to them if they need it when you can?"

"Do I have to, like, raise my right hand?" Paul asked.

Jack smiled. "No, you're not taking an oath, just promising you will try to be the best person you can be."

"Oh, okay." He looked around at the faces again. "Yes. I don't mind doing that."

"Welcome to BOTW," Jack said.

Everyone in the group stood and went over to Paul, shaking his hand. For his part, Paul was more or less flabbergasted. He'd never been so welcomed in any place in his life, not even his own home.

"Now," Jenny said. "It's time to add your name to the wall." She handed Paul a marker, and he walked slowly to the wall with all the signatures. After signing his first and last names, he turned to the others, who applauded as if he'd just done something amazing.

Paul rejoined the group and sat in his seat, feeling a blush creep up his neck.

Jack said, "So, Paul, tell us about yourself."

He took a deep breath and let it out slowly, doing his best to keep the nervousness from taking over.

Jack interrupted before Paul could speak. "And Paul, tell us everything, even the ugly stuff."

He took another cleansing breath and said, "I'm Paul Hanson, and I was in a fire. That's why I'm scarred up. The scars go pretty much everywhere. People at school make fun of me and bully me. Either that, or they ignore me because some of the kids have told people not to be my friend."

He heard a slight gasp from someone. He'd had his head ducked, looking at the floor, and he looked up to see who had gasped. It was Michelle's friend. From the look on her face, she felt truly bad for Paul and what he had to deal with every day.

"We'd never do that," she said. "That's awful."

Paul glanced at the boy sitting next to him. His face told him he knew of the promise to beat up anyone who became Paul's friend. He couldn't tell if the guy was going to defy the bullies or not.

As he looked around the room again, he noticed Michelle's friend was looking at him. "I heard about that," she said. "I don't care what those bullies say."

Paul smiled. "Thanks, but I wouldn't want you to get harassed because of me."

"My mom's a teacher at the school. They won't bother me."

The guy next to him said nothing, and Paul wondered if he might do his best to avoid being Paul's friend. He couldn't blame him if he did. Who needed trouble from guys like the bullies at the school?

There were eleven kids there that night, and each of them introduced themselves to Paul and said a little bit about themselves.

The boy next to Paul was Andy. He said he recognized Paul from school and talked about how he liked to play computer games and watch TV. He also liked to go to shoot baskets at a local park at an outdoor court but only by himself. There was no invitation to join him, and Paul wasn't surprised by that either.

After a general discussion of how things had been going in their lives since the last meeting, they separated into two groups, the girls in one of the smaller rooms and the boys in the other.

Once they were separated, they talked more about their lives. Jack reminded everyone that what was said at the meetings stayed in the meetings, and that sharing the troubles discussed in the meetings with anyone who was not a member of BOTW would be dealt with.

"The only thing you can tell others is if Jenny or I lose our minds and do or say something inappropriate," he said in conclusion.

Paul felt this was mostly said for him since the others had been there many times before and knew the rules. Mostly, Paul figured there was nobody for him to tell anyway.

It turned out that three of the boys had fathers

who were in prison, including Andy. All of them were in for selling some kind of illegal drugs, with Andy's father having the additional charge of armed robbery for holding up a liquor store.

Paul's father wasn't in prison, at least as far as he knew, but since it wouldn't surprise him if he was, he could understand how the boys might feel, though none of them seemed particularly close with their fathers. That was another thing Paul could identify with.

When it was Paul's turn to talk, he mentioned this about his father. He talked about how his father didn't even know where he was and Paul preferred it that way. He pulled up one leg of his shorts and showed the boys some scars where his father would burn him, saying, "These weren't from the house fire."

Several of the boys could identify with Paul's trouble with his father.

One of the boys lived alone with his dad. His mother had been killed in a car wreck. He said his dad wasn't that bad but he missed his mom. She had been gone two years now.

When the meeting ended, Paul had a better grasp of how he wasn't alone in the situations he faced in life, that others had faced similar problems. It was funny how he always thought his problems were unique to him. Now he had learned that wasn't really the case.

After everyone left and they were in the car heading home, Jenny asked, "So, what did you think of your first BOTW meeting?"

"I liked it."

She flashed her warmest smile at him. "That's great! I think you'll find there are a lot of kids willing to be friends with you there. Just remember, we don't advertise who is a member. Some of the kids don't want everyone knowing they're members, since it's for troubled teens, and they don't want the stigma of being identified in that way."

"I won't say anything to anyone," Paul said.

That night, he considered how he could ask Andy to come over to hang out that Saturday. He planned to ask the kids who like to play Dungeons and Dragons if they wanted to come over and hang out and play games and felt maybe Andy might want to join them.

All he could do was ask.

19

The next day at school, Paul again approached the boys who liked playing Dungeons and Dragons. He sat down, and the boys looked nervously around the cafeteria.

"I won't stay," Paul said. "I just wanted to invite you guys to come over to my house this Saturday and play some games or something." He made a show of looking around the room himself before adding, "Nobody has to know."

"Where you live?" one of the boys asked.

"In that big house down at Chambliss Point."

"I know the one. You live there?"

"Yeah. I'm staying with a couple, Jack and Jenny Turner. They sort of took me in."

The other boys looked at each other, and one said, "We'll think about it. What time?"

"How about ten? You can stay through lunch."

"And the people you're living with don't mind?"

"No. They suggested it."

Again the boys looked at each other, and the same guy said, "We'll let you know."

Paul stood and walked back to where he usually sat at the table alone but noticed someone was sitting there. He started to look for another empty table then realized it was Andy.

Sitting, he said, "Are you sure you want to be seen with me?"

"What those guys could do to me is nothing compared to what I've dealt with."

"Really?"

"Really. Besides, I'm sort of in the same boat. Nobody wants to be with me much, either, except the kids from BOTW."

Paul said, "Listen, I'm having a sort of get together at my house Saturday. You wanna come?"

"Sure. Who else is coming?"

"Maybe those four guys that I was talking to," Paul said, indicating the nearby table where they sat.

Andy thought a moment and said, "Okay. What time?"

"Ten."

"I'll ask my mom, but I'm sure she'll let me."

As they sat talking, the girl who had mentioned at the meeting that her mother was a teacher at the school came by and sat down. Paul tried to remember her name, but he couldn't. She had said it only once during the meeting when she introduced herself for his benefit, but now her name escaped him.

"What's up?" she asked.

"Just talking," Andy offered. "What's up with you?"

"I saw you two over here, and I thought I'd invite myself into the conversation." She smiled at them.

"Paul is planning a get-together for Saturday," Andy said.

"Oh?"

"Yeah," Paul said. "I'm hoping to get some guys

together to play Dungeons and Dragons or something."

She smiled. "Are girls invited?"

Paul and Andy exchanged looks. "It's sort of a guy thing," Paul said. He was shocked she wanted to come over. It wasn't like he was some star athlete or something.

"Oh, that's cool," she said. "Just thought I'd ask."

"No problem," Paul said. "By the way, I'm embarrassed to say this, but I forgot your name."

"Melody. Melody James."

Paul suddenly realized why he couldn't remember her name. She was friends with Michelle, the older girl who had been the first to speak to him at the meeting, and he recalled thinking the names were so similar he might get the two girls mixed up.

"Aren't you friends with Michelle?" Paul asked.

"Yes, but she's older and goes to the high school."

"I hope I don't get the two of you mixed up. I'm kind of bad with names sometimes."

"Just remember my name isn't like me. I can't sing a lick. Michelle, though, she's in her school chorus. So just kind of think of us as opposite to our names." She grinned. "So her voice is melodious; mine isn't despite my name."

Paul laughed and said he'd try to remember that, and Melody excused herself. "I'll let you guys get back to talking about your get-together."

As he and Andy continued talking, Paul soaked in the friendship being offered. It wasn't like the BOTW meeting, where the kids were expected to talk to each other. This was a choice Andy had made. Added to that was the fact that Melody had stopped by to say hello, too. It all made Paul feel good—better than he had in a while.

When he arrived home that afternoon, he did his homework and played with the dog until Jenny got home. She noticed the good mood he was in and asked about it.

"I actually made some friends at school today."

"Oh? Who?"

"Well, it's only Andy and Melody, but the guys who were going to play Dungeons and Dragons might come over Saturday as well."

"Will Melody be joining in?"

"No. I just want it to be guys. Having one girl over would seem too much like having a girlfriend."

Jenny grinned at him. "Don't knock it."

"I'm not 'knocking' it. I just know she isn't interested in me like that."

"You might be surprised. Not all girls are into finding the handsomest guy around. A lot of us look for guys who are just nice."

"Jack's handsome, though."

"Yeah. I got lucky, but to be honest, I was a little nervous when we first started dating. I was afraid he might turn out to be a jerk behind all that handsome."

"He told me you met when you worked at the courthouse."

"Yep. And yes, I have to admit it was his looks that attracted me first, but again, looks can be deceiving."

"You love him a lot, don't you?"

"More than breathing."

"Can I ask you a personal question?"

"You can ask," she replied, hinting that she didn't obligate herself to answer.

"Why didn't you guys have kids?"

Her smile disappeared. "I'm infertile."

"Oh. Sorry."

"It's okay. You didn't know. Anyway, that's why we started Bridge Over Troubled Water. It sort of allows us to parent lots of kids. Small children are always easy to love. Teens, not so much. We felt they needed our love the most."

"You love the kids in the program?"

"Yes."

"How can you love people you barely know?"

"Because we go into it knowing we will love them. It's like the best teachers. They know they will love their students, and the students recognize that in them."

Paul considered this and realized it was true. He had known from the first day of classes in years past that a certain teacher was kind and loving and truly cared. It was almost like an aura they put off. He could feel that same aura in Jack and Jenny.

"Why didn't you adopt?"

"We considered it but never went through with it. Besides, who's to say we might not still adopt someone?"

He thought they were too old to adopt a baby but didn't say it. He didn't want to hurt her feelings.

When Jack arrived home, he also noticed Paul's good mood. When Paul shared the reason why, he said, "That's great. I told you there were kids in school who would be your friend, no matter what influences tried to stop them."

Saturday arrived and Paul paced nervously, wondering if any of the boys would show up. He knew Andy would. They had become fast friends at school. He wasn't sure about the other boys. They had told him yesterday they would try, but that was all the commitment he could get from them.

A few minutes before ten that morning, Andy arrived, greeting Jack and Jenny before settling down with Paul.

Andy took out a deck of cards and showed Paul a few tricks. He was very good with his hands and could cut the cards into three stacks with one hand. The tricks were amazing as well.

About fifteen minutes past ten, two of the other boys, Nathan and Ken, arrived. When they sat down with Paul and Andy, Nathan said, "Mark and Steve can't make it." He didn't explain why, and Paul didn't need an explanation. He couldn't blame them, really. The threat of being bullied was enough to keep them away.

The boys spent time playing Dungeons and Dragons as well as enjoying an impromptu magic show from Andy, who performed about a dozen card tricks.

After lunch, they sat in Paul's bedroom and talked.

"Can I ask you something?" Ken said.

"Sure."

"How did you get out of the fire?"

Paul told them about going to the window

seconds before the explosion that propelled him through the window and into the yard, where he somehow had the presence of mind to roll around to smother the flames.

"Do you miss your mom?" Nathan asked.

"Sometimes, but to be honest, she wasn't the best mom in the world. Jenny is much better."

"How was she not the best mom?" Andy asked.

"Well, besides never letting me do anything fun, she would hit me a lot. In that way, she and my dad were alike."

"Lots of parents hit their kids," Ken said. "Mine don't hit me, but I know it goes on."

"She would use the buckle end of a belt. I'd show you the scars, but they're just part of the landscape now."

"Wow," Ken said. "You had it bad."

"Yeah," Paul said.

"I'm sorry that happened to you," Nathan said. "I mean all of it, the beatings, your dad, the fire. Everything."

"Thanks."

They sat in silence for a while until Nathan said, "You didn't start the fire, did you?"

Paul looked at him. Why would he ask that? Had he heard something?

Before Paul could answer, Nathan said, "Sorry. I shouldn't have asked that."

"I didn't start it." He indicated the scars on his face. "Why would I do this to myself?"

Nathan didn't answer, but the thought that maybe Paul had been attempting suicide crossed his mind.

Andy said, "Things are getting too heavy. Let's go outside and play with the dog or something."

They all agreed, and the rest of the day went well, with nobody bringing up the fire again, except once.

Nathan came up to him while Andy and Ken were involved with the dog and said, "I'm sorry, man. I didn't mean to be rude."

"That's okay," Paul said. "I guess it's a question a lot of people have."

20

When he got home, Nathan called Mark. "Hey, man. You should have come to Paul's. We had a great time. He's really a nice kid."

Mark had known Paul before the fire and knew he was a nice kid, but he had other reasons for not going. Reasons he didn't want to discuss with Nathan or anyone else.

"That's cool. I just don't want to strike up any friendship with him."

"Why not?"

"I just don't. What all did you do there?"

"Played Dungeons and Dragons and Clue. Another kid was there named Andy. He does card tricks, and not easy ones. He's a whiz with a deck of cards. Then we had lunch and talked in Paul's room before going outside to play with the dog."

"What did you talk about?" Mark asked.

"Just stuff in general." Nathan paused. He hadn't intended to tell Mark about the question he asked Paul, but he knew Mark would have asked the same question. He'd been interested in that fire since it happened.

"I also asked him if he set the fire. I've heard that the detective investigating the arson asked some of the kids he used to hang out with a lot of questions about Paul. They said it sounded like the detective thought Paul may have set the fire."

"Who are 'they'?"

"One of the kids the detective questioned."

"They think Paul set it?"

"I guess. But he says he didn't, and I believe him. Like he said, why would he do that to himself?"

"I suppose so."

Nathan could tell Mark didn't want to talk about this, so he changed the subject. "The dog was cool, too. He'll, like, chase a ball you throw until he's ready to drop. We all took turns throwing it because our arms would get tired before he got tired of chasing it."

"Yeah, dogs are weird like that. Listen, my dad wants to take me camping next weekend. You wanna come?"

"I'll ask my folks," Nathan said, aware that Mark had purposely changed the subject. He was at a loss as to why Mark didn't want to talk about Paul. Then it hit him.

"You know that those guys at school won't ever know we were hanging out with Paul today, right?"

"Yeah, I know that."

"Then why do you sound so reluctant to talk about him?"

"I just don't want to, okay?"

Mark was getting upset, so Nathan dropped it.

"Okay, fine. I'll drop it. Where does your dad want to go camping?"

They continued the conversation for several more minutes before disconnecting the call. When they did, Mark went to his bedroom and lay on his bed. It was his favorite place to do some thinking as he stared at the poster of a girl in a bikini on his ceiling.

His mind went back to what he'd seen the night of the fire. He couldn't tell anyone about it because he wasn't supposed to be out. It was in the middle of the night, and his parents would ground him big time if he admitted to being out wandering the streets at that time.

He had sneaked out just to walk the streets. He hadn't done anything illegal other than break curfew for kids his age. It wasn't like he had gone out to do drugs or even smoke cigarettes. He'd just gone out and wandered because it made him feel like an adult or something. He wasn't even sure now why he had done it, but he had.

He had wandered over to the street where Paul lived. Not because Paul lived there or anything. It was just where he ended up.

As he walked along what he thought was a deserted street, he saw something that would later make him sorry he had come out that night of all nights.

It was dark with no moon out that night, so he couldn't make out who it was, but someone small was outside Paul's house. The door was open, and he had come outside and grabbed what looked like a gas can before taking it inside. The door closed, and Mark moved on.

The next morning, he'd heard there had been a fire and that Paul was seriously burned and his mother had died.

With horror he realized it must have been Paul with the gas can. He couldn't be 100% sure it was

Paul, but who else could it be? It was a guy, and he didn't seem large enough to be an adult.

Let Nathan and the others think Paul was a nice kid. He'd seemed nice before the fire, but it had turned out he had killed his own mother. Mark figured he must have meant for both of them to die in the fire, but Paul had lived. Now, Mark wondered if he might finish the job he'd started. Mark didn't want to be around for that. He even wondered if he might be interrogated by the cops if Paul finally committed suicide.

Now, Mark was caught between the proverbial rock and a hard place. If he came forward with what he knew, Paul would be arrested and he himself would end up grounded for at least a month. Heck, his parents might take some kind of steps to make sure Mark was unable to leave the house at night or something, though he wasn't sure what that could be. Keyed locks on the doors that he didn't have a key for? He wasn't sure, but he didn't want to find out.

If he didn't come forward, he would have to deal with the guilt of knowing, but he felt he could handle that. At least that would be better than making his parents not trust him anymore.

He would have to keep his mouth shut and hope the cops figured out what had happened. From what he'd heard, they were on the right track.

He'd just let them handle it. It wasn't his problem to solve. Besides, what if it wasn't Paul? Okay, it didn't seem conceivable it was anyone else, but since he couldn't see who it was, it might have been someone else, even if the odds of that were one in a million. It was possible that some deranged kid had some kind of grudge against Paul or even his mom and had broken into the house to set it on fire.

He wasn't sure.

The thoughts of his night out stayed with him the rest of the day, as they did whenever he had reason to think of them.

Yes, he'd keep his mouth shut. He saw it as his only option. *Just shut up and deal with the guilt and let the cops do their job* had become his go-to conclusion on the matter.

21

The following Tuesday morning, Bob made the decision to ask Jack if he could help locate Howard Hanson. He knew that his investigator, Tom Gordon, was capable. Like Jack, Bob had known Tom since childhood. He'd even arrested him once for possession. He now felt that Tom's complete turnaround was nothing short of miraculous.

Placing the call to Jack's office, he sipped his coffee and hoped for the best. He needed to speak to Paul's father, but the budget-strapped department lacked the funds to send Bob to Opelika, and he lacked the time to go there.

When the call was answered, he was put through to Jack after a short wait.

"Hello, Jack. I was wondering if I could ask a big favor."

"How big?"

"Think Montana."

After a second of silence, Jack asked, "Okay, what is this Montana-sized favor?"

"Well, you know that the budget here at the department isn't exactly the same size as Montana, right?"

"More like the population of Montana."

"Right. Well, I need to find Howard Hanson, and I'm not having any luck using the phone to do that."

"And why would I want to help you find Howard

Hanson? Paul never wants to see him again."

Bob had his own suspicions about why that was but kept them to himself. If Jack knew Howard might be able to provide some evidence that incriminated Paul, he wouldn't lift a finger to help him. He wanted to be honest, but that rarely helped in an investigation. "I have no intention of telling him where he can find Paul. I just have to ask him some questions about their time in Opelika. Besides, if Paul isn't the arsonist, he's the next most likely person."

"Bob, once you identify yourself as a cop in Denton, he'll know where he can find Paul."

"Jack, his dad hasn't made a single effort to find him yet, and it's been nearly a year. My guess is he doesn't want to know where he is, especially if he'd heard that his ex-wife is dead. I didn't learn much, but what I did learn said he wasn't interested in the responsibility of raising a teenage boy."

"Okay, you have a point there. What have you found out?"

"He's a regular guest of the Opelika PD, or at least he was. Since he's not been a guest for nearly a year, though, I'm thinking he split for parts unknown after his wife left him."

"That makes sense. I take it you want me to send Tom up to Opelika to have a look around and see if he can find out where Howard is now, am I right?"

"I always did say you were a smart guy."

"Not always," Jack said, a reminder they were not friends when they were in school together.

"Okay, but I have since we grew up."

Jack knew better than to ask if the department

might assist with the cost of the trip. This would be his financial responsibility if he did it.

"How do you see this helping Paul?"

"I'm not really sure it will, but it's worth a try. Who knows? Howard Hanson could incriminate himself."

"He didn't even know where they were."

"That we know of," Bob said. He didn't want to say it, but the truth was that he felt Howard Hanson might be able to help identify Paul as the likely arsonist.

Jack considered this and said, "I'll get back to you. Let me talk to Tom and see what his schedule looks like."

"That's all I can ask," Bob said.

"And Bob?"

"Yes?"

"I'll do this only if I can be in the room when you interrogate Paul's dad."

Bob considered this. "Are you going to act as his attorney?"

"If I have to. Do you think he might implicate Paul as the arsonist?"

"I doubt it. Mostly, I think he'll clam up and tell me zilch. And that's only if I can find him."

After hanging up, Bob considered what he'd done. He didn't like involving Jack in helping to possibly point the finger at Paul, but he had a crime to solve. If the kid was guilty of killing his mother, charges needed to be filed. He hoped Paul hadn't started the blaze that killed his mother and severely injured him, but so far, he was the only suspect, and if enough facts lined up, Paul would be arrested.

At least he would have a good lawyer, Bob said before turning up his mug of coffee to drain the last of it before pouring himself another cup.

Jack called Tom and asked, "So, what are you working on today?"

"I'm finishing up with the Griggs investigation. You should have my report this afternoon."

"Great. I need you to go to Opelika."

"In Alabama?"

"Is there another Opelika?"

"I don't know. What do you need me to do there?"

"It's sort of a missing person thing. If you can drop by my office this afternoon around three, I can tell you more."

"I'm guessing you need me to find Paul's father."

"You'd be right in that guess."

"No problem. I'll bring my report on Griggs when I come."

"Great. I'll see you then."

After disconnecting, Jack thought about all he'd done to help Tom. It was not allowed for an ex-con to become an investigator, either in private practice or for a business such as Jack's law offices, but it helped that Jack had been a law partner of a man who was elected to the state legislature, Chuck Shelton.

Chuck had helped get an exception for Tom. The biggest problem with ex-cons being investigators was that investigators usually carried a gun. Chuck had managed to get a measure passed that would allow a person to work as an exclusive investigator for a law firm if a gun was never in their possession. The cons had to also go three years without an arrest and have three recommendations from "people who had demonstrated that he or she was a trusted member of the community." As a well-known attorney and a state legislator, Chuck had been one of Tom's supporters. So had Trisha, Chuck's wife, who was also a judge in Denton. Jack, of course, had been the third author of a letter of recommendation.

What these investigators could do legally was limited, but none of those limitations prevented Tom from doing his job.

Tom arrived at 3:00 that afternoon and entered Jack's office, handing him the file he had completed.

"So, what can you tell me that would help in finding Paul's dad?" Tom asked as he sat across the desk from Jack.

Bob had emailed him what little he'd found out about Howard. He shared that with Tom, along with information on how Howard had earned money.

"He sounds more like a kid earning spending money," Tom said.

"Yes, I'd say he's not a very responsible individual. You should check some of the local bars, especially those near where he lived. They might not have seen him in a while, but they may be able to put you in touch with guys he might have known."

"You don't have any names of acquaintances?"

"No. Paul said his mom wouldn't allow them to

come around, so he doesn't know any of their names."

"Anything else?"

"When do you need me to leave?"

"Is tomorrow morning too soon?"

"Nope. Just gotta clear it with Sadie." Sadie was Tom's wife, who had also been central to helping Tom clean his life up. "I do know that Lynda and her husband and kids are coming for a visit this weekend and staying through Monday. I'm looking forward to seeing them, especially the grandkids, but I don't think what I have to do in Opelika will last long. I should be able to be home by Saturday."

Lynda, Tom and Sadie's oldest daughter, was living in New Orleans with her family. She was a professor at Tulane in the English department.

"She doesn't have to teach Monday?"

"She gave her students an assignment that is so involved she gave them a day off from class to work on it."

"How nice of her to do that."

Tom grinned. "I imagine they had to talk her into it. She doesn't cut them much slack. You want me to drive or fly?"

"Drive. The country air will do you good."

Tom left the office and went home to tell Sadie about his trip.

"Will you be home by Saturday?" Sadie asked. Her face told him the answer better be yes.

"Absolutely, even if I have to go back after Lynda and the crew leave."

He packed and the next morning left for Opelika. The drive was pleasant, if boring. He chose to take the rural roads instead of heading up to Montgomery and turning northeast on I-85. He enjoyed less traffic, even if it did take a bit longer to drive to the town on the edge of the border with Georgia.

When he arrived, he found a motel and checked in before heading to find the house where Howard Hanson had lived. After driving by there, he would visit the police department to get a mugshot. Tom would want to recognize Howard if he ran into him at a bar or something.

Driving by the house, he stopped and walked up to the door. Knocking, he waited for someone to answer, but nobody was home. Tom had expected this but felt it was worth a try.

He left his card wedged in the door with a note written on it that said, "Important you call."

He just wanted to find out if the current resident had known Howard. He doubted it, but it was certainly possible. Later, when the man who lived there called back, he had nothing important to share and claimed he'd moved to Opelika from Atlanta and had never met Howard Hanson.

He set his GPS to take him to the local police department and parked in the visitors' parking area. As he entered the building, he strode up to the desk and told the officer there that he was looking for Howard Hanson, who had once been arrested by the Opelika PD.

"What do you need from us?"

"His mugshot."

"And what is this in regards to?" the officer asked.

"I'm actually doing this to help the Denton, Florida, police. They want to ask him some questions is all."

"Must be important questions to send a private detective up here."

"I don't know. I actually work for a local attorney who is friends with the detective looking for Mr. Hanson."

"Wait here," the officer said. She rose and walked through a door behind her. Another officer, this one with sergeant stripes on his lapel and sleeve, stepped out with her a moment later.

"You need a mugshot?"

"Yes."

"Can I see some credentials?"

"Sure," Tom said and held out his license for inspection.

After reading it, he handed it back. "Who's the detective you're working with down in Denton?"

"Detective Bob Ebert."

"Okay, hang on a sec. You want a closeup of the face or the full mug shot?"

"A closeup would be great if you have it."

"Only take a minute. I'll be right back." The sergeant went back through the door he'd entered through and was back in about five minutes.

"Detective Ebert vouched for you. I'll just need to print his mugshot. Be about two minutes."

"Thank you," Tom said and waited as the sergeant left again and returned a few minutes later, holding out a printed photo of Howard Hanson's latest mugshot. It was a blowup of the original, bringing his image so close Tom could see only his head, but it was enough, probably better than the full picture since it provided a better image of his face.

"Good luck," the sergeant said. "And if you find him and he's not in Opelika anymore, don't bring him back here."

Tom smiled and said he wouldn't. He left the department and sat in his car for a moment, memorizing the face of Howard Hanson.

The face was not extraordinary in any way. His dark hair was combed straight back, and it appeared he used some kind of hair oil. Howard's face had stubble from not shaving, but no beard or mustache. There were no details about his height or weight, which usually accompanied mugshots, but then he'd not asked for those details. A picture was enough for what he needed to do.

Starting his car, Tom drove to his hotel to get some rest before going out to scout some of the bars near the house where Hanson had once lived.

22

After freshening up after a quick nap, Tom drove to the bar closest to the house where the Hansons had lived. He located the bar using Google by searching for bars near the address. The bar was a dive called Jerome's. As he entered, he looked around to see if he recognized Howard, but he wasn't one of the eleven customers there that evening.

Before coming here, he had conducted a search on Facebook for any Howard Hansons who had lived in Opelika. He found Howard there, but the account had not been touched for two years, with the most recent post having occurred twenty-six months ago. Similar searches of other social media platforms had yielded nothing.

Sitting at the bar, he ordered a club soda and sipped it. His past problems with substance abuse did not allow him to drink anything else. As he drank, the bartender eyed him. Tom could tell that most of the other customers were regulars, so a newcomer would at least be the subject of some curiosity.

Tom signaled the bartender to come over, and the man stepped over to where he could talk for a moment with Tom.

"Whatcha need?"

"Are you the owner?"

"Yeah." The man eyed Tom with more than

curiosity now. It was bordering on suspicion.

"My name is Tom Gordon—"

"I don't need no bartenders."

"That's good because I'm not looking for a job. I'm looking for a person."

"You a cop?"

"Nope." Tom figured a little lie wouldn't hurt. "I work for an attorney down in Florida, and I'm trying to find a guy who inherited some money."

The curiosity returned to replace the suspicion. "How much money?"

"Enough to send me up here. He used to live near this place, and I figured maybe you'd know him. Story goes he liked to drink."

"Nothin' wrong with that."

Tom smiled. "Keeps you in business, eh?"

The bartender smiled back, his manner approaching jovial. He was likely figuring that there was money in information. "You got that right. What did you say your name was?"

"Tom. Tom Gordon. And yours is?

"Jerome. Jerome Mason." He waved his hand at the bar's interior. "Welcome to my palace."

Tom took another sip of his club soda as Jerome continued eyeing him. Tom knew what he was waiting for, so he obliged. "I'm looking for a guy named Howard Hanson. You know him?"

"I might." The answer was meant to prompt talk of payment for the information Jerome could share. "How much is it worth to you to find him?"

"Well, I'm not at liberty to pay you for any information, but if you can lead me to him, I'll be sure to tell him you were responsible for helping me find him so he could get the inheritance. And I'd suggest a little payment to you as a reward would be the right thing to do."

Jerome shook his head. "Not good enough. That guy wouldn't give me a cent, not even for a beer."

"Then you do know him."

"Maybe," Jerome acknowledged.

"Why do you say he wouldn't give you a cent?"

"Let's just say I know what kind of guy he is. Besides, I don't buy your inheritance story."

Tom considered this and nodded. "Okay, I'll level with you. There's a possibility he committed a crime, and anyone who knows where he is but doesn't share that information could be considered an accomplice after the fact."

"So you are a cop."

"Of a sort." Again, a lie wasn't a bad idea in this case. Tom was already wishing he had used an alias.

"What kind of crime?"

"Arson."

"Really? His son's bedroom caught fire once."

"It did?"

"Yeah. So did the school. I remember wondering about that since the bedroom had caught fire."

"What did the police find out about that fire?"

"Don't ask me. I don't know about it other than he came in one day talkin' about how his boy set fire to his bedroom."

"What can you tell me about Howard?"

Jerome looked disgusted and said, "He was a customer. Came in here a lot and left drunk a lot, too. I've not seen him in months, though. His old lady hightailed it with the kid, and he came in one night to celebrate his freedom. I asked him if maybe she'd been cheatin' on him and had left with her new boyfriend, and that made him mad. He started talking about how she had been actin' suspicious and maybe I was right. I wished I hadn't said anything like that because he was gettin' riled up. I guess he was fine as long as he didn't think she was shackin' up with another guy, but now he was getting really angry about it."

"What happened then?" Tom asked.

"Finally, he says, 'I'm gonna find her, and she and her boyfriend are gonna regret ever makin' me look like a fool.' Then he got up and stormed out. Haven't seen him since."

"And that was months ago?"

"Yep."

"And you have no idea where he went?"

"Not a clue."

"Did he have anyone he would hang out with? Anybody who's in here right now?"

Jerome looked around. "Nah, he didn't hang out with any of these guys. I mean, they kinda knew him, but that's all. He was mostly a loner. Kept to himself for the most part and drank his beer. That was about the most he ever said to me in one night."

"Mind if I chat with some of these folks in here?"

"I don't, but they might. Don't start no trouble. They don't want to talk, you stop asking. Got it?"

"No problem."

Tom figured a group question was more expedient. "Excuse me," he said above the sounds of chatter in the bar. "I'm looking for someone who used to be a customer here. Does anyone know Howard Hanson?"

"I *did* know him."

Tom looked at the man who had answered. He was a short, balding man who carried most of his weight around his middle.

"Do you know where he is?"

"Nope. He had a buddy, though. I do know that. Best buds, they were."

"What is his name?"

Zack. Don't know his last name. I used to see the two of 'em down at the Striking Spare."

"Let me guess. That's a bowling alley."

The man smiled. "Kinda catchy, ain't it?"

"You never saw them together in here?"

"Nah. Zack liked whiskey, and Jerome's got nothing but beer."

"For not knowing his last name, you seem to know a lot about him."

"I talked to them once at the lanes when I was at my bowling league. I mentioned this place, and Zack said he didn't drink beer and that was all Jerome served. It was one conversation."

The man turned back to his beer in obvious dismissal of Tom.

"Anyone else know Howard? Or Zack?" Tom called out to the room.

"No better than Lenny, there," one man said, indicating the short, balding guy.

Everyone in the bar, including the man who'd spoken, returned to their beer and conversation, dismissing Tom as effectively as Lenny had.

Tom turned back to Jerome. "I don't suppose you know Zack's last name, do you?"

Jerome shook his head. "Nope." He turned and moved to refill Lenny's beer.

Tom left money on the bar for his club soda and a tip and left. Climbing into his car, he took out his phone and Googled Striking Spare. It was a ten minute drive.

Arriving at the local bowling alley, he hoped he would find someone who might know either Howard or Zack.

He sat at the bar in the rear of the bowling alley, figuring he would go about things the same way he had at Jerome's. Hit up the bartender with questions before moving on to the other customers.

This place was busier than Jerome's had been. There were at least two dozen people sitting at the bar or in the booths that lined the far wall and the wall to the right as he entered.

When the bartender came by, he ordered another club soda. After being served, he said, "I'm looking for someone. I understand he frequents this bar."

"Who?"

"Actually, it's two people. One's named Howard Hanson, the other, Zack. I don't know his last name."

The bartender eyed him, obviously deciding whether to talk to Tom or not. Finally, he said, "I don't know anyone named Howard, but I know a Zack. I don't know his last name, though. He just stops in a couple times a week."

"Any regularity with his visits?"

"What do you mean?"

"Like does he come in every Friday evening? That sort of thing."

"Not that I've noticed. He's just a customer who stops in once in a while."

Tom held out Howard's picture. "This is Howard Hanson. Do you recognize him?"

The bartender gazed a moment at the picture. "That's a mugshot, isn't it?"

"Yes."

"Are you a cop?"

"Nope. Just trying to find him."

"Why?"

"He can help me with something."

The bartender figured out that Tom wasn't going to share what the reason was. "Well, I don't recognize him."

"You sure?"

"Positive."

"I do know he came in once with Zack," Tom said.

"Maybe it was when I wasn't working."

"How long have you worked here?"

"Two years in August."

Tom finished his club soda and placed a ten on the bar to cover the cost of the club soda and a very generous tip.

"Thanks for that small amount of information, anyway," he said and left.

It was getting to be supper time, so he stopped at a diner and ate before heading to his hotel. As he ate, he decided to search for "Zack" and "Opelika" on his laptop once he was settled into his room, figuring there must not be too many guys with that name in such a small city.

When he did the search, he found three people whose internet footprint matched his search. He found a Facebook page for one of them. The picture of the man showed someone around Howard's age, and Tom was hopeful that this was the Zack who had been Howard's friend in Opelika.

He clicked on "Friends" to see if Howard Hanson might show up in that list. He did, and he knew this was the Zack he was looking for. Tom began to look through the posts Zack had made on Facebook. They were mostly jokes and comments about general topics, but they were recent.

He checked the "like" emojis to see if perhaps Howard had "liked" one of Zack's posts. Tom knew a lot of people didn't post a lot on their own Facebook pages but interacted through others' posts there.

On the seventh post he looked at, he had success. Howard Hanson had given a post a thumbs-up emoji. The date on the post was less than two weeks ago.

Howard Hanson was still friends with Zack, whose last name was Gregory.

Looking at Zack's "About" page, Tom found that Zack enjoyed outdoor activities such as fishing and hunting. He also listed another bar in Opelika as a favorite: Bottoms Up.

Tom was too tired to go there now after the drive and everything he'd done that evening, so he showered and climbed into bed.

He would try to find Zack tomorrow.

23

Tom woke the next morning and opened his laptop. He searched whitepages.com for Zack Gregory in Opelika and easily found his last known address. He showered and dressed before going to a Waffle House nearby for breakfast. After that, he used his GPS to find Zack's address.

The combination sand and gravel driveway was empty, and after he knocked, his suspicions were confirmed that nobody was home. The barking of a dog inside told him that someone lived there.

Taking out his phone, he checked Zack's Facebook page again to see if his workplace was mentioned. When he found it there, he wondered if people understood how easy it was to track them through their social media pages. They supplied the information themselves. All that was necessary was opening their page and reading what was there.

According to his Facebook page, Zack worked at a Firestone Tire dealership. When he arrived there and went inside, he asked the man behind the counter if he could speak to Zack.

"You a cop?"

"Nope. I have some money that his friend Howard Hanson owes him."

"Howard? I haven't seen him in months."

"You know Howard?"

"Well, I know who he is, but that's about all. It's

not like we were friends or anything. Not surprised he owes Zack money, though."

"So, can I speak with Zack? I won't keep him long."

"You could if he was here, but he quit."

"How long ago was that?"

He considered and said, "Three or four months ago, I'd say. Just walked in one day and said he was outa here."

"Any idea where I can find him?"

"Have you checked his house?"

"Over on Oak?" Tom asked, seeing if he had the correct house.

"Yeah."

"Yeah, I checked there. Nobody inside but his dog."

"Oh, yeah. Rufus. You don't wanna mess with that one. Zack leaves him inside during the day to make sure nobody breaks into his place."

Tom wondered what anyone would want to steal. It didn't look like a house that would hold anything of much value. "So, you know where he works now?"

"I don't, but let me check with some of the guys in back." He disappeared through a swinging door at the back wall behind the counter and was gone for maybe a minute. When he returned, he said, "Larry says he works for the Michelin place over on Walker."

Tom smiled and thanked the man. As he was leaving, the man called after him. "When you see him, tell him Jimmy says hi."

"Will do."

Ten minutes later, Tom was pulling into the parking lot of the Michelin dealership. When he entered, he recognized the man who greeted him as Zack from his Facebook photo.

"What can I do for you?"

"Zack Gregory?"

The man's appearance changed instantly from friendly to suspicious. "Who wants to know?"

"My name is Tom Gordon. I'm investigating something that happened down in Florida."

"What kind of something?"

"Doesn't matter, really."

"Matters to me."

"I'm representing someone who lost a relative in an act of arson."

"What does that have to do with me? I ain't been in Florida for two years."

"It doesn't actually concern you at all. I just hope you can answer a question for me."

"Can't stop you from askin'."

"What do you know about the fire that happened at the home of Howard Hanson?"

"You think I set it?"

"Not at all. I just wondered if you knew what happened there that caused his son's room to be damaged by fire."

"It was a small fire. Didn't really do any damage other than some smoke. What? You think Howard set it or something?"

"I don't really think anything. I'm just trying to find out what started it."

"Well, Howard didn't set it."

"I didn't say he did. Again, I'm just asking if you

knew how that fire started."

Zack considered Tom with great suspicion, as if he thought Tom was lying with every statement. After a moment, he said, "The kid started it."

This was the answer Tom feared most. "How do you know that?"

"Howard told me. Said the kid was playin' with matches one day and set a big box of comic books on fire. Howard put the fire out before it could catch beyond that. Like I said, nothin' but smoke damage. Course, the comic books didn't do too well, though."

"What did Howard do to punish his son?"

"Heck if I know. It's not like I'm interested in how he disciplines his kid. That's none of my business. All I know is what Howard told me about the fire."

"Do you know if he called the fire department?"

Tom knew the answer to this was no, but he wanted to see if Zack would make something up, which would lend the lie to what he had said.

"Naw. Howard said he put the fire out. Figured a little paint would cover the whole thing up."

"Did he paint the room?"

"I guess he did. It's not like I went into his kid's room. Don't think I ever set foot in it, in fact."

"Where is Howard now?"

"I don't know."

"He's a friend of yours on Facebook. You don't know where he lives?"

"No. He left Opelika and I haven't seen him since." Tom could see that his knowledge that Howard was a friend on Facebook bothered Zack.

"Have you received any calls from him? Anything like that?"

"No. I think you should leave now, but first, maybe you should know about the other arson in town."

"What other arson?" Tom wondered if Bob Ebert had heard about that and not shared the information with Jack. It was likely something he'd withheld for now.

"The school. Maybe Howard's kid decided to burn the school down after seein' how easy it was to light a fire."

"Do you have a reason to think that he did?"

"No. I just think you're barkin' up the wrong tree thinking Howard set any fires. Only a kid would set fire to the school."

Tom wondered if this was true. He would go to the library and read up on this arson in the newspaper's archive there.

"Now, if you don't mind, I got work to do," Zack said.

"Okay," Tom said and left, his stomach in knots.

He was in no hurry to pass this information along to Jack. He would be more disappointed than Tom was.

Driving to the local library, he began searching the electronic archives of the local newspaper. He entered "school fire" in the search engine, and the story popped up immediately.

The fire had been set in the middle of the night and had burned several rooms. Despite the fact that the fire had been set inside the building, Tom was suspicious that there had been no alarm going off that someone had entered the building illegally. That was also a concern from the local police, according to the article.

As he read, Tom was surprised to learn that there had been other arsons in the town prior to the school being burned. Two houses and a bar had also been set ablaze by someone in the past year or so. There were no suspects, at least not at the time the story had been printed.

He found articles on the other fires as well. While it was true that if a school was set on fire that it was likely the work of a student, why would a kid set fire to a bar? The two houses, which were next door to each other, had been empty. The newspaper story said they were owned by the same couple as rental properties but were empty at the time of the fires.

This would take more investigation. He needed to look into these fires as well to find out what he could. He certainly didn't expect to find the arsonist, but perhaps what he could discover would help Paul.

24

Tom arrived at the courthouse to look into the identity of the owners of the two houses that were burned nearly a year ago. The pictures of the two homes showed total destruction, with pieces of timber sticking up like the blackened bones of some enormous beast and little else. The fire inspector had been certain they were arson, and the police suspected teenagers who had set the fires for kicks.

After providing a clerk with the address of one of the properties, he was able to find the names of the couple who owned them, Jacob and Cecilia Dabney. They lived in Auburn, the neighboring city of Opelika and home to the university.

He did some more research and found a phone number for the Dabneys. He called and Cecilia Dabney answered.

"Hello?" The voice sounded like that of an older woman, perhaps in her seventies or eighties.

"Is this Cecilia Dabney?"

"Yes. Who is this?"

"My name is Tom Gordon. I'm doing some investigating that involves the arsons in Opelika in the past year."

"Are you with the police?"

"No, ma'am. I'm a private investigator. I'm looking into an arson that could be connected to the ones that burned down your houses in Opelika."

"Oh, dear. Was anyone hurt?"

"Sadly, yes, ma'am. That's why I'm investigating."

"How can I help? We don't know who did it."

"Yes, ma'am. I was just hoping to find out a few things about the fire and some of the people you knew who might have decided to do something terrible like that."

"Well, I'm not sure I can help. All I know is the fire was set by someone, and we had to rebuild with the insurance money. But we didn't set it. We're not criminals."

"No, ma'am. I definitely don't believe you or your husband either set the fires or caused them to be set. I was just wondering if you might have suspected anyone of doing it."

"No, not really. Both houses were empty at the time. One was for rent and the people who lived in the other house were out of town. They were newlyweds. That was the first house they lived in as a married couple. They'd gone to Atlanta to visit her parents, I believe, so it wouldn't have been them."

"Yes, ma'am. Do either you or your husband have enemies?"

"No! I can't think of anyone who would do something like that."

"I ask because it's odd that both of the houses burned in the arsons that occurred recently in Opelika were both owned by you."

"I see why you think someone didn't like us, but for the life of me, I don't know who that could be. The police figured it was a couple of teenagers getting their kicks. It's sad some kids do that kind of thing just for fun, but it happens."

"Yes, ma'am. What about people who might have done work on the houses recently? Was there any kind of dispute about pay?"

"No, certainly not. Anyway, we only had one person who did any work for us, and he only mowed the lawn of the vacant house until we could get it rented. It's hard to rent a house with overgrown grass and weeds in the yard."

Tom felt the hair on the back of his neck react to that news. "Who did the mowing for you?"

"A local man. He came recommended by a friend."

"Do you remember his name?"

"No, but we paid him by check. Let me look at the check register and see."

"Would you? That would help me a lot."

"You don't think the man who mowed the grass started the fire, do you? Why would he? If the house burned down, he would lose the work."

"Yes, ma'am, but it's worth a try. If it's a certain person, it could shed some light on this."

"You mean you have a suspect in mind?"

"Not exactly a suspect, ma'am. Just someone whose name has popped up in regards to the arson in Florida I'm looking into. Sometimes, arsonists don't care about what they burn. It's about the thrill of watching the fire burn. Other times, it's a revenge kind of thing. Maybe he had a gripe with you that he didn't tell you about."

"I see. Well, let me get my check register for the time of the fire and I can call you back. I don't want to make you wait while I look."

"Yes, ma'am. Just please, be sure to call me back when you find out his name. If not, I'll be calling again later today. I need to get back to Florida."

"Certainly. I'll find it as soon as we hang up and call you back."

Tom drove to a local diner and went inside for a cup of coffee while he waited for Mrs. Dabney to return his call. Just as the waitress set the cup in front of him, his phone rang. The number for the Dabneys showed up in the screen.

"Hello, Mrs. Dabney," Tom said.

"Yes, I found the man's name."

"Excellent. Thank you, ma'am. What is it?"

"Howard Hanson. I remember he used to bring his son to help him sometimes. Cute boy."

"When did you first hire Mr. Hanson to mow the lawn?"

"A little over a year ago, I think. After your call, I called my husband. He remembers him, too, but not his name."

"Does he know where Mr. Hanson is now?"

"Not that I know of. Would you like my husband's cell number? He's at a friend's house. They went fishing this morning."

"That would be great," Tom said, taking out a pen and grabbing a napkin to write on.

She gave him the number, and Tom thanked her.

Disconnecting, he phoned Jacob Dabney.

When he answered, Tom said, "Mr. Dabney, my name is Tom Gordon. I spoke to your wife about your houses that burned down, and she says she spoke to you about my call."

"Yeah, she spoke with me. Do you think you know who did it?"

"Honestly, sir, I can't be sure right now about that, but I am interested in the fellow you had mowing the grass there."

"Yeah, I don't remember the guy's name, if that's what you need. I just remember it was Howard something. I'm getting old and don't remember stuff like that much anymore. I used to have his phone number. I put it under lawnmower in my phone's contacts. That's why I don't remember his name."

"You no longer have his phone number?"

"No, I deleted it."

"That's too bad," Tom said. "I'm wondering if he had any kind of beef with you about anything."

"Actually, your call to my wife made me think of something. I hired him to do some extra work around one of the houses. His work was shoddy, and I had to hire someone else to redo what he did. I refused to pay him."

"Did you tell that to the police?"

After a short silence, he said, "Honestly, I don't think so. I didn't really think about it until my wife called me and said someone was asking about him. It never crossed my mind he would do something like that anyway. I figured if he did anything, it would be to steal something to get his money."

"I take it he was not happy about doing the work and not getting paid for it?"

"You could say that, but it wasn't like he swore revenge or anything. Just yelled and stormed off."

"And that was the last you heard from him?"

"Yep. Good riddance, I say."

"What about his son. Your wife mentioned he would come help his dad mow the lawn."

"What about him?"

"What is your memory of him? Was he polite? Did you feel you could trust him?"

"Sure. I mean, he was a kid. He'd say hi and things like that. I can't say I trusted him, exactly. I just didn't distrust him. Know what I mean?"

"Yes. Do you have any idea where Howard Hanson is now?"

"Nope."

"Okay, thank you, Mr. Dabney."

"If you find out Hanson set fire to my houses, will you let me know?"

"Sure thing. I suspect the police will be the ones who contact you about that. You might want to call them and tell them what you just told me."

"I'll do that. I'd like to get the insurance deductible and lost rent from him if I could. I'd take a pound of flesh, but the cops won't let me do that."

"I understand your anger, sir," Tom said. "Thank you for speaking with me."

"No problem. Good luck."

Tom didn't bother explaining that he was mostly interested in finding out if Howard Hanson might be someone who used arson as a tool of revenge. It would be up to the local police to pin any Opelika arsons on Hanson.

Tom drove to the location of the bar that had been burned down. Now, it was an empty lot. Across the street was a small hardware store, and he stepped over there and entered.

A man behind the counter greeted him. "Mornin'! What can I do for you?"

Tom indicated the empty lot across the street. "Wasn't there a bar across the street that burned down?"

The man chuckled. "A little early to be lookin' for a drink, ain't it?"

Tom laughed along with him. "No, I'm just looking into the fire."

"You a cop? I figured they stopped lookin' into that months ago."

"No, I'm not a cop, either local or otherwise. I'm just being asked to look into the arsons that happened up here about a year ago."

"You some kind of private eye?" He could tell the man was impressed, as if it might be a very interesting job to have.

"I'm a private investigator, yes."

"No kidding?"

"No kidding."

"Well, ain't that somethin'? So you're investigating that fire?"

"Along with a couple of others."

The man, whose name was Eddie according to the name stitched on his shirt, swore and added, "What can I do to help?"

"I was just wondering if you were a customer of the bar when it was open?"

Eddie laughed. "Does a cat have a climbin' gear?"

"I take it you were a customer?"

"Hey, man. After a long day, ain't nothin' like a cold brew to wet the whistle. Know what I mean?"

Tom did know what he meant. Along with taking and selling drugs, he'd been a heavy drinker before converting to the man he was today. "That I do," Tom said. "Did you know any other of the regulars there?"

"Some of 'em. You thinkin' one of the regulars burnt Smitty's down? Why would they do that? I mean, it ain't like there ain't other bars to go to, but why burn down Smitty's? I tell ya, I was kinda sad when it burned. Now, I gotta drive a half mile to get my end-of-the-day beer. Before, all I had to do was cross the street."

Tom considered Eddie. He was exactly like the people he used to hang out with when his life centered on drinking and doing drugs. He could tell Eddie had a sense of humor and was outgoing and friendly. In a way, Tom liked him, but he was also glad he didn't hang around with guys like him anymore.

"Did the owner have any problems with any of the customers? You know, like something happened that made a customer angry right before the fire happened?"

"Not that I know of. Any one in particular you're thinking about?"

"Well, there is one guy I've heard might have some information about at least one of the other fires, though there's no proof he did anything wrong."

"Who?"

"Do you know a fellow named Howard Hanson?"

"Snake? Sure! I know him."

"Snake?"

"Yeah, that's what I called him. He had this tattoo of a snake coiled around his right arm, with the head being his hand. If he put up his hand with the four fingers all held together and the thumb underneath, it would look like the snake was about to bite." Eddie demonstrated, holding his hand up as if he had a sock puppet on his hand with the "mouth" open.

"So, he was a regular at Smitty's?"

"Yeah, but he didn't set that fire. No way." He leaned a bit closer to Tom and said, "To be honest, I always figured ol' Smitty burned it down for the insurance money. He wasn't gettin' any younger, and the insurance was probably more than the profit he'd make on the place for the next three years. Regular customers keep you in business, but it's the ones wandering in that really turn a profit. And Smitty's had mostly nobody new wandering in."

"Did you tell that to the police?"

"No way, man. Who am I to put the suspicions on Smitty? He's a nice guy. And if you tell them I said that, I'll deny it and say you musta got the wrong idea."

Tom made a locking motion over his mouth, and said, "I'm just looking for information about the fire. Just wondering here. How sure are you that Smitty did the deed himself?"

"On a scale of one to ten? Eleven. But like I said, I wouldn't say that to the cops."

Tom had to wonder at the truth of that statement. He felt that if push came to shove, Eddie would tell anyone who would listen. After all, Tom could be investigating for the insurance company for all Eddie knew.

Figuring he had all he could find out from Eddie, Tom said, "Well, thanks for talking to me about this."

"Sure thing. I guess you don't need any tools or anything, huh?"

"Not today, but thanks." He was about to leave when something occurred to him that Eddie had said. Turning back, Tom said, "One more thing, if you don't mind."

"What's that?"

"You said you know Howard Hanson, or Snake as you call him. You ever hear from him?"

"I got his email. You want it?"

Tom couldn't believe the luck. Even Zack, Howard's good friend, didn't say he had Howard's email. Of course, he could have, but he'd said he hadn't heard from him in months. He could have been lying—probably was—but now here was a guy happily volunteering that information.

"Sure, if you don't mind."

Eddie gave it to him, and Tom jotted it down, repeating it to make sure he had it right.

"Yep. That's it."

"I don't suppose you have his phone number, do you?"

"I did, but he said he had to get rid of the phone. Couldn't afford one anymore."

Tom could understand that. Cell phones were a luxury to those who made little money, and Howard was certainly among them. Then it occurred to Tom that Howard may have had to give up the cell phone when his wife left him. She was the primary breadwinner in the family, and it was likely he could no longer afford one, not even a burner.

"What do you know of his wife and son?"

Eddie shrugged. "Only that he had one of each. He rarely talked about them until she left him. Then he was really angry. Snake wasn't the kind of guy who took being left by a woman well. I told him he was better off without them."

"What did he say to that?"

"He said 'maybe so,' but it still ticked him off that she hightailed it to Florida."

Tom was speechless for a moment before he said, "He knew she was in Florida?"

"Yeah. Said she went down there to where one of her friends lived."

"Did he name the town?"

"Naw. Just Florida, but I figured he knew the town since he knew what friend she moved down there to be close to."

Tom smiled. This was more than he'd bargained on. So Howard Hanson knew where his wife and son were. That was big news that could change everything. Perhaps he had sought some revenge on his wife and son.

Tom left the hardware store and stopped by the local school that had been set fire to.

He was brought into the office of Ms. Reddy, one of the assistant principals and asked about the fire.

"Yes," Ms. Reddy said, "we always suspected one of the students, though we have no proof of it."

"You mean a particular student?"

"Yes."

"What's the student's name?"

"I think I'll keep that to myself until I know more about why you're here. Like I said, we have no proof, so it would just be my opinion anyway. But there's plenty of circumstantial stuff to suggest it was him."

"Well, I am here looking into a series of arsons in Opelika that happened within a short span of time, including the school fire."

"And who are you working for?"

"An attorney in Florida, Jack Turner."

"Is he defending someone in an arson?"

"Not exactly. He just sent me here on a sort of fact-finding mission in case charges are filed."

Ms. Reddy eyed him. "We had a student back then who had gotten into some trouble with one of the teachers. It was the teacher whose classroom was where the fire was started."

"And did the police look into your suspicions?"

"They did, but without more, they couldn't charge the student."

"I understand that the alarm system didn't work that night."

"No, it worked. It's just that the motion detectors are in the main halls, not in the classrooms. The classroom where the fire started was on the ground floor and had windows. Apparently, the boy—or I guess I should say the person—who started the fire broke out one of the windows and climbed in."

"There's no alarm to signal such a break-in?"

"No. We're not a rich school district. We're lucky we have what we do. There are cameras in the hallways, but not in the classrooms. Other than that, the classrooms with windows are vulnerable. The school board feels that being able to limit damage to a single classroom is sufficient reason not to do more with the alarm system."

"I thought all schools now had full security systems."

"Not all of them. We're an older building. New ones have that stuff included in the construction costs. We have what we have."

"Since I am not with the police and won't take this information anywhere else other than my employer, could you tell me the name of the student you suspect did this?"

"You have to understand this is only a suspicion. There were no prints left behind or anything like that. The boy can't be arrested for this because other than suspicions, we have nothing."

"I understand. I just want to know if it's the same boy my employer is helping out."

She seemed to consider her options before saying, "Okay. I'll tell you his name, but that's all I'll do."

"That's all I ask."

"Paul. Paul Hanson."

His reaction must have told her this surprised him. Her voice when she said her next words said she knew the answer to her question.

"That's who the lawyer is dealing with, isn't it?"

Instead of answering, he said, "Why do you suspect him? What happened with the teacher?"

"I'm not at liberty to say. It involved something that Paul was punished for."

Ma'am, I promise not to tell anyone you said anything. I just want to know if it was truly something that could have led to Paul setting fire to a classroom."

She eyed him before speaking. "I could lose my job for telling you."

"Only if I tell someone you said something."

"You might. All I can tell you is that it was serious enough that a student might do something in anger to the teacher involved. It meant he would likely have to repeat the class."

"We can subpoena his discipline records."

"That's up to you."

"What if I get his legal guardian to tell you it's okay to tell me?"

"Who's the legal guardian?"

"Jack Turner, the attorney in Denton I work for."

She opened her computer's search engine and verified that Jack was a lawyer in Denton. She called the firm's phone number she found on the internet, identified herself, and asked to speak to Jack, placing the call on speaker.

"This is Jack Turner?" Ms. Reddy asked.

Tom heard Jack's voice say it was.

"Mr. Turner, are you the legal guardian of a young man who used to live in Opelika, Alabama?"

"Yes. Are you with my investigator, Tom Gordon?"

Ms. Reddy looked at Tom. "Yes."

"Yes, I am the legal guardian of Paul Hanson, who used to live in Opelika. I understand you are an assistant principal at his school there?"

"How do you know that?"

"You identified yourself when you asked to be connected to me."

"Oh, I forgot. Yes, I'm Ms. Reddy."

"How can I help you, Ms. Reddy?"

"Do you give me permission to talk with Mr. Gordon about Paul's discipline records while he was attending our school?"

"Absolutely."

"Okay, thank you. I suppose that will suffice."

"You have permission to tell Tom anything regarding Paul."

"Thank you."

She ended the call and turned to Tom. "He was caught cheating on a big exam. It would have guaranteed he failed the class, given his average in the class at that time. It was a math class, so to advance to the next level, he would have to take it again the following year."

"What was his defense on the charge of cheating?"

"He said he wasn't cheating, but the problems that were on the test were in plain view when the teacher walked by. Someone had given them to him, apparently, and they had been worked out ahead of time."

"Did the teacher see him using the work that was, as you say, 'in plain view'?"

"He didn't have to. The mere fact they were there was reason enough to charge him with cheating on the test."

"How would he get the problems in advance?"

"Who knows? Kids these days have phones to take a picture of an exam paper. We believe one of the students who took the exam the day before shared the picture with Paul, and Paul worked them out ahead of time with help from his textbook or maybe someone else. He would likely have earned a lower grade on the exam without such help.

"Was he allowed to complete the exam?"

"No. He was removed from the room and given a zero."

Tom felt sick to his stomach. He rose and said, "Thank you for your time, Ms. Reddy."

She shook his hand and Tom left. He wasn't looking forward to telling Jack about this.

He stayed that night in his hotel, phoning Jack and filling him in on what he'd found out. There was a possibility that Howard had set the fire. He knew where his ex-wife and son were living and had not been happy that she had left him.

Then again, it was equally possible that Paul had set the fire. Tom could see a scenario in which Paul had intended to die in the fire himself before changing his mind. After all, the can of gasoline had been left outside his mother's bedroom, but her room was across the hall from his own, so essentially, the gas can was also left outside his own bedroom.

Jack took the news well, all things considered. He told Tom to return to Denton the next day and come to the office when he arrived in town.

They had things to discuss.

25

Tom drove back to Denton and arrived in the early afternoon, stopping for a bite of lunch before going to Jack's office. He knew he should have gone straight to the office but wasn't looking forward to the conversation they would have about Paul or his father.

As he entered, Jaz, Jack's secretary and sister-in-law, told him to go right in. As he entered, Jack looked up and said, "So, it wasn't good?"

"Not entirely. The fact that Paul's bedroom had burned and a friend of Howard's said Paul started the fire won't go well for him. Add to that the suspicions of the administration of the school that Paul set the fire that damaged the school, and it tends to point an even bigger finger at Paul."

"Then again, we have the fact that Howard worked for the owners of the two houses that burned and had a beef with them over money. That's certainly a motive."

"That seems to be all we have on him. Motive. No other proof or even evidence that could lead to an arrest. Paul has a lot more evidence against him for the arson of the house where he lived with his mom."

Jack sat back and laced his hands behind his head, something Tom recognized as his thinking posture. He was silent for a moment before saying,

"Bob Ebert is going to want to know what we found out."

"He didn't pay us," Tom objected.

"No, but he asked for a favor, and I said I would send you up there to find out what you could."

"Jack, we'd be providing information that would likely lead to Paul being arrested."

"I know. That's the problem. Frankly, I figured you would find out something that would point the finger at his father."

"Well, Howard did know Paul and his mother had moved to Denton."

"And you can bet I plan to introduce that as an alternate theory of the crime."

"But we have no proof he was anywhere near Denton on the night of the fire."

"Yes, that's a problem," Jack said and heaved a sigh. "Rock, meet hard place."

"What are the chances he'll be tried as a minor?"

"Somewhere between slim and none. He's certainly old enough to know setting fire to a house is a crime, especially an occupied one. It will appear he knew he would likely kill his mother."

"But why? Why would he do that?"

"It's possible he wanted to die in the fire but didn't and didn't want his mother around to deal with it."

"That's ridiculous."

"Is it? He's fourteen. His logic isn't necessarily going to lean toward mature thought. In fact, it's very likely it wouldn't. He wouldn't want his mother left to deal with the results, at least at this young age, he wouldn't." He continued sitting with his hands clasped behind his head. "At least, that's what the prosecution could say, and we have to figure out a way to contradict that or at least provide reasonable doubt."

"What about the email address for Howard Hanson?"

"Yeah. It's also odd that Paul never gave it to us or mentioned it before."

"Maybe he doesn't know it," Tom said. "I mean, it's not like he kept in touch with his dad."

"True, but it will just be something else suspicious about Paul."

"Did Bob ever ask about that?"

"No, but he wasn't really looking for the dad until recently. Searching for him was probably more of a 'check the box' kind of thing."

"So, what are we gonna do, boss?"

Jack stared at his phone. "If we don't tell Bob what we found out and he finds out later we knew, it'll look even worse for Paul."

"How will he find out later?"

"If we say we don't have any information, he'll likely go up to Opelika himself on his own dime, even if he has to take vacation days to do it. I know Bob. He won't rest until he knows everything about their lives in Opelika that he can learn. You found this out in a couple of days. I'm sure Bob could do the same. If they talked to you, they'll talk to Bob."

"Jack?"

"Yes?"

"What if Paul did it?"

"I've been thinking that since we talked on the phone. If he did do it, he has more psychological problems than I suspected, especially if the suicide attempt theory is the correct one."

"He's been seeing a psychiatrist to deal with the aftermath of the fire, though, right?"

"Yes, in addition to living with a woman who's a clinical psychologist, which helps."

"Has he done anything that suggests he might still try to kill himself?"

"Nope. Not yet, anyway."

"How's Jenny going to take this?"

"Not well."

"So, are you going to call Bob?"

"Yes. I'm just not looking forward to it."

"I understand that," Tom said, thinking of how he had put off this visit when he arrived back in Denton. "You gonna call Jenny first or Bob?"

"I'd prefer neither, but I'd rather tell Jenny face-to-face."

"You want me to go while you phone Bob?"

"No. Sit tight. I may need to ask you a question if he asks me something."

When he had Bob on the phone, he said, "Hi, Bob. It's Jack Turner."

"Jack! How are you. I was just thinking about you and wondered when you would call."

"Yes, I have some news to share with you."

"I'm listening," Bob said.

Jack explained everything Tom had found out in Opelika, including the information about Howard and his problems with the people who owned the two houses that had been burned down, as well as the fact he knew where his ex-wife and son lived. He emphasized that in the hopes that Bob would think Howard was more likely to have set the fire.

"That doesn't look good for Paul, I'm afraid. In fact, it's possible, even probable, that he did this."

"And it's possible his father did, too."

"That's true. Do you know of anything that would put him in Denton on the night of the fire?"

"No."

"Jack, I'll hold off on arresting Paul while I consider what you've told me. If I do arrest him, though, I'd prefer you bring him in. I don't want to arrest him and have to take him out of your home in cuffs."

"It's not a solid case you have against him, Bob."

"I don't know. You say one guy says Paul set fire to his bedroom. Sounds like he has done this before."

"There's no proof that Paul did that, though. Just some hearsay."

"If we can find Howard Hanson, it won't be hearsay."

Jack thanked his instinct that had told him to withhold Howard's email address from Bob. He'd intended to tell him if Bob leaned toward Howard as the arsonist, but he hadn't.

"When are you going to make a decision as to whether to charge Paul in this?" Jack asked.

"It will be a few days. I know Paul isn't going anywhere, and I need to talk to my superiors about it first. I can't say I'm hopeful that Paul won't be brought up on arson and murder charges. To be honest, I like the kid, but my job is my job. You understand that."

"All too well," Jack said.

They said their goodbyes and Jack hung up.

"They're going to charge him?" Tom asked.

"Probably," Jack said.

Tom cursed under his breath, and Jack said, "Ditto."

26

On Wednesday of that week, Mark knew he had to tell someone about what he saw the night of the fire. They had been getting friendlier with Paul, and Mark wanted no part in the newly formed group. He saw Paul as a guy who had murdered his mother and brought on the problems he now faced because of his appearance. The guys who had told everyone to steer clear of Paul mostly ignored their friendship with him. Mark figured they didn't care that some of the school nerds were friends with Paul, or they had stopped caring altogether due to what Mark considered their limited attention span.

As they sat at their usual table that morning, Mark knew Paul and Andy would not arrive for at least ten minutes. He took a deep breath and interrupted the conversation that had already begun about a chess tournament that Nathan and Ken wanted to take part in.

"I have something I need to tell you guys," Mark said.

The other boys looked at him. Mark's face told them it was serious.

"What is it, man?" Nathan asked. "You look like you might be sick."

"It's Paul."

"What about him?" Steve asked.

"I think he set the fire that killed his mom."

"You're crazy!" Ken said. "Why would he do something like that? Besides, he got hurt bad in the fire. Seems like he wouldn't have done that to himself, don't you think?"

Mark took another deep breath and said, "I understand all that. I think it's crazy too, but I can't ignore what I saw that night."

"What are you talking about?" Nathan asked.

"I snuck out that night and was just walking around. I ended up over where Paul used to live with his mom." He hesitated, trying to focus on what he'd seen. "I saw someone small, like a kid, going into Paul's house with a can of gas. They say that's what exploded in the house that killed Paul's mom and injured Paul."

"Are you saying you saw Paul go into his house that night with a gas can?"

"I guess. I mean, I don't know who it was, but it wasn't a big person. He looked like he was Paul's size. Who else would it be?"

"Dude, you have to tell the cops about this," Nathan said.

"Are you crazy? My parents would ground me for a year or something for sneaking out in the middle of the night."

"So? You can't keep this to yourself."

"Well, I haven't. I told you guys."

"Yeah, finally," Steve said.

"Really, man. You have to call the cops and tell them, even if you don't tell them who you are," Nathan said.

Ken looked at Nathan as if he'd just suggested Mark try to do a backflip off the table and said,

"They won't believe him if he does that. They'll just figure he's a kid trying to start trouble or something."

"I guess," Nathan said. "But, still. This is serious stuff. This isn't something like seeing Paul take a candy bar in a store without paying for it. This is murder. He killed his own mother, for Pete's sake."

"Or some other kid did it," Steve added.

"Who would do that? You think there's some kid running around Denton thinking, 'Gee, I think I'll murder someone by setting a fire in the middle of the night'? Get real."

"I guess. I don't know," Steve said. "This is bad."

Nathan looked at Mark and said, "You have to tell them, Mark. You know you can't go through life like this, knowing you saw something that was evidence in a murder case. Even if it wasn't Paul, you need to tell someone. You'll survive whatever punishment your parents come up with."

"I don't know, man. This is going to be bad."

"And dying in a fire isn't?"

Mark wanted to leave but knew he couldn't. Instead, he sat back and said, "I shouldn't have even mentioned it to you guys."

"No, you were right to tell us, though I wish I didn't know," Nathan said. "Now, you have to tell the cops."

Mark looked at them. Each face implored him to do what they all knew was the right thing. "Maybe I can get them not to tell my parents."

The other boys knew that was impossible but agreed with Mark that he might be able to do that.

None of them mentioned he would likely be called to testify in a trial.

Just then, Paul and Andy arrived at the table.

"What's up?" Andy asked them.

They all looked at Paul and Andy before Nathan said, "Nothing much." Then he looked at the other boys and said, "I have to go. I have to talk to one of my teachers about something."

Mark said, "What are you going to talk to a teacher about?"

"Nothing important, really. I mean, it's not like I'm going to tell them some kind of big secret. I have some questions about class. That's all."

The boys all saw Paul as a murderer now. They liked Andy, but he'd have to figure out whether he wanted to be with them or Paul.

Ken said, "Yeah, I have to go, too."

Then one by one, they all left the table, using lame excuses.

Paul was left there with only Andy. The actions of the other boys were confusing. They had all seemed happy to be with Paul the past two days of school, even ignoring the warnings not to be his friend. Mark had seemed distant, but the others had welcomed him and Andy into their little group of friends.

"That was weird," Andy said.

"Yeah. It's almost like they decided we weren't welcome anymore."

"Actually, it was exactly like that."

Paul sat at the table, looking as abandoned as he was. Andy, it seemed, was his only true friend.

The rest of the day went like any other day, with

the exception that all four of the other boys would see Paul and ignore him. The message was clear. Either they had been threatened again and had decided to sever the friendship, or they had all decided Paul was unwelcome for some other reason. In either case, the result was the same.

Paul had one friend now.

How long would it be before Andy abandoned him, too?

That afternoon when he arrived home from school, Mark felt as though the world was coming to an end. He would have to break his promise to himself never to tell what he saw. The other boys had made it clear that they would be forced to abandon him the way they had with Paul if he didn't do the right thing. He knew they were right, but that didn't mean he had to enjoy having to do it.

He sat for several minutes, working up his nerve before lifting their house phone's receiver. He was about to press 9-1-1 when he remembered that the number was only for emergencies. This was important, but not like an emergency where the cops needed to get to a car accident or something.

Instead, he dialed 4-1-1 for information. Once he had the number to the Denton Police Department, he dialed the number he'd written on a sheet of his notebook paper.

A woman answered, and he said, "I need to talk to someone investigating the fire that happened about a year ago. It's the one that killed Paul Hanson's mother."

"May I ask why you need to talk with the

detective in charge of that case?" the lady asked.

"I have some information. I saw something that night."

"Umm, how old are you?"

"Fourteen."

"Are you sure this is for real? It's a crime to file a false report on a case."

"It's real. Believe me, I've thought about this a lot. I need to get it off my chest. I saw something that may help solve who set the fire."

"Okay, hold on. I'll connect you with Detective Ebert."

After a moment's wait, a man answered the line. "Detective Bob Ebert. May I ask who this is?"

"Do I have to give you my name?"

"You don't have to, but it would certainly help. Besides, you're just a kid, really. The officer who spoke with you before told me you're only fourteen. If you give me your name, it will help me believe you."

For a moment, Mark considered giving him Nathan's name but knew that would come out as soon as the detective talked to Nathan, which was sure to happen sometime in the next day or two.

"Mark. Mark Lewis. I go to school with Paul Hanson."

"Are you a friend of his?"

"Well, I kind of was, but I don't think I will be after this."

"What do you have to tell me about this case?"

After a moment's silence, Detective Ebert added, "Son, I don't have a lot of time to just sit on the phone here. Are you going to tell me or not?"

Mark's sudden tears surprised him, even though he knew they shouldn't have. "I'm scared."

"Why?"

"When my parents find out what I've been keeping secret and how I found out, they're gonna kill me."

"Maybe they won't be happy, but then again, they will probably be proud you decided to come clean about it. That's how most parents are, anyway."

"Okay," Mark said, doing his best to stop crying. Then he told the detective what had happened that night.

"Do you think it was Paul?" Detective Ebert asked.

"I don't know. It just wasn't someone big."

"Could it have been someone else?"

"I guess it could have been, but who else would have done that who wasn't big like an adult?"

On his end, Bob was unhappy that this would lead to arresting Paul. He couldn't ignore all the evidence that suggested he was guilty of setting the fire. It wasn't ironclad, but it was enough to indict him for arson and murder. He figured the district attorney might drop the charge to manslaughter in the first degree, but that was up to him.

After he finished jotting down the notes from the call, which he did despite the fact the call was recorded, he said, "Thank you for calling this in, Mark. You've been a tremendous help here." He asked for Mark's address and jotted that down.

"Will your parents be home tonight?"

"Yes, sir."

"Fine. I'll be stopping by to discuss this further. You might want to tell them yourself before I arrive."

"What time will that be?"

"Probably around seven. Give you time to have supper."

"I don't think I'll be eating anything tonight," Mark said, and Bob's heart went out to this kid who had been saddled with this for about a year now.

"Okay, I'll be there around seven. Don't worry, Mark. I'll speak to your parents about not being too hard on you for this."

"Thanks," Mark said. "Bye."

"Bye, Mark," Detective Ebert said and hung up.

He would have to call Jack, but he'd wait until after talking with Mark in person. He wanted to look into the boy's eyes as he told his story again, and he wanted to make sure the story didn't change at all from what he'd said on the phone.

27

That evening, Bob stopped by the home of Mark Lewis. His parents' faces told him they already knew why he was there. Once he was seated in their living room, Mark came in and sat on the sofa with his parents, facing the detective.

"Mark, tell me again what happened."

"I snuck out the night of the fire. I wasn't really going anywhere. I just thought it would be cool to walk around town that late."

"Why did you end up in the neighborhood where Paul Hanson lived?"

Mark shrugged. "I don't know. I was just walking, not paying much attention to where I was going. Like I said, I was just enjoying being out that late."

"And what did you see as you approached Paul's house?"

"I didn't even know it was his house. I didn't really know Paul at the time."

"Okay. What did you see?"

"There was this person outside the house. It was dark, so I couldn't see his face, but he was carrying a gas can and he went inside. I wondered who it was since I figured it was another kid. He wasn't real big."

"Can you guess how tall he was?"

Mark shrugged. "I don't know. Maybe about my

height. I'm not sure. I can only say he wasn't real tall or big."

Bob watched Mark's face as he told his story. It was the same one he'd told before, which wouldn't be hard to remember well enough to retell several times, but he looked as though he was telling the truth. He looked into Bob's eyes for the most part, and he obviously wasn't happy to be having to do this.

"What did you see after that?"

"Nothing really. I just kept walking. I tried to stay in the shadows because I didn't want whoever it was to see me. Like I said, I was doing something I knew I'd be in trouble for if I got caught.

"If you thought it was another kid, why would that worry you? It's not like a kid is going to turn you in for breaking curfew."

"If it was someone I knew from school, he could—you know—hold it over me."

This rang true to Bob. Kids were into simple blackmail if it could serve their purposes. 'Do this or I tell your parents' could be a powerful motivator to cause Mark to keep to the shadows. Mostly, Bob was asking about this to see what Mark would say in response. If Mark were lying, he might make up a more elaborate answer. People who were lying tended to do that to make their stories sound more believable.

"Why did you wait so long to come forward?"

"I didn't want to get in trouble with my parents. I figured you would solve it fast, but you didn't." Mark looked at Bob accusingly, as if blaming the detective for having to confess to sneaking out.

"We're going to punish him for going out at night and for waiting so long to come forward," Mark's father said.

Bob looked at him. "I wouldn't be too harsh. After all, he did come forward on his own eventually."

Mark's father looked at his son. "Maybe, but he should have come forward when it happened."

"I agree with you there," Bob said before turning back to Mark. "And you're certain you can't identify who it was you saw with the gas can entering the house?"

"No. I just believe it was a kid, so it had to be Paul."

"Thank you, Mark. If we arrest Paul for this, you should be prepared to have to say this in court. Are you willing to do that?"

Mark looked at his parents, whose stern looks told him the answer to Bob's question. He shrugged. "Yeah, I guess I have to."

"You'll feel better about this once you've testified," Bob said.

Still looking at his parents, Mark said, "Everyone at school will think I'm a rat."

"Or they might think you're doing the right thing," his mother said.

Bob thanked them for their time and left. Taking out his phone, he called Jack. "I have news, and you're not going to like it."

"What?" Jack asked.

"We have a new witness, and I regret to say it looks like Paul is the arsonist. I need you to bring him in."

"A witness? After all this time? You've got to be kidding, me, Bob."

"Nope. A kid from the school said he snuck out that night and saw 'someone small' with a gas can go inside the house."

"Someone small could be anyone who's not large, Bob. That doesn't necessarily mean it was Paul."

"No, but with the print evidence and everything else, I think we have enough of a case to arrest him for arson and murder."

Silence greeted Bob for a moment before Jack said, "Okay. Can we do it in the morning?"

"Sure. I'll be in around eight."

"We'll be there by 8:30."

"I'm sorry, Jack."

"Yeah. Me, too."

They disconnected the call, and Bob drove to the station to complete the paperwork on the interview and went home.

The next morning, Jack and Paul entered the police station and were directed to the detectives' squad room to speak with Bob. Bob rose from his chair when they entered and indicated they should have a seat across from him.

Bob looked at Paul and said, "Paul, I'm sure you know why you're here."

"Yes, but I didn't do it."

"Paul, you are under arrest for arson that resulted in the death of your mother, Amber Hanson. You have the right to remain silent. If you give up that right, anything you say will be taken down and used against you in a court of law. You have the right to have an attorney present during questioning. If you want an attorney but cannot afford one, one will be appointed before any questioning. Do you understand these rights as I have explained them to you?"

Bob knew that reading Paul his Miranda rights was more of a formality to abide by the law. Jack was his attorney, and he was sitting right there.

"Yes, I understand."

"I'd like to have the arraignment as soon as possible, Bob," Jack said. "I want to be able to take him home today and not have him placed in a cell."

"I'm sure we can arrange for the arraignment. I've notified the DA, and they're willing to do that for you, but it will be up to the DA and the judge as to whether Paul gets to go home with you today. That's not my call, you know."

"Yes." Jack wasn't concerned about bail. He could post whatever was necessary. His home itself was worth over a million dollars.

"You want to tell me your side of this?"

"I didn't do it," Paul said. He indicated his scarred face. "Why would I do this to myself?"

"Well, you could have forgotten something and went back inside to retrieve it, believing you had time before the house exploded. Or you could have been attempting murder/suicide but lived through it."

"But I rolled around to put the flames out."

"Then either you changed your mind about suicide or it was the former reason, or something like it. Then there's the fire that happened in your bedroom in Opelika."

Paul stared back at Bob. "How did you know about that?"

"Investigation, Paul. We don't only look around Denton for clues." He didn't mention that it was Tom who had found this out.

"You think I started that?"

"Someone in Opelika says you did. Says your father told him you did."

"Again, that's hearsay, Bob," Jack said.

"Not if we can find Paul's father to testify."

"My dad started that fire. It was an accident."

Jack put his hand on Paul's arm. "That's okay, Paul. Save it for the trial."

"But I don't want there to be a trial," Paul said, tears welling and starting to spill over his eyelids.

"I'm sure the DA will give you an offer. Considering we have the prints and the fire in Opelika, not to mention the fire at the school where you are the prime suspect as well, you might consider the offer they give to avoid a trial."

"You have no proof of that," Jack said.

"No, but we're going up there to see what else we can find out about it."

Paul was shocked. "I'm the prime suspect in the school fire?"

"Yes, but we will need to investigate that further. The truth is, Paul, you're in some serious trouble, even beyond the charges here in Denton."

Paul looked at Jack, his eyes pleading.

"It's okay, Paul. We're going to fight this."

Bob's phone rang and he answered. When he hung up, he said, "We can step across the street to the courthouse. The judge is ready to arraign Paul."

When they entered the courtroom, Judge Mitchell Godwin was waiting. Only the court reporter and the judge were in the room, and Jack was grateful for this.

The case was announced, and Judge Godwin looked at Paul and Jack. "How do you plead?"

"Not guilty," Paul said. He was aware of how this went from watching shows on TV.

The judge turned to "Red" Miller, the Assistant District Attorney whose real name was Julius, who had been given this case, probably this morning. He and Jack knew each other well. "We're okay with ROR, Your Honor. The suspect lives with his attorney and his wife."

"He's living with you, Jack?"

"Yes, Your Honor."

"And I suppose you will guarantee his presence at trial?"

"Of course, Your Honor."

Judge Godwin slammed his gavel and said for the record, "The suspect is released to the custody of his guardian and attorney, who has guaranteed the suspect will not flee the jurisdiction."

As they left, Jack said to Bob, "I'll be in touch."

"Thanks. You know I wasn't hoping for this."

"Yes, I know that."

Jack and Paul rode home in silence. Jack wanted to allow Paul time to absorb everything that had happened. On the short drive, Paul mostly looked out the window. Jack heard a few sniffles and knew Paul was crying.

When they arrived at the house, Jenny was there. She had taken the day off after going in to make the necessary arrangements for the rest of the day. This would allow her to spend time with Paul when he got home. He would not be going to school.

When they were inside and seated in the living room, Jack said, "You mentioned something to Detective Ebert about how your father started the fire. Could you tell me about that?"

"My dad converted my room into a meth lab. I slept on the sofa. All my clothes were in a dresser in a corner of the living room or hung in the coat closet just inside the front door."

"So there was a fire in your room because of the meth lab?"

"Yeah, though nobody's going to believe me when I tell them."

Jenny said, "Your dad wasn't exactly a model citizen."

"Still, they'll just think I'm saying that to blame him."

"Did you have any friends over who can verify your bedroom was actually the living room?" Jack asked.

"No. It wasn't like the couch was made up like a bed."

"And you never had to go into the dresser for something when a friend was over?" Jenny said.

"No. The rare times I had a friend over, it was only for a few minutes while we got a drink or something. They weren't really allowed in the house. My dad was afraid they'd see the lab and know what was going on and turn him in."

"Did your dad make a lot of money cooking meth?" Jack said.

"I don't know. If he did, he didn't spend it on me or my mom."

Jack decided to change to another topic Tom had learned in Opelika. "The school says you had been a problem with the teacher whose classroom was burned."

Paul was silent for a moment, prompting Jack to say, "You want to tell me about that?"

"Yeah. We didn't exactly like each other."

"And there was a particular incident that happened right before the school fire?"

"Yes. I was given a zero on a big exam because the teacher said I cheated. It meant I'd probably have to take the class again, and that's what happened."

"Did you cheat?"

Paul hesitated before answering. "You won't tell anyone?"

"No. It wouldn't matter now, anyway. You've suffered the consequences for that."

Paul looked at Jenny, who shook her head to show she wouldn't tell anyone either. "Yeah, I cheated. This guy gave me the answers before class. It was a multiple-choice answer test. We had to show our work, but the teacher never really checked that, so I could just do some figuring and end up with the right answer. I even purposely put the wrong answer on two questions to make it look like I didn't cheat. But then when they looked at my exam paper after he accused me of cheating, they saw I hadn't really known how to do the problems. I just ended each one with an equal sign and the right answer, at least for all but those two."

"Did the other kid get in trouble?" Jenny said.

"Yeah. He was suspended, too, but he didn't get a zero on his exam because they couldn't prove he'd cheated to get his answers. And besides, he was good at math."

"There were a few other arsons in Opelika back then. A bar and two houses. You know anything about them?"

"No."

"They might think you burned the bar because your dad spent time in bars."

"They can think what they want, but I didn't do that. I never set a fire intentionally. Besides, if he was at the bar, he wasn't home, and that was a good thing. If he wasn't home, he couldn't hit me or burn me with a cigarette or something."

Finally, Jack settled on the most damning evidence for discussion.

"There's a kid at your school who says he was out that night and saw what looked like you going into your house with a gas can."

Paul paused a moment, thinking, and said, "Who said that?"

"I don't know yet, but I will."

"What was he doing out that late? The fire happened in the middle of the night."

"He apparently snuck out that night. He just happened to walk past your house before the fire."

"Why would he wait this long to come forward with this?"

"I'm not sure, but we'll be able to question him and find out everything in his story and try to punch holes in it. Still, it is true that someone went into your house and left the gas can in the hallway outside your bedrooms. He truly could have seen that."

"Whoever it was, it wasn't me."

Jack had the feeling Paul was being truthful, but if that were the case, who had burned down the house? Did Paul have an enemy at school who had broken in and set the fire?

"We're going to do whatever it takes, Paul. I can't promise anything, but I will work as hard as I can on this case."

"You win a lot of your cases, don't you?" Paul asked.

"A fair number of them. To be honest, most people arrested for a crime are guilty, but sometimes there are extenuating circumstances that come into play."

"What's that?"

"Extenuating Circumstances? It means there's more to the story than meets the eye. Things that are involved that create less guilt than committing a crime with malice toward a victim." He paused before asking, "Are there any extenuating circumstances here? Did you set the fire but feel you had a good reason to do that?"

"No!" Paul said, nearly shouting. "How many times do I have to tell you that I didn't do it?!"

"That's the last time. I'm sorry, Paul, but I have to be sure I have all the information to help me defend you. It could get ugly, and if I know everything that I can know, I will be able to see if I can find out who our arsonist is. That would be the best outcome."

"Okay. I just get tired of being suspected. I want the trial to get over with so everyone will know I'm innocent."

Jack smiled. "Good. I'm glad you feel that way because that's how every defendant who's truly innocent of the crime he's been charged with feels. They don't want it to linger. They want it over with."

"Well, that's how I feel. I'd be okay with having it tomorrow."

Jack chuckled, hoping that would help lighten the mood in the room. "I can't make it happen that soon, but I think a trial this summer isn't out of the question."

"The sooner the better," Paul said.

"I have to go back to work. I have a new case that needs my attention," Jack said.

"What case?" Paul asked.

Jack smiled at him. "You've forgotten already?"

Paul smiled back, his first smile of the day.

"Paul?" Jenny said.

"Yes?"

"I want you to know that we love you, no matter how this turns out."

He smiled at her. "Thanks."

"I'll be home this evening, and I'll catch you up on what we're doing on your case, okay?" Jack said to Paul.

"Okay."

As he left, Jack noticed Paul didn't look very sure of the outcome. But then, neither was he.

28

When he arrived at his office, Jack called Tom and asked him to stop in when he had a chance.

"What do you need, boss?" Tom asked as he sat.

"We need to find Howard Hanson. I figure that email address might be the key."

"You want me to email him?"

"Actually, I want you to send two emails. One today after I look at it, and the other near the start of the trial. Maybe a week before it's scheduled to start."

"What makes you think he'll reply? Shoot, he might not even open it."

"Because the subject line on the one you send just before the trial will be 'I apologize and want to pay you after all.' You're going to create an email account under the name Jacob Dabney. If you have to assign some numbers because there's already a Jacob Dabney on the email server, choose some that make up a date, as if it's a birthday, like jacobdabney0617. Once you've done that, write the email and tell him you feel bad that he had worked those hours but hadn't made anything for his efforts, even if they were unsatisfactory. Just say you want to send him $50 to cover the time he spent on that job. Tell him you need an address for where to send the money."

"Isn't that illegal, like phishing?"

"No. Phishing involves pretending to be someone else to get something of value from the email's recipient. A mailing address is not something of value. It's just information. Besides, I intend to give him the $50, so he's benefiting, at least in a small financial sense."

"Okay. You think he'll reply?"

"Yes, I do. It's $50. He might come back with a counter offer. If he does, haggle some, but don't make him think you're not going to send anything. We need an address where he lives now so we can bring him in to testify at his son's trial."

"But you don't have a checking account in Dabney's name."

"We'll give him cash."

"And you don't want me to send that email yet, right?"

"Not that one. We'll do that a week before the trial starts. That's the great thing about email. He could travel anywhere, and his email address will follow him."

"What if he never checks that email account?"

"That's why you're sending him another email from another fake account that says he owes you money. He won't ignore something like that. Use a subject line that will anger him, and use a function that tells you if the email was opened. That way, even if he never answers, you'll know he opened it. Once you've written that email, let me approve it. Then you can send it."

"I'm on it," Tom said.

Tom went to the small office he used at Shelton and Turner and sat at the computer. After opening an email account with a service that featured email tracking and creating an account in a false name, he created another email account under the name of jacobdabney1016.

After typing the first email from the first fake email account, he saved it and began the second one from the fake Jacob Dabney. This one required more care. He would have to sound sorry that he hadn't paid Howard but not so sorry that it sounded fake.

Taking a swallow from his club soda, he typed, "Dear Howard." No, that felt too familiar. Dabney would not likely call him by his first name in an email, even an apologetic one. He backspaced and began again.

Dear Mr. Hanson,

I've been talking it over with my wife, and I feel bad that I didn't pay you for your time when you did that work for me that I found unacceptable. I found someone who knew you and he gave me your email address. Yes, I still feel the work was not good, but I feel bad that I did not at least give you some money for your time. It was, after all, time you could have spent doing something else to make money.

With that in mind, I want to pay you some money for the work you did. I do not have an address for you, but I do know from searching for you that you no longer live in the Opelika area, so I will be mailing you the money.

If you will reply with your current address, I will mail you $50 to at least pay you for the time you spent working for me on that project, even if I wasn't happy with the results. I think it's only fair, and my conscience has been bothering me.

Apologies,

Jacob Dabney

Tom read the email several times. He hoped Howard Hanson would believe the nonsense expressed in the email, but he also figured that when he saw the $50 figure, he would be inclined to believe it. Not believing it meant he might be saying goodbye to an extra fifty bucks.

He printed what he had, including the email about Hanson owing money to a fake person, and went to Jack's office. He was busy for the moment, so he sat with Jaz and talked.

"How's Rick?" Rick was Jaz's husband and Jack's older brother who had disappeared from Jack's life for many years.

"Doing well. Still building houses and enjoying working outside and staying sober."

"That's great. Sadie wanted me to ask if the two of you would like to come for supper this weekend. Nothing special. Just food, friends, music, and maybe some cards."

"Hearts?"

"Sure, why not?" Tom said.

"I'll talk to Rick. I'm sure he'd be up for that."

"Great."

At that moment, Jaz's phone buzzed. She answered and said, "Okay." Turning to Tom, she said, "You can go in now." At that moment, the door to Jack's office opened, and one of the attorneys who worked for Jack exited, smiling at Tom as he did.

"Come on in, Tom," Jack said.

After taking his seat, Tom passed the printed emails to Jack, who read them.

"These look fine, Tom. You can send the one about Howard owing money. I'll let you know when to send the other one."

"No problem," Tom said.

Returning to his office, Tom opened the email Jack wanted to send and pressed the send button.

Now, all there was to do was wait for the verification it was opened to come through.

That evening, he checked the email that he'd created for that purpose and found it had been opened about a half hour after being sent. There was a reply, and Tom opened it.

The reply only said, "I don't know you and I don't know what you're talking about." Then Howard added a warning about what he would do if contacted again, cussing and threatening him while doing so.

Tom smiled. Checking the time-stamp that showed when Howard had opened it, Tom saw it had taken about thirty minutes for him to open the email. It was indeed an active email account, and he would receive the other email from the fictional Jacob Dabney when it was sent. The subject line alone would guarantee he opened it, and the prospect of money would guarantee he would answer, if only to request a higher payment. If he did, he would reply agreeing to something at least moderately more than $50 while not making it seem like too much, which could easily raise Howard's suspicions.

Tom phoned Jack. "The fish is on the line," he said.

"Great. We'll send the other email about a week before the trial. I'll make sure he comes to court if I have to send the local cops to pick him up to ensure he honors the subpoena."

Tom hung up the phone and told Sadie that Rick and Jaz would probably be coming for dinner that weekend.

29

Paul wasn't allowed to return to his school after the arrest. He would be treated differently by everyone now. He knew that although the law said he was innocent until proven guilty, that wasn't true for most of the people around him.

The day after his arraignment, he was enrolled in what was called an alternative school. It sounded harmless, but like most things with simple names, it was more than it seemed. Alternative schools were for students who the school authorities felt were not suited to be with the regular population of kids. Paul considered it to be the solitary confinement or even the death row of the school system.

Sure, there were plenty of kids who needed to be separated from the general population of students because they could become dangerous, but he certainly wasn't one of them. If allowed to return to the school he had been attending, he would act and behave as he had—no better but no worse.

When Jack pulled up in front of his new school, he followed Paul inside to help him get to where he needed to go. They stopped in the office and were greeted by a woman who smiled and welcomed them, but Paul suspected she was not being genuine. He felt she was just doing her job but that inside she was wondering what kind of terror this student might cause.

Paul was shown where his classroom was. There were only five other students in the class, all his age. Apparently, the teachers moved from room to room and the kids stayed where they were to cut down on being possibly unsupervised in the hallways.

Paul had sometimes considered school to be like a prison, but this made those other schools seem like a party. The windows were even covered with chain link fencing to prevent people from breaking in—or out.

None of the students in his class did anything to welcome him, of course. Mostly, they looked at him as if he had just dropped in from some planet where the creatures who lived there were covered in scars. They also avoided him, as if whatever had caused his scars might be contagious.

Paul sat at a desk and uttered an aloof goodbye to Jack as Jack did his best to be positive about this development. Paul's behavior suggested that nothing positive was happening in his life.

The rest of the day passed with no communication from anyone. The teachers did their best to engage Paul, but realized early on that Paul was not going to respond other than to do what he was told. The teachers in his final two classes didn't bother to attempt to engage him in conversation, so Paul figured word had spread that he wasn't a friendly sort and that attempting conversation for now was fruitless. Paul figured they were just giving him time to adjust. They didn't seem like bad people, but he still wasn't interested in getting to know anyone there.

He was taken home by bus, and once he was walking home from the stop, he made a decision. It wasn't much of a plan. Even he recognized that, but he couldn't stay there and continue attending a school like the one that he'd just spent the day hating. He'd learned a word in his old school recently that described his situation: intolerable. He'd felt a kinship to that word as soon as he saw it.

Life was intolerable, but he didn't want to end it. Instead, he would change it. He was going to run away, carrying out the plans he had before the fire.

Reaching the house, he took out his key and let himself in. He had hoped that neither Jack nor Jenny had found it necessary to come by the house because they forgot something, and he was glad neither of their cars sat in the driveway. He would have to work fast to make sure they didn't show up while he packed.

Going into his room, he pulled a few of his clothes out of the drawers and stuffed them into his backpack.

Once the clothes were packed, he stopped in the kitchen and packed a few bottles of water and some snacks and left the house. He began walking to the highway. He would cross the bridge and then attempt to thumb a ride toward Wharton and beyond.

He would spend the night under an overpass and move on the next morning. He wanted to get into Alabama and possibly settle in Mobile, a city large enough to get lost in and not be found.

As he walked, he drank his first bottle of water while thinking of Jack and Jenny and all they'd done for him. He was sorry to leave them, but what he had to do was obvious now. He would likely be convicted of setting the fire that killed his mother and scarred him. He couldn't let that happen. It was another incentive for running away.

The first person to stop for him took him as far as Wharton. It was a fairly big town compared to Denton, but as he walked attempting to thumb a ride, nobody picked him up. He wondered how much his scars were the cause of that.

Night fell and the chances of getting a ride grew slimmer. A teenager thumbing a ride during the day could be seen as a kid trying to get somewhere to meet friends. At night, they turned into a danger, and again, his scars would add to that belief.

He noticed a bridge about a mile ahead. He could stay under the bridge.

When he arrived there, he climbed up to where the town side of the bridge met the ground and dropped his bag. He opened a second bottle of water and drank it while munching on a power bar he'd taken from the house and making plans.

When Jenny arrived home at 5:30, it was well after Paul should have gotten home. She was concerned but not worried. He may have found someone to go into town with and have fun playing basketball or something.

However, when she went upstairs and found his room a scatter of clothes, concern twisted into worry.

She called Jack, wondering if he might know something about this.

"Hi, hon," Jack answered.

"Jack, do you know why Paul's clothes would be strewn about his room?"

"No. He's not home?"

"No, and I'm worried. It looks like someone tossed his clothes all over the room. They're on his bed, on the floor, along with his school books and the other things he kept in his backpack. It's a mess. That's so unlike him."

"Check for his favorite t-shirt."

"The one with the picture of the dog on the front?"

"Yes."

"Hang on." She went into Paul's bedroom and searched for the shirt. She knew it was clean. She'd washed it in the last load of laundry and had put it in the dresser herself. After a moment, she said, "It's not there."

"Okay," Jack said, "I think he might have run away."

"Oh, no!"

"Yes."

"Should we call the police?"

"I'd rather try to find him ourselves, but there's really no choice. The worst part is it will make him look more guilty."

"Jack, he's barely fifteen. Guilty or innocent, they assume the worst will happen."

"True, but the police and the DA won't see it that way."

"Do you think they'll remand him into custody?"

"It's possible, but I'd be willing to have them put the ankle bracelet on him instead."

"Same here. What should we do?"

"I'll call Bob and let him know. At least he'll listen when I tell him this isn't proof Paul's guilty."

"But will the judge?"

"Good question."

They disconnected, and Jack phoned Bob.

"What is it, Jack?" Bob said when he saw his caller ID.

"I'm afraid I have bad news."

"What?"

"I think Paul ran away."

"Oh, Jack, that's not bad news. That's terrible news."

"I know."

"Any idea where he might have gone?"

"Anywhere but north. He wouldn't go back to Opelika, but east or west would make sense."

"What about a friend?"

"He only has a few, and only one that he might look into staying with, but he's a member of BOTW and would call me if that happened."

"You sure?"

"Yes. I'll call his house anyway to make sure."

"Okay. Any idea what time he left?"

"I assume he came home after school and left. The alternative school would have called Jenny if he wasn't in a class."

"That's true," Bob said. "That means he's been on the run for a few hours."

"He's not 'on the run,' Bob. He's only recently turned fifteen. He's just scared. Kids that age always expect the worst outcome, regardless of what may have really happened."

"You may be right, but I'm not sure the DA or the judge will see it that way."

"We're agreeable to attaching an ankle monitor."

"They might go for that," Bob said.

"I hope so. I'll let you know if we hear from him."

"That sounds good. I'll send out a BOLO."

"Okay, but stress he is not dangerous. He's just run away."

"Don't worry. I will."

They disconnected, and Jack thought about how much time Paul had had to travel. If he'd managed to thumb rides, he could be in Alabama by now.

Paul grew bored sitting under the bridge and decided to at least walk for a while until he grew tired enough to sleep. He could find another place to camp for the night down the road. Now, though, he had to walk.

Shouldering his backpack, he set off once more. He had walked a few miles when his journey ended.

A police car pulled up in front of him as he walked. The bubble lights flashed on and bathed the area in an eerie shade of blue.

The officer approached. "Are you Paul Hanson?"

It was then Paul knew that his idea was fated for this from the moment it occurred to him. He'd admitted to himself that it wasn't well-planned, and deep inside, he probably knew that he would be found sooner or later. Still, this was much sooner than he thought.

It was over. He would have to go back to Jack and Jenny and try to explain why he did this. He didn't want them to think it was because of them. In fact, they were the only reason he'd had misgivings in the first place.

"Yes," Paul said.

"Your folks are worried about you. Climb in. I'll take you home."

Paul considered his words: folks…home. It hit him that this was truer than he'd ever thought it was before. He began to cry, sure that the officer thought it was because he'd been found, and in a way, the officer was right, just not in the way he probably thought.

As they drove, the officer called in that he'd located Paul and was taking him home to Denton.

When he climbed out of the police car with his things, Jenny and Jack rushed to greet him. Jenny held him in a strong hug while Jack waited his turn. That Jenny was crying only made Paul feel worse.

Jack thanked the officer and followed Paul and Jenny inside. When they were seated in the living room, Jack spoke first.

"We'd like to know why you did this."

Paul let everything out then. His misery at his new school. His fear of what would happen at his trial. How much he hated leaving them but didn't see any other way to deal with these problems.

"I'm just scared," he said when he'd finished.

"Paul, running away is never an answer. It's just leaving one problem for an even worse one, and the original problem is still there."

"Okay." Paul could think of nothing else to say.

"We have to appear before the judge again tomorrow. Hopefully, he'll probably just make you wear an ankle bracelet that will monitor where you are at all times," Jack said.

"Okay," Paul said. What else could he say? It wasn't as if he could refuse. He was sure doing that would ensure he stayed in jail until the trial.

Jenny said, "Are you really that unhappy at this school?"

"Yes. It's awful. I don't even have Andy and Melody to talk to."

Jenny looked at Jack and said, "Do you think we could hire a teacher to homeschool him?"

Jack said, "What would you think of that, Paul?"

He considered it and said, "That would be okay. It would be better than having to put up with going to this alternative school."

Jenny said, "I know some retired teachers. I'll make some calls and find one who's able to take this job."

Paul said, "You mean you're going to pay someone to teach me? Like a private tutor or something?"

"Yes," Jack said. "We don't mind. We want what's best for you."

Paul hung his head. "I'm sorry. I didn't mean to worry you." He spoke so low that they almost couldn't hear him.

"We forgive you, but please, don't do it again, okay?" Jack said.

"I won't."

Jenny started calling some of the teachers she knew who might take the job of being Paul's full-time homeschool teacher. On her second call, she found the perfect person. Ms. Livingston was happy to take on the job, but she insisted that they meet in a public place, at least until she got to know Paul better.

After talking with Jack, Jenny called Ms. Livingston again. "How about Jack's office? He has an empty office you can use."

"That would be fine," Ms. Livingston said.

Arrangements were made for her to start the following day.

Jack made a conference call to Red Miller, the prosecutor in Paul's case, and the judge who had allowed Paul to be released to him and Jenny. After some discussion, it was agreed that Paul would have to wear an ankle monitor. This was not the usual way such things were handled, but with Jack being a local attorney and also Paul's guardian, the process was streamlined a bit for everyone's sake. Jack took Paul to the police station that night to have the monitor set and activated.

30

Jack had to leave early the next day to drive to Tallahassee on business, so Jenny took Paul to his first day of school with Ms. Livingston. As she drove, Jenny could see that Paul was happier to be going there than to the public school. Ms. Livingston had taught math and science for thirty years. She had also read and traveled widely and had written a few books about her travels. These showed an ability to teach English and social studies as well.

"Paul?" she asked when they had left the house.

"Yes?"

"There's something I want to tell you."

"What?"

"I want you to work on giving more people the opportunity to love and accept you for who you are."

"Most people are mean to me, and only because I have these scars."

"Yes, and you need to give them the chance to get to know the real you. That you're not your skin. Who you are is inside you, not outside."

"I know, but they won't give me a chance."

"Andy did. And Melody. Michelle was nice to you, too, as were the other kids at BOTW."

"I guess."

"If you give up on people, you give up on life."

"But I keep getting my feelings hurt, and they make me mad with how they act."

"I understand, but you need to think about something. Over half the anger and even more of the hurt feelings in the world are the result of misunderstood intentions."

"Huh?"

She smiled at him before looking back at the road. "We often attribute a meaning to what someone does or says that isn't correct. For instance, if you were to approach Andy and ask if he wanted to come over and play games and he just said no without explanation, you might think he didn't like you anymore or that someone had talked him into not spending time with you. You would go away angry and hurt. Then later, you might find out he had an argument with his mother. Or worse, someone close to him had died and he wasn't ready to talk about it and just wanted to be left alone. In the moment, he may not consider how his answer to you might be taken. You'd have your feelings hurt and be angry at him because you misunderstood his intentions. It happens all the time with people. Every day."

"I see what you mean."

"Can you try to give people more than one chance?"

"Yes. I guess so."

They arrived at the office and Ms. Livingston was waiting outside. She stepped over to greet them. Paul had thought she would be really old since she had taught for so long, but she looked to be only in her fifties. That was old as far as he was concerned, but not as old as he'd imagined her to be. The thought of what Jenny had said in the car came to him, and he realized he had formed an opinion without waiting to find out anything about Ms. Livingston. He'd also thought she might be really strict with him, and he might be wrong about that, too. She seemed like a nice lady who was eager to teach him.

"Hello, Paul," she said as she approached with her hand out to shake. "I'm Ms. Livingston. I'm happy to be able to teach you."

He shook her hand and looked at her smile. It was genuine and indicated she had meant what she said. She was happy he was here.

"Nice to meet you," Paul said.

"Thank you for doing this," Jenny said.

"No problem. I'm happy to earn a little on the side, and I'm sure working with Paul will be a pleasure."

"I need to get to work myself," Jenny said. "Jack or one of his employees will give him a ride home."

Hugging Paul, she said, "Bye, Paul. Try to enjoy yourself."

"I'll try," Paul said, hoping he would.

"Come on in and we'll get started," she said, placing a warm hand on Paul's shoulder and leading him into the building. "You don't need to bring a lunch anymore. We can go out for lunch, but it will have to be something inexpensive. They're paying me well, but not well enough we can go to fine restaurants."

"You sure?"

"Yes, I'm sure. I have to eat, too, you know, and

I really don't want to have to bring a lunch every day, and there are a number of places that serve healthy food."

He smiled at her and they entered the office that would serve as his classroom for now.

"Do you have a laptop?"

"Yes," he said, opening his backpack and taking it out.

"Good. I want you to write something for me so I can get to know you better. Talk about your life. Talk about what you like to do for fun. Talk about some of the things that bother you, and talk about your life before you moved to Denton. You don't need to tell me anything you aren't ready to share, but I want to get to know you. I want to get to know who you are."

"Okay." He sat a moment as she removed her own laptop from her bag and began typing on it.

Ms. Livingston noticed his wondering glances and said, "I'm doing the same thing. I want you to get to know me, as well."

"Oh." He started typing and decided to tell her everything he could about himself. His likes and dislikes. His fears. His family. His inability to make friends because of his scars. Everything.

He typed for nearly an hour before stopping. She had stopped before he did, telling him to take however long he needed.

When they were finished, they exchanged laptops and read about the other.

As Paul pored over what she'd written, he began to realize they would get along well. She talked about how insecure she had been as a teenager and how the first time she had to give a speech in front of class in sixth grade, she had stumbled through it while her entire body shook with fear, and she'd thought she was going to throw up in front of the class. She talked about her late husband and how much she missed him. She talked about how she loved to travel and wanted to take a cruise around the world someday.

By the time he had finished, he knew more about her than he ever thought he would.

When he looked at her, she had tears in her eyes.

"I'm so sorry these things have happened to you, Paul."

"It's okay, really. I mean, they happened. I can't change that."

"True. Do you have any questions for me?"

"Yes. Don't teachers have to stand in front of a class and talk every day?"

She smiled. "Yes, Paul. You see, I got over that fear. I realized that if I wanted to be a teacher, I would have to conquer that fear, and I wanted badly to be a teacher."

"How did you get over it?"

"By facing it. By meeting it head-on. The only way to get over your fear of doing something is to do it and realize it wasn't as bad as you thought it would be. You see, in my case, I was afraid the kids would judge me and my performance in the speech, not to mention I feared a bad grade on it from the teacher. Fear was controlling me instead of me controlling my fear. When I realized a couple of things, it helped me overcome it."

"What kind of things?"

"First, we are judged by those around us every second of every day. Some judgments are harsher and are done by harsh people. You see, the kids in my class who were going to judge me harshly weren't going to change their assessment of me whether I did well or not. Those who would judge me kindly would do so regardless of how well or badly I did when I spoke in front of the class."

"What else?"

"I realized that the fear was giving me the bad grade that I so wanted to avoid. I decided that it didn't matter if I did well or not, I had to overcome that fear, so I would volunteer to speak in front of the class whenever I could. When I found that I was still breathing and my friends were still my friends afterward, it gave me the ability to lose that fear."

"Wow. I never thought of it like that."

"Fear is both your best friend and your worst enemy, depending on its effects. Fear of burglars in the night is a good thing because it makes us lock our doors and keep our homes and lives safe. Fear of getting in a bad car wreck makes us slow down and be careful driving. Those are good fears to have.

"But fear of doing something that makes you better as a person is a bad fear. Those kinds of fears are your worst enemy. They keep you from doing things you should do. There are people who fear going outside their homes, and while it's right to be wary of people who might harm you, allowing that fear to take over your life is bad. Imagine the fun you would miss by never going out, not to mention that's not good for your physical health, either."

"Did Jenny tell you to talk about this with me?"

"No. I used to talk about it with my students as well. I'd tell them that fear is the great immobilizer. And sometimes being immobile can get you hurt or killed, like a deer that freezes in the headlights of an oncoming car."

"I never thought about that."

"But you will now, I'm sure," Ms. Livingston said.

"Do you have any questions for me?" he asked.

"Yes, but I'll find those answers as we interact. Besides, being an adult allows me to see the pain beneath the words and doesn't require me to ask as many questions."

"Okay, just don't get hurt or angry from misinterpreting something I say or do."

"What?" she asked, sounding confused.

Paul explained what Jenny had told him that morning.

She smiled at him. "Don't worry, Paul. I'll make sure we understand each other."

As the school year wore on, they grew close. It turned out to be the best school year he'd had, but the trial hung over him like storm clouds on the horizon, always present and always threatening.

31

The weeks passed, and the fear was always somewhere in the back of his mind. That fear wasn't like Ms. Livingston's fear of public speaking. He couldn't practice facing the trial the way she had practiced facing her fear. As the date of the trial approached, Ms. Livingston told him there wasn't anything he could do about it anyway, so worrying wouldn't help.

That advice helped a little but not enough. He kept worrying enough that he often lost sleep because of it.

When the date for the selection of the jurors was getting close, Paul asked Jack if he had to be there for that, and Jack said he did. Paul was disappointed. While he looked forward to having it over with, he wasn't looking forward to sitting day after day at the defense table while hoping the jury believed him. Sitting through jury selection, or what Jack called *voir dire*, would just be more sitting and watching the proceedings that would determine the rest of his life. Paul wasn't looking forward to that.

Jack had asked him if he wanted to testify, telling him he didn't have to if he didn't want to. Paul had insisted he testify, and Jack agreed that it would be useful in this case. Apparently, it was rare for a defendant to take the stand in his defense, but Jack felt Paul would do fine with preparation.

"I want the jury to see what kind of person you are. I know it's a sensitive subject for you, but I don't want them to judge you by your scars."

"Neither do I."

When jury selection was only a week away, Paul could feel the worry and stress ramp up. The school year had ended two weeks before the trial. The judge had agreed to wait until then so Paul wouldn't miss any school. Paul wondered if that was more a personal favor to Jack than concern about Paul's education.

It also surprised him that Jenny had spoken to Ms. Livingston about continuing as Paul's teacher for the next school year. Paul asked Jenny, "What if I don't live here anymore? What if I'm in prison?"

"I have faith you will be here. Jack's a good lawyer, and hopefully, he can convince the jury that you're innocent."

"I am innocent."

"I know, but right now, whoever will sit on the jury doesn't know that. It's up to Jack to convince them."

"Jack and me," he corrected.

She smiled at him. "Yes, and you. But don't put all the weight on your shoulders. It's Jack's job to bear that burden."

He still hadn't slept well that night, but it did help that she had so much faith in Jack.

Two weeks before *voir dire*, Jack called Tom and told him to send the fake email from Jacob Dabney.

By the time the trial was about to begin, they still

had no reply. This worried Jack. What if he'd decided to change his email address? That address would still accept emails, but if Hanson wasn't reading them anymore, they wouldn't be able to find him. It was important that they find his location.

As they headed to the courthouse to begin perhaps the most crucial part of the trial, *voir dire*, Jack shifted his mind to thoughts of what kind of jurors he sought. While a young mother would likely be sympathetic toward Paul, she also might have a problem with the charges leveled at him. He would have to be careful to seek someone who could feel sympathy rather than worry or fear.

Jack had told Paul about Kelly Poole, the attorney he had hired years ago fresh out of Florida State University's Law School. Among other things, she was his jury specialist. In fact, she was the first attorney he and Chuck Shelton had hired after they became law partners. She could read people better than he could, and her help had assisted in choosing a jury that was good for them on a number of occasions.

As they arrived in the courtroom, Kelly was already seated at the defense table. She was busy looking over the jury pool, the list of citizens who had received notice to report for jury duty today. Both Jack and Julius "Red" Miller, the prosecuting attorney, would question them about their lives and beliefs prior to either rejecting them or accepting them. They each had a total of only four preemptory challenges for the seated jury of twelve plus four alternates. A preemptory challenge was a "rejection without cause," so care in their use was vital. Use them up before questioning a potential juror you definitely did not want on the jury, but that you had no acceptable cause to reject, and you'd be stuck with that juror, possibly destroying your case. Such things happened all the time, and Jack was nearly manic in his desire to get it right. He always sweated out that last preemptory rejection because it was the last one available to him.

Paul sat beside Kelly as court was called to order. He had little to do other than watch the proceedings, and again he wondered why he had to be there that day. The judge entered and sat in his high seat that overlooked the courtroom.

As Jack went about the business of defending Paul, Paul considered how this judge was older than the one who had arraigned him. He was heavyset with fine whisps of white hair styled in a combover and had a white mustache and wore thick-framed glasses. He reminded Paul of a movie actor he couldn't place.

When the judge was seated, Paul noticed his name plate sitting on the top of his high desk. It read "Judge Reilly." Paul wondered what his first name was before thinking how stupid it was to be wondering that when his freedom was on the line. Then he realized that might be why he was wondering about it. This man would play a major role in what happened to him from this point forward.

As the potential jurors were called into the courtroom and introduced to everyone, Kelly watched their faces and body language. Which ones were serious? Which were afraid or timid? Which ones looked too anxious to be on the jury? Who seemed too young? Too old? All of these traits and more were important to identify in a potential juror.

The serious ones would likely take everything that happened in the courtroom as important and would pay attention without drifting off.

Those who were timid or afraid might have trouble making up their minds in deliberations. They could also be swayed easily if they were thinking of acquittal and a more forceful personality was pushing hard for guilty.

The people who longed to be on a jury could go either way, depending on other factors, such as prejudices and beliefs. Too often, these types were anxious to convict someone for their own reasons.

Age tended to indicate many factors that could come into play. An eighty-year-old could grow tired, just as a twenty-two-year-old could grow bored. It certainly wasn't always the case, but all of these factors came into play during *voir dire*. It was a gamble, and Jack constantly reminded himself that the stakes he played with were the lives and freedom of his clients.

They spent the entire day choosing a jury. Jack used his final preemptory challenge when seating the last juror, which instilled a sense they had a good jury. The jury consisted of nine women and seven men. The twelve jurors that would deliberate would be named at the end of the trial just before deliberations to make sure the four who would be alternates, which were chosen at random, still paid close attention to the trial. Jack prayed the final twelve would be those he felt the best about.

Red had used all of his preemptory challenges as well, but his last preemptory challenge had been used when seating the fourteenth juror. They were lucky in that one woman Jack and Kelly felt particularly good about was the fifteenth to be seated. Jack believed Red wanted to challenge her, but he had no good reason to do so other than he thought she might lean more toward acquittal, which was not a good reason for rejection, though it was basically the only reason attorneys cared about.

As he packed to go home and polish his opening statement for the hundredth time, Jack asked Kelly what she thought of their day's work.

"I feel pretty good about it, especially numbers four, seven, and fourteen."

"I guess we'll know how we did soon, but I agree with you. Those look good, and I think we have a solid jury for the defense."

During *voir dire*, Paul sat quietly, not fully understanding the importance of choosing the correct jurors. The questions asked of the potential jurors were fairly repetitive, and Paul considered it boring. He felt it didn't matter one way or another who was on the jury. They would all lean towards conviction from the outset because so many people thought the police wouldn't charge someone without good reason. In the end, it would depend on his and Jack's ability to overcome those feelings and convince them he was innocent.

When they arrived home, Jack told Jenny about how good both he and Kelly felt about the jury.

"You ready to start setting things right

tomorrow?" Jack asked Paul.

Paul looked at him and did his best to smile. "Sure," he said, though he didn't convince them or himself.

That night was another sleepless one for Paul. Jack was up until after midnight working on final touches to his opening.

Tomorrow really was the first day of the rest of Paul's life. He prayed the rest of his life would turn out well.

32

Paul again sat at the defense table next to Kelly, who sat next to Jack so they could whisper during the trial to discuss what was happening.

The formality of the room made him even more nervous than he already was. It looked much like the courtrooms he'd seen on TV, and it intimidated him. He wondered if that was done on purpose to make the defendants feel uncomfortable. If so, it was working. He wanted to run out the door and keep going, but he'd tried that already, and that had led to having to wear the ankle monitor that kept track of where he was at all times, as though he really might be a dangerous criminal.

Jack and Kelly were leaning close together and talking too quietly for him to hear them, so he looked around the courtroom to see if there was anything that made him feel less nervous.

As he searched for what was not there, he thought about the days and weeks leading up to today. Jack had told him they were trying him as an adult, not a minor. He told him that in Florida, fourteen-year-olds could be tried as adults if they committed certain crimes, among them arson and murder or manslaughter. According to the District Attorney, being fourteen at the time of the fire is old enough to know that starting a fire that would likely kill someone asleep in the house would result in murder, especially considering the placement of the gas can. He believed Paul's age should not be a "get out of jail free" card, since trying him as a minor would mean he would be free in just a few years.

Paul had considered this and had to agree with the District Attorney. This wasn't like being forced to be a lookout for a gang member selling drugs on a street corner or something. Whoever had started the fire had done it to kill him and his mother. It was premeditated murder. Even Jack agreed that it was, and Jack hadn't been surprised Paul was being tried as an adult.

Jack's phone rang, and he pulled it out. Glancing at the screen, he smiled as if he'd expected the call.

"Hey, Tom," Jack said as he rose and walked over to a more deserted area of the room. Paul watched him as he talked on the phone to whoever was calling, and a large smile appeared on Jack's face. Whatever it was about, it was good news.

A man in a sheriff's uniform stepped forward and called out to the room, "Order in the court. Court is now in session in the matter of The State of Florida versus Paul Hanson. Please rise." Jack quickly ended the call, silenced his phone, and returned to the defense table just as the judge entered from a door behind the bench.

"Be seated," Judge Reilly said and announced to the room as if they didn't already know, "We will be hearing the case of The State of Florida versus Paul Hanson, a minor defendant who will be tried as an adult. A word of warning to everyone present: I do not tolerate outbursts of any kind in my court. If you are unable to demonstrate the decorum these proceedings deserve, you will be removed from the room and not allowed back in unless you appear before this court in a legal matter. Do I make myself clear?" He looked around the room at those attending, which were surprisingly more than Paul had expected.

"You may be seated," the judge said, and everyone sat. The sound of the people taking their seats made Paul think of a sigh of relief.

Paul was already afraid of the judge. The man reminded him of a mean dog that had been chained up for most of his life and would strike out at anyone who so much as bothered him.

Paul supposed the judge was satisfied that everyone understood his warning—Paul certainly had—and the judge turned to the attorneys seated at the two tables at the front of the courtroom.

"Is the prosecution ready to proceed?"

"Yes, Your Honor," the prosecutor said.

"And the defense?" the judge asked.

"Yes, Your Honor," Jack said.

"Would the bailiff bring in the jury," the judge said, and the man in the sheriff's uniform stepped through a door to the judge's left and returned a moment later with sixteen people, who filed into the jury box and sat.

As they entered, Paul heard Kelly whisper to Jack, "What was the call about?"

"I'll tell you later," Jack said, smiling.

The prosecutor, a man Jack had told him went by the name Red, began to speak to the jury.

"Ladies and gentlemen, thank you for serving on the jury in this matter. I have a job to do, and so do you, and to be honest, none of us wish to be here."

Red turned and looked at Paul before continuing. "As we discussed yesterday, the defendant is technically a minor, but the nature of the crime dictates we try him as an adult, which is allowed if the defendant was at least fourteen at the time the crime was committed. You might consider him a nice person, and he might be most of the time. However, we intend to prove that he decided to set fire to his home while his mother was asleep inside, knowing it would result in her death.

"We will prove he planned this. He himself bought what he would need to start the fire and ensure it didn't burn itself out before spreading through the home, eventually igniting a can containing gasoline that he'd set outside his mother's bedroom door. His intention was to make the can explode, killing his mother.

"We will show he was having trouble adjusting to life alone with his mother and fought with her about his lack of freedom to do what he felt boys his age should be allowed to do. Was she a strict parent? Possibly. But that's her prerogative. She was raising her son in the way she thought best, just as I'm sure every person in this courtroom would do.

"It should be obvious that Paul Hanson did not escape the results of his deed. His face, and indeed much of his body, are covered in scars. He was not yet fifteen at the time of the fire, which occurred more than a year ago. He spent a long time healing from the wounds that were inadvertently self-inflicted.

"Now, why was he still in the house when the can exploded? I'm sure you will ask yourself that, but we will have an expert in the psychological growth of teenagers testify how that could happen.

"It was basically an error on his part, and we will show how that could happen. If any of you know or are the parent of a teenager, you will likely see how a person his age could make such a mistake.

"We will bring in an expert on fires and arson who will testify to how the fire was started and how and why it spread so rapidly.

"We will have a detective testify what he found out during his long, detailed investigation, and what he found out shows that the defendant is guilty of arson and murder.

"The complete truth is we don't know the exact reasons the defendant set his house on fire, but we can speculate what they might have been given an informed opinion.

"We will present an eye witness who will describe the person he saw that night carrying a gas can into the house late at night. A description that matches the defendant, who as far as anyone can tell is the only person alive who matches the description *and* was there that night.

"We believe you will find that even though we lack a clear motive that only the defendant can tell us, it is clear, ladies and gentlemen, that it was the defendant who started that fire."

The prosecutor sat and Jack rose to stride over to the jury box. He brought his chair with him and sat. He had used this tactic a number of times. It was something he had learned years ago from Trisha

Shelton, who had defended Hank Pittman, the man who had become like a father to Jack. Sitting in front of the jury gave them a sense they were equals and a lot alike. It had worked for Trisha that day as it had for Jack several times since. He saved the tactic for those cases where he felt he could get the jury's sympathies for his client.

"Good morning," he said. "I, too, thank you for your service here. Without juries, the legal system of the country would collapse. Your job, though, will be easier than the prosecutor says it will. What you will hear from him and his witnesses will boil down mostly to innuendo. And while defendants have been found guilty with only circumstantial evidence, I truly doubt that will be the case here.

"Paul Hanson, my client, was just a boy when this happened, and he's little more than that now. He was as much a victim of that fire as his mother was, except that she did not have to suffer the agony of the painful treatment for deep tissue burns, nor does she have to face a world that judges by appearances and not character.

And that's essentially what you have here, ladies and gentlemen. Appearances. There will be some testimony that will appear damning to my client, but once you consider what really happened, you will see that the truth is far different from what the prosecution will try to make you believe it is.

"The prosecution believes nobody matching the description of the person carrying that gas can could be anyone other than my client Paul. That simply isn't true. There could have been many who fit the description you will be given. Their witness did indeed see someone enter the home with a gas can, but as with any description that doesn't definitely identify the person, that description could match any number of people, and even someone with a motive to start the fire that evening."

As Paul listened, part of him kept thinking that Jack sounded as though he was grasping at straws. His theory, though good, was mostly about how it could have been someone else. Paul knew that Mark, one of the boys at school, had been the one who saw someone enter Paul's house. It hadn't been Paul, of course, but how could they convince anyone it wasn't him?

As Jack ended his opening remarks, he sat next to Paul, who looked less than impressed.

Kelly leaned close to Jack and asked again about the phone call. "It looked like good news," she said.

"Oh, it was. Better than good, actually."

Paul joined the conversation. "What?"

Jack smiled at Paul, wondering how to put this to him.

33

The day before opening arguments, Tom had received a reply to the email that said the fictional Mr. Dabney wanted to pay Howard another fifty dollars. Howard's reply, though, required a response, so he called Jack.

"You're not going to believe it. I finally got a reply from Howard Hanson."

"That's great news! Better than great. Sure took long enough. Did he provide a mailing address?"

"Yep. You want me to read his reply to you?"

"Sure."

Tom cleared his throat as if he were about to address Congress and began to read the reply. "Mr. Dabney, I have to say I'm surprised by your email. I don't know who's giving out my email address, but I guess it's okay since you want to pay me what you owe, but you really should make it $100. I worked hard no matter what you thought. It was good work but I don't want to haggle about that. I could try, but then you might decide not to send anything, and I really could use the money right now. Anyway, my address is 427 Eisenhower Street in Pensacola, Florida 32501. I expect the money within a week."

"Pensacola?" Jack said. "Then he moved down here. Pensacola isn't that far from Denton."

"Nope. And he's strapped for cash right now, which isn't a surprise."

"Alright, I want you to go to that address with a subpoena. Tell him you're willing to follow him here and put him up in a nice hotel. He'll probably go along with that to enjoy the nice room and maid service if nothing else. Tell him we'll pay for his food while he's here, too."

"You're willing to do that for this guy? He's a creep. He burned his own kid with cigarettes."

"I'll do whatever I have to in order to get him to be here when I need him."

"What if he won't testify? What if what he will say isn't good for our case?"

"Then I won't call him to the stand, but I still want him here. Besides, if I can use him just to create reasonable doubt, I might still call him to the stand."

"It's your dime," Tom said and left for Pensacola, stopping on the way for lunch.

When Tom arrived in Pensacola, he went to the house and knocked. When nobody answered, Tom wondered if Howard had skipped out, but he doubted that would happen, given the fact that money was being sent to him at this address.

After several hours, Howard still had not arrived home. Tom began to wonder if perhaps he was out tying one on with the anticipation of an extra fifty bucks.

Tom left and checked into a local hotel, deciding to return the following morning in the hopes of meeting Howard Hanson. The subpoena was locked in Tom's glove compartment. He returned the next day just as Jack was arriving at the courthouse for opening arguments and the start of the trial.

When he pulled up to the small house, Howard was leaning into his car, getting something he'd evidently left inside. Tom grinned to himself as he watched Howard, seeing what they hadn't known.

After watching Howard go back inside the house after getting something out of his dilapidated car, Tom placed his call to Jack.

"You're not going to believe this," Tom said after Jack had answered.

"What?"

"I'm sitting in front of Howard Hanson's house and just saw him retrieving something from his car. The man is short, Jack, like maybe Paul's height. And he has a wiry build, though a bit more muscular than Paul."

Jack thought back to the mugshot of Howard Tom had been given.

"The mugshot was a closeup," he said, the problem dawning on him.

"Yep. Just his face and head. The height chart lines can be seen behind his head, but not the numbers indicating how tall he is."

"That is great news. Thanks, Tom. I have to go now, though. Court is being called to order."

"Later," Tom said and disconnected the call. As he approached the front door, he saw there was no doorbell and knocked.

Howard opened the door a crack and said, "Yeah?"

"I've been authorized to give you fifty dollars in cash as payment from Jacob Dabney."

Howard's eyes widened. "You brought it here?"

"Yes."

Now, Howard's smile replaced the wide eyes. "Thanks, man!"

Reaching into his sports coat, Tom withdrew an envelope with fifty dollars and the subpoena. He handed both to Howard.

Taking them, Howard asked, "What's this?"

"It's a subpoena to appear in court in Denton. I have instructions to escort you to a nice hotel there and put you up for a few days."

"What do you mean 'hotel'?"

"Just what I said." Tom could see Howard suspected something else was afoot. "No, this isn't another way of saying 'jail' or anything like it. I really am going to put you up in a nice hotel in Denton while you wait to testify."

"Testify about what?"

"Your son, Paul."

"What about him?"

"He's on trial for murdering his mother. You don't watch the news?"

"Never cared much for that."

Tom could see that the news his son was on trial for murder was a surprise, if not a shock. "He's suspected of setting his house on fire, killing his mother. Weren't you informed she had died?"

"No." Tom could see the lie as if it were a physical thing exiting his mouth. He certainly knew of his ex-wife's death, whether he'd been told about it or not.

"Well, as I said, I'm supposed to either follow you in your car or drive you there myself."

"What could I possibly have to say about the fire?"

251

"We need you as a witness to say Paul would never do such a thing. You're sort of a character witness."

"Oh," Howard said, and his look told Tom he could go either way in the character witness department. Of course, Tom didn't mention that a father as a character witness was rarely given much weight. It was just something to tell him to get him to come to Denton. He would find out the real reason once he was on the stand. A stay in a nice hotel on the beach was an added incentive.

Tom looked at the car in the driveway. "Can that car make it to Denton?"

"Sure. It runs better than it looks."

"I can wait in my car while you pack something."

"Are you lying to me? I'll make you pay if you are."

"No, sir. I'm telling you the absolute truth. You can even call the hotel to check that there is a reservation in your name. My boss is willing to support you while you're there, even buying you meals you can eat in the hotel's restaurant."

"What hotel?"

"The Denton Marriott."

"The Marriott? Really?" Howard was looking as though he'd just hit the lottery. It was one of the nicer hotels on the beach in Denton.

"Yes, sir. Now, if you could pack a few things, we can be on our way. I have to check you in because they will need a credit card for payment, and I doubt you want to pay for it."

Howard glanced around as if someone might be

watching them and said, "Give me ten minutes."

He closed the door and Tom went to wait in his car. Eleven minutes later, Howard came out, waved at Tom, and backed out.

Tom followed him to the Marriott.

As Paul stared at Jack, waiting for an answer about the phone call Jack had received earlier, he wondered what kind of good news Tom had shared. "Well?" he said.

Jack leaned over to Paul and said, "You're not a very tall kid. How tall are you?"

"Five-two."

"Was your mother particularly short?"

"I don't know. She was something like five-seven or eight."

"That's about average for a woman. So, tell me, where did you get your short stature?"

"Huh?"

Jack cut to the chase. "Why didn't you tell me your father was a very short man, like maybe about your height? And thin and wiry?"

"How did you know that?" Paul asked.

"Tom found out. That's what the call I received was about. Tom has found your father. So why didn't you tell me?"

"I didn't think it was important."

"Why not?"

"Because he couldn't have been here. He didn't know where we were."

Jack winked, "Oh, but he did. Now we just have to prove he was here the night of the fire."

"You knew he found me and didn't tell me?"

"He found you a long time ago, before the fire."

"Why didn't you tell me?"

"I didn't want you to worry."

"How long have you known?"

"Not that long."

"Do you think he started the fire?"

"I do indeed. It's not going to be easy to prove it, though, but I plan to give it my best. At least, I think we might be able to show reasonable doubt."

When Tom and Howard arrived at the Denton Marriott, Tom escorted Howard inside and checked him in before following Howard to his room, needing to verify that he liked it and wouldn't be changing rooms, though he mentioned nothing of his reason for escorting him to his room with a view of the Gulf.

As he left, Tom stopped at the desk, asking to see the manager.

"Yes, sir? How may I help you?" the gentleman said as he approached.

"I work for Mr. Jack Turner, the attorney in town. We have an important witness in room 517, Howard Hanson. I need to be notified immediately if he attempts to check out." He handed the manager his card and thirty dollars. "Will that be a problem?"

"Are you responsible for his bill?"

"Yes."

"Then no, there will be no problem with that."

"Thank you. Please leave a message on his room information that gives my number to call immediately if he checks out. If your employees need an excuse to have me here, they can say that a problem came up with the credit card used to check him in, so they need me there to check him out."

"We will handle it, sir," the manager said.

Tom thanked him and left.

Tom drove to Jack's office once the trial had ended for the day and caught Jack up on everything.

"He's in 517?"

"Yes. You going to visit him there?"

"Yes, but only briefly. I don't want to get into what I might ask him once he's on the stand. Still, I think it wise to at least stop in and see him."

When Jack did stop by, Howard seemed to have little time for small talk.

"I'm hungry. That guy said you'd pay for my meals here?"

"Yes."

"Mighty nice of ya. I'm headed there now. Want to join me?"

"Sadly, I don't have time for that this evening. Perhaps another time. I just wanted to say hello and thank you for being here."

"No problem, captain," Howard said with a smirk. Jack allowed the familiar term, as if they were great friends, to pass.

"Tom will come by every evening to check on you and make sure you don't need anything. I would ask that you not stray from the hotel property. They have most anything you could want or need here, and if you need something they don't have, Tom will buy it for you." The promise of not making Howard pay was intended to make sure he didn't decide to go anywhere else. The Marriott offered all the pleasures of a nice vacation that Howard could want, other than a woman's company.

Following opening remarks earlier that day, the prosecution continued its case. Red had called Joe Sissler to the stand and had gone over the details of the fire that proved it was arson. Jack's cross examination was short.

"Did you find evidence as to who set the fire?"

"I understand they have fingerprints from—"

"You don't need to talk about the fingerprints, sir. That's not your area of expertise," Jack said, interrupting him. "I just wanted to know if the fire itself somehow indicated who had started it? Did you find proof that would tell us who the arsonist was?"

"No. Fires aren't able to do that."

"That's what I thought. Thank you, Mr. Sissler."

By this time, court had to be adjourned because the judge had a conflict that had arisen the day before. They had gone home.

Jack knew that Red would call Detective Bob Ebert to the stand the next morning. Jack's cross of him would be more involved.

34

Jack had taken Paul home when court had adjourned for the day. When he arrived home later that evening, Jack filled Paul in on the plans for his father. Paul's reaction was not as good as Jack had thought it would be.

"He's coming here? To Denton?"

"Yes. In fact, he's already here, but don't worry. He has no idea where to find you and likely wouldn't do anything if he did. We've put him up at the Marriott and are paying for his meals, so he's probably not going to do anything that might mess up that situation."

"Wouldn't he skip out if he thought you were going to make it look like he could have started the fire?"

"He might if he knew that. I haven't told him what we're going to ask about on the stand. He thinks he's here to help exonerate you. Sort of as a character witness."

"That's tricking him, isn't it?"

"Sometimes in legal cases, it's necessary. As you suggested, if he knew we were going to make it look like he may have set the fire, he'd disappear. I doubt disobeying a subpoena would bother him in that case.

"Okay," Paul said, but Jack could tell he was still worried.

The next morning as they drove to the courthouse, Paul asked, "Will my dad be in court today?"

"No. We won't need him until the end of the trial. He's the last witness I plan to call to the stand. Until then, he can enjoy his little vacation, which he should. It may be the last days of freedom for him."

Jack noticed that this news helped ease Paul's mind. He relaxed visibly for the rest of the drive.

"How long have you been worried about if he would be in court today?"

"Since you told me you'd brought him here."

"Paul, Jenny mentioned that she told you about the source of most misunderstandings. When you are worried about something and knowing everything would help ease the worry, ask about it."

Paul looked at him for a moment before answering. "Okay."

When the trial was called to order, Red called Detective Ebert to the stand.

"Detective, are you the lead detective investigating the fire that killed Amber Hanson?"

"I am."

"The fire inspector, Mr. Sissler, testified that he found a charcoal lighter fluid can at the scene, sealed it in an evidence bag, and handed it over to you. Is that correct?"

"Yes."

"And what did you find out about that can of charcoal lighter fluid?"

"It had the defendant's fingerprints on it."

"And did you find any other fingerprints on that can?"

"No."

"Mr. Sissler said that charcoal lighter fluid was used as an accelerant in the fire. Do you have reason to doubt his findings?"

"No."

Red considered a legal pad on the podium as if verifying something.

"Did you do any further investigations concerning that can of charcoal lighter fluid?"

"I went to the convenience store nearest the home and asked if the defendant had recently purchased a can of charcoal lighter fluid."

"And what did you find out?"

"I talked to a clerk who recognized the defendant as a frequent customer. She told me that the defendant purchased a can of charcoal lighter fluid."

"And when did he make this purchase?"

"A few days before the fire."

"Did you find a grill that used charcoal at the scene?"

"No."

"Did that make you suspicious regarding the defendant's possible guilt in the arson?"

"Yes."

"Was there any other evidence you found in which the defendant's fingerprints led you to believe he had started the fire?"

"Yes. His fingerprints were on remnants of a gas can we found at the scene."

"Is this the same gas can Mr. Sissler testified had been placed in the hallway outside Amber Hanson's bedroom door as she slept?"

"Yes."

"What conclusions did you come to regarding this can of gasoline?"

"Mr. Sissler told me that the can had not been full but had contained enough gasoline to cause a large explosion. I decided that whoever had placed the gas can outside Ms. Hanson's bedroom had intended for it to explode in the fire."

"Did your investigation find other evidence that the defendant might have started the fire?"

"We found out that the defendant's bedroom had been burned when he lived in Opelika."

"Was the Opelika fire department called to put that fire out?"

"No. It was contained and the fire was put out with a home fire extinguisher."

"So the defendant was not successful in burning his house down that time?" Red said.

Jack stood. "Objection."

"Withdrawn," Red said, holding his hand up in a gesture of accepting fault, but he knew the damage was done. He'd implied Paul had attempted to burn his house down with his parents inside before.

"Were there other suspicious fires in Opelika when the defendant lived there?"

"Yes. Two houses and a bar were set on fire, and someone set a fire in a classroom at school."

"Did the defendant know the teacher whose classroom was burned?"

"Objection! The defendant is not even a suspect in that case," Jack said, standing. As he did, he looked at the jury and could see the damage was already done.

"Sustained."

Red moved on to another question. "Did your investigation of the fire at the defendant's home in Denton find anything else?"

"Yes. One of the defendant's classmates came forward and told me he saw someone matching the defendant's appearance enter the house in the middle of the night with a gas can."

"Okay, Detective, you don't need to explain what he told you. We will be calling that young man to the stand later to testify as to what he told you. I just wanted to establish that you were told this. After this classmate told you about seeing someone matching the defendant entering the house with a gas can, what did you do?"

"At that point, I called the attorney for the defense and asked him to bring the defendant to my office to be arrested for murder and arson."

"You were already aware that Mr. Turner was the attorney for the defendant?"

"Mr. Turner is also the defendant's guardian."

Red continued with questions that solidified what had already come out in Detective Ebert's testimony. Finally, he said, "Thank you, Detective." Grabbing his legal pad, he returned to his seat.

Jack rose and approached the podium. As he did, Judge Reilly asked, "Mr. Turner, do you anticipate a lengthy cross-examination?"

"Maybe only thirty minutes, Your Honor."

The judge checked his watch and said, "Okay. We can hold off on lunch, then."

The truth was that his cross of Bob could take longer, but Jack didn't want to allow the jury to spend their lunchtime contemplating what they'd heard without hearing at least some of the cross-examination.

Approaching the podium, Jack asked, "Detective Ebert, would it be possible for someone else to have placed that gas can and started the fire in the middle of the night?"

"Of course. The person could have worn gloves when handling the gas can."

"So, simply finding the defendant's prints on the can's remnants isn't absolute evidence that he did it, correct?"

"That's correct."

"Is the same thing possible regarding the can of charcoal lighter fluid?"

"Yes."

"You testified that there was no charcoal grill at the residence. Did you ask the defendant about that during your investigation?"

"Yes."

"And what did the defendant say was the reason for purchasing the charcoal lighter fluid?"

"He claimed he had planned to run away and needed it to start a campfire."

"If he were planning to run away, then why kill his mother?"

"I don't know."

"It's a good question, though, isn't it? Do people the defendant's age generally decide to murder a parent when they've decided to run away?"

"Not generally, but it's not impossible."

"Is it impossible that someone else committed this crime?"

"No, but the evidence points to the defendant."

"Detective Ebert, did you go to Opelika to investigate the other fires?"

"No."

"Who did?"

Ebert adjusted himself in the chair, as if it was becoming uncomfortable. "Your investigator did so."

"Did the Denton PD hire him for that purpose?"

"No. You did it as a favor."

"Why did I do this?"

"You felt it would be helpful to find the defendant's father since you believed he might have started the fire in this case."

"Did my investigator find anything else out that could possibly point the finger at someone else as the arsonist?"

"Yes, the two houses that burned were owned by a couple who would hire the defendant's father to do odd jobs and mow the lawn."

"Did it turn out the defendant's father ended up having a dispute over money with that couple?"

"Yes, according to your investigator."

"You didn't look further into this?"

"Shortly after receiving this news, the defendant's classmate came forward to tell me he saw someone matching the defendant's description entering the house in the middle of the night with the gas can. I felt that was enough to arrest the defendant, taking the other evidence into consideration."

"Okay, Detective, regarding the person seen outside the house on the night the Denton fire was set, have you ever arrested a man who might, in the dark of night, be mistaken for someone the defendant's age because of a slight build?"

"I haven't actually encountered that myself."

"But is it possible?"

"Of course."

"It didn't occur to you that this may have happened? That the arsonist was actually an adult but slight of build and not very tall?"

"Not when considering the other evidence."

"What about another classmate of the defendant? Is it impossible that one of them had a grudge and wanted to settle it using violent means?"

"No, but generally, kids don't take things like fingerprints into consideration. They often don't think straight when committing a crime, especially one that would likely lead to the murder of one or more people. They generally make a lot of mistakes, such as the defendant could have regarding that same evidence. If a classmate had done this, his prints would likely be on the evidence."

"Likely?"

"Yes."

"But not absolutely, correct?"

"Yes, that's correct. Nothing is absolute."

"And my client's guilt is not absolute, either?"

Ebert squirmed again. "I guess so, but I was reluctant to arrest him on this, which you're aware of, so I didn't arrest him without sufficient evidence to do so."

"Why were you so reluctant?"

"Because I had a hard time thinking he did this. He seems like a good kid, but teenagers can fool you sometimes."

"But don't you generally discover something that makes them seem, well, less of a good kid? Something that has nothing to do with the crime, such as seeing them being cruel to someone else? Something like that? After all, you said kids his age tend to make mistakes. Wouldn't that be especially true if they thought they weren't being observed?"

"I suppose so."

Jack had scored minor points with this, so he moved on to another line of questioning. "Detective, is there an explanation for the fire in the defendant's bedroom other than arson?"

"Of course."

"You said that the police did not investigate this fire since they were unaware of it. Correct?"

"Yes."

"Why do you suppose his parent or parents didn't want the fire to be investigated?"

"Maybe they didn't want their son accused of arson."

"Is it possible there was another reason, such as not wanting the police inside the home?"

Red stood and objected. "Your Honor, are we going to have to hear of every possibility here?"

"It goes to an alternate theory, Your Honor," Jack said. "The prosecution brought up the fire in Opelika. I'm just pointing out that such a fire does not necessarily mean the defendant set the fire."

"Overruled," Judge Reilly said.

"It's possible."

"Have you ever encountered adults who would do almost anything to keep the police from entering their home?"

"Of course."

"Have you ever discovered that the reasons for that were to prevent the police from discovering some kind of illegal activity?"

"Yes."

"Did you ever interview the defendant regarding that fire?"

"No. The evidence we have is related to this fire in Denton, not the fire in Opelika. It just demonstrated a possible pattern of behavior."

"A possible pattern?"

"Yes."

"Not a definite one?"

"No."

"If the fire in his bedroom in Opelika was never investigated, isn't it possible that it is only being assumed that the defendant started the fire?"

"I suppose so."

"Because there is zero proof that the defendant started that or any other fire in Opelika, including the fire at the school, correct?"

"Yes, that's correct."

Jack managed to barely go beyond the thirty minutes he had said he needed for his cross-examination. When he was done, the judge announced a recess for lunch.

Jack felt he'd done a good job so far, especially in getting it on the record that a small adult could have committed the crime, as well as the suspicion of Paul's father.

After lunch, he knew that Red would be calling Mark Lewis.

35

At lunch, Jack called Tom to see if he'd made progress with the task he'd been given. Tom was spending his day going from one cheap motel to the next to see if he could find anyone who recognized the picture of Howard. Jack knew he hadn't found anyone because he would have received a text at least if he had. Still, he wanted to get an idea of his progress.

When Tom told him they had found nobody so far, Jack said, "Well, all we can do is keep trying." They badly needed to place Howard in or near Denton on the night of the fire.

"What was that about?" Paul asked after Jack had disconnected the call.

"We're trying to locate someone who can place your father in Denton the night of the fire."

"You really think he might have done it?"

"He's always been my number one suspect."

"Why?"

"Who knows? The fact is people do terrible things to others for a variety of reasons, and all of the reasons are selfish. So to answer your question, if he did it, he did it for some horribly selfish reason that I would never truly understand."

They ate their lunch and returned to the courtroom.

Red called Mark Lewis to the stand.

When he was sworn in, Judge Reilly leaned toward the witness stand and said, "Young man, do you know the difference between a lie and the truth?"

Mark swallowed and said, "Yes, sir. Of course, I do."

"Do you know that if there is only a small part of a lie in what you say, the entire statement is a lie?"

"Yes, sir."

"Do you know that lying under oath is called perjury, and it's a felony? You could go to jail for lying under oath."

Jack suppressed a smile. It was unlikely that young Mark Lewis would have to worry about jail if he committed perjury, but the judge was simply making sure Mark understood the gravity of what was happening."

"Yes, sir."

Judge Reilly glared at Mark a moment before turning back to Red. "Proceed. Let the record show that the witness is aware of the importance of telling the truth on the stand."

Red approached the podium and flipped to a page of his legal pad.

"Good afternoon, Mark. Are you familiar with the defendant in this case, Paul Hanson?"

"Yes. He goes to my school. Or at least he did."

"Has he ever asked you to lie for him?"

"No."

"Do you like him?"

Mark shrugged. "I'm not, like, a friend of his. We don't hang out together. Never did. We just…know each other."

"So, you would have no reason to come forward and tell us something you saw in order to get some kind of teenager revenge on him. Is that right?"

Red was leading his witness, but Jack didn't object. He knew what Red was trying to accomplish with this line of questioning, and Jack had no problem with it.

"You mean would I lie to get him in trouble?"

Jack smiled at how Mark had turned the leading question into one that was better phrased and wondered if Mark might become an attorney one day.

"Yes, would you lie to get him in trouble?"

"No, sir."

"Do you recall the night Paul's house was set on fire?"

"Yes."

"Did anything happen that made it memorable for you, other than someone's house burned down and a woman was killed?"

"Yes."

"What happened to make it particularly memorable for you?"

"I snuck out that night and was walking around town." Mark glanced at the judge, who was eyeing him. "I wasn't doing anything, really, just walking around because I thought it was cool to be out that late."

"What happened while you were walking around town?" Red asked.

"I was sort of wandering, you know, with no particular place to go in mind, and I ended up in Paul's neighborhood."

"What happened then?"

"I was walking and I saw this person. He was going inside Paul's house, and he was carrying a gas can."

"What did you notice about this person?"

"Well, it was dark, so I couldn't see his face or anything. Besides, he was facing away from me."

"Did you notice anything about this person?"

"He was small. Like a kid."

"Do you mean like a small child or someone more your age?"

"Someone more my age, like a teenager, but not very big."

"In your opinion, is the defendant a large person?"

Mark looked surprised by the question. "No. In fact, he's kind of small when you compare him to a lot of the guys at school. He sometimes got teased for that."

"Did the person you saw entering the house that night with a gas can look anything like the defendant?"

"Well, only his size. Like I said, I didn't see any details."

"To clarify, then, are you saying the person you saw was about the same size as the defendant?"

"Yes, as far as I could tell."

"The next day when you heard there had been a fire and that a woman had died and a classmate had been severely burned, did you think of that image of the person entering the house with a gas can?"

"Yes."

"Did you suspect the defendant?"

"Objection," Jack said, standing. "Calls for an opinion."

"Sustained," Judge Reilly said.

"But are you sure it was someone small, like the defendant?" Red asked.

"Yes."

"Why didn't you come forward with this story earlier?"

"I didn't want to get in trouble with my parents, and I felt the cops would be able to find who did it without my help."

"Why did you finally come forward?"

"I got to feeling guilty for not saying anything. It had been a long time but they hadn't arrested anyone yet."

Red smiled at the jury and returned to his seat. Jack stood and approached the podium.

"Good afternoon, Mark. You state that you were unable to see any features of the person you saw entering the house. Does that mean it could have been an adult, just one of small stature?"

"I guess."

"Did you notice if the person was wearing gloves?"

"No. I really kind of hurried by and hoped he wouldn't see me since I was out that late and could get in trouble."

"Even another kid your age?"

"Sometimes kids can sort of blackmail you if they have something on you they could tell someone else."

Jack nodded. "Yes, that's true. Did you immediately think it was another kid?"

"Well, I guess. He was short."

"Do you remember what he was wearing?"

"No."

"Anything else? A limp, maybe, or some other way of walking that would set him apart from others?"

"Not really."

"Have you ever seen a small man in public from behind?"

"I don't know. I guess I have."

"Would you say it was easy to mistake that man for a kid?"

Mark shrugged. "I guess that could happen."

"What about a woman? You ever see a man from behind walking down the street and thought it was a woman because he had long hair?"

Mark chuckled. "Yeah."

"So would you say that sometimes looks can be deceiving? That we often see something and think it's something else until we get a better look?"

"Objection," Red said as he stood. "Counsel is leading the witness."

"Withdrawn," Jack said. Just putting the idea in the collective mind of the jurors was all he needed to do, and he'd accomplished that.

Jack took his seat as he said, "Thank you, Mark." He glanced at the jury. Their intense looks told him they had paid close attention to his questions and Mark's answers.

Red stood and said, "Your Honor, I regret that my final witness has been unavoidably delayed. He can testify first thing tomorrow."

Judge Reilly looked unhappy with this

development. He had already had to shorten one day because he himself had to be somewhere else on short notice.

Scowling at Red, he said, "It's unavoidable?"

"Yes, sir. He had a family emergency."

Still scowling, he said, "Then, I suppose we will have to adjourn until tomorrow morning at nine o'clock sharp."

After court was adjourned, Paul asked Jack if he thought things were going well.

"That will all depend on Tom's success at finding someone who can place your father here the night of the fire."

Tom spent the day looking for a motel clerk who would recognize the picture of Howard. By four o'clock, he had not found anyone who recognized him. He'd covered all of the cheaper motels in Denton and had started asking about him at some of the same type of motels in Wharton.

At the twenty-fourth motel on his journey, he finally found someone who recognized him.

The woman had the look of someone who took no nonsense from anyone. She seemed capable of violence if the situation called for it. She bore no nametag, so Tom introduced himself, hoping she would reciprocate.

"Hi, I'm Tom Gordon." He smiled at her, but her response was mostly blank.

"Yeah? If you need a room, we're full up."

"No, ma'am, I don't need a room for the night. I'm actually local." He pulled out the picture of Howard and held it up.

"Do you recognize this man?"

Without spending any time looking at it, she said, "Am I supposed to?"

"I don't know, but we suspect him of setting a fire that killed his ex-wife and nearly killed his young son."

This information got her attention. "Really?"

"Yes, ma'am. Could you take a good look and tell me if you recognize him as a former tenant?"

"How long ago was this?"

"Quite a while. A little over a year."

She looked back at Tom. "And you expect someone to recognize him after that long?"

Tom shrugged. "We have hope."

"Who's 'we'?"

"My employer and I."

"And who would that be?"

"I work for Jack Turner. He's an attorney."

She brightened. "I know Jack Turner! Well, not really know him, but I definitely know who he is. He's a nice guy! Represented my cousin's son when he was arrested for drug possession. Managed to get him probation instead of doing time."

"Yes, ma'am. He's defending this man's son, but we don't think the boy did it. We're fairly positive this guy did it."

She bent over the image and Tom could see her doing her best to find any memory of him.

"You know, he does look kind of familiar." She continued studying the picture.

"Wait a minute! I remember him! He paid with a credit card that was declined. Then he tried to pay cash, but I told him he'd have to go get a gift card to pay since we have to have a card on file in case of damages to the room."

"Could you check a date and tell me if he stayed here that night?" Tom felt his adrenaline spike.

"I don't remember his name."

"But I do," Tom said and provided the date and Howard's name.

Fifteen minutes later, he sent Jack a one-word text: Bingo.

36

That evening after getting the name of the motel and the woman Tom spoke to, Jack went to meet her. She owned it and lived in the quarters attached to the office with her teenage daughter. The teenager was working the front desk.

"If you need a room, we're full," she said as Jack entered.

"Thank you, but I don't need a room. I need to speak to Ms. Hogan."

The girl looked at Jack and stepped to the doorway leading to the living quarters. "Mom?!"

A moment later, a woman in her mid-forties came out and immediately recognized Jack. "Mr. Turner!"

After some conversation, he remembered the son of Ms. Hogan's cousin and asked how he was doing.

"Much better than he was. He understands how close he came to being in jail for a while."

Jack moved the conversation to what she had told Tom about Howard, asking if she would be willing to testify that he had been a guest of her motel on the night of the fire.

Jack was surprised that she didn't hesitate to reply. "No problem. When do you need me there?"

Jack considered this and said, "Can you be ready tomorrow? It's possible that you will be questioned by the prosecutor before you testify since you aren't on my witness list, and the judge might give the prosecution time to get from you what you intend to testify to in court. Given that I'm only using you to show that Mr. Hanson was in town the night of the fire, the prosecutor may choose to allow you to testify without your deposition. If he wants to depose you, then I might not be able to put you on the stand until Monday."

"I can do that," Ms. Hogan said.

"Great!" Jack said. "I have to make it official for the judge since you're not on my witness list, so I have a subpoena to give you."

"That's fine," she said. "I'd be there with or without it."

"Thank you, Ms. Hogan," he said. "I won't keep you any longer."

"My pleasure, Mr. Turner! It's the least I can do since you helped Aiden without charging an arm and a leg."

The next morning, which was Friday, Jack informed Red that he had a witness who wasn't on his initial list. Word was sent to the judge about this, and he requested them to come into his chambers.

"What's this about a new witness, Jack?" Judge Reilly said, his displeasure on full display.

"I apologize for this. I only found out about her yesterday."

"And what will she testify to?" Red asked, equally disturbed but likely putting an extra layer of distress on for the judge's benefit.

"All she will say is that Howard Hanson was in town the night of the fire."

"So?" Red said. "I take it you found him, then." Jack had put Howard on his original witness list in the hopes of locating him before the trial.

"Yes, we have. I intend to offer him as the possible arsonist in this case."

Red issued a short burst of sarcastic laughter. "What? He walked on his knees or something?"

Jack said nothing in response to this. Red and the judge would both immediately see the merits of his defense the moment Howard entered the courtroom. He was the only person in the room who knew Howard's stature since the investigation had not gone far enough to find out any real particulars about Howard other than his previous city of residence and his minor scrapes with the law there. No physical description had ever been attained.

Judge Reilly looked from Jack to Red and back to Jack. "Is that all she is going to testify to?"

"Yes, she has records from her motel that show Howard was a guest the night of the fire."

Red asked, "Where is the motel?"

"It's the Beachside in Wharton," Jack said.

Red and Judge Reilly exchanged a glance, and the judge said, "Any objections, Mr. Miller?"

"I suppose not," Red answered, a smirk on his face. Jack was looking forward to how Red would look when Howard stepped into the courtroom.

"Do you need time with this witness before she testifies, Red?" Judge Reilly asked.

"As long as that's all she is going to testify to and she has the records to prove it, then no."

"Alright, Jack. The witness is allowed, but if she starts testifying to anything else, I'm stopping it."

"No problem."

Judge Reilly turned to Red. "Is your witness here today?"

"Yes, he's here."

"Then let's get this started. I want a full day today. Jack, who is your first witness?"

"Ms. Hogan, the lady we've been discussing."

They returned to the courtroom, and Jack stepped through the entry doors to let Ms. Hogan know she would testify today, but not until after the prosecution's last witness, a psychologist.

"That won't take long," Jack said. He anticipated having few questions, if any, for him on cross. Given what he knew Red was asking of the psychiatrist, he would likely have only a couple of questions himself.

When court was called into session, Judge Reilly told Red to call his next witness.

"The state calls Dr. John Schuler to the stand."

A deputy at the front of the courtroom leaned out of the doorway and called Dr. Schuler into the courtroom.

After being sworn in and taking his seat, Dr. Schuler cleared his throat and stated his name for the record when asked.

"Dr. Schuler, you are an expert in the psychology of adolescents, is that correct?"

"Yes."

"I have called you here today to discuss some things that might confuse the jury regarding the behavior of the defendant the night the fire was set.

I'm sure the jury is wondering about a young boy setting a fire that ended up badly injuring him. Is such an action plausible?"

"Yes, the adolescent brain sometimes doesn't consider other outcomes. If a young teenager set the fire—and I'm not saying the defendant is guilty, only that it's possible—then he may think he has much more time than he actually has to get out of the house. He may have discovered that the fire spread far more quickly than anticipated and found himself trapped. It's also possible that he intended to be a victim of the fire as well. He may have been thinking of a sort of murder-suicide."

"So what you're saying is that it's possible the defendant either misjudged the time he had to vacate the house, or he may have been trying to commit suicide in addition to killing his mother in the fire. Is that right?"

"Yes."

"Thank you, Dr. Schuler."

Jack rose. "Dr. Schuler, is it also possible someone else could have set the fire and the defendant is just another victim of the arson?"

"Of course."

"Regarding suicide, would a teenager who had told others he planned to run away have decided instead to kill himself and his mother?"

"Objection!" Red said, standing.

Jack responded, "Your Honor, the prosecution has said Dr. Schuler is an expert in adolescent psychology, and he brought up the idea of suicide with the doctor's testimony."

"But, Your Honor, there is no evidence that the

defendant told anyone he intended to run away."

"Your Honor," Jack countered, "I didn't say that he had. I only asked if such a situation existed, would a murder-suicide be likely."

The judge considered this before ruling. "Overruled," Judge Reilly said. "The witness may answer."

"I don't see that as likely, but it is absolutely true that a teenager might misjudge the speed at which a fire would spread. That would be true regardless of whether or not he planned to run away. Even adults make such misjudgments regarding a fire."

"Thank you, sir," Jack said and sat in his seat as Dr. Schuler stepped down from the witness stand and left. He was unhappy that the witness had added that last part to his response, but it had already been mentioned in his testimony, so it wasn't much of a blow to what he was accomplishing with that question.

Judge Reilly turned to Red. "Your next witness, Mr. Miller?" he asked, knowing the answer.

"The prosecution rests, Your Honor."

Turning to Jack, Judge Reilly said, "Call your first witness, Mr. Turner."

"The defense calls Ms. Linda Hogan to the stand."

Ms. Hogan entered, a ledger held snugly against her left side, and was sworn in. Jack approached the podium and said, "Thank you for being here today, Ms. Hogan. I only have a few questions for you."

She smiled at him and nodded. Jack could see she was nervous, but he also knew that the best cure for that was beginning the testimony. Once someone was into a rhythm, they generally relaxed. He would open with some conversational questions to ease her nerves a bit.

"Ms. Hogan, are you the owner and operator of the Beachside Motel in Wharton?"

"Yes."

"How long have you owned it?"

She considered this and said, "Eleven years last March."

"Do you keep accurate records of your visitors?"

"I have to. It's the law."

"Did you bring the records for the date in question with you today?"

She held up the ledger she'd brought in with her. Jack said, "You'll have to answer, Ms. Hogan, so the court reporter can record your response. It's like the records of your guests at the motel. It's the law." He smiled at her and a chuckle ran through the jury and the few people in the courtroom, mostly reporters from the local media.

"Sorry. Yes. I have it here."

"Could you open it to the date of March 18 of last year?"

She did so, flipping pages to find what she needed.

"Have you found the date?"

"Yes."

"Is there a Howard Hanson listed as staying in your motel that night?"

"Yes."

"And do you recall him?"

"Actually, I do. He was rather belligerent about having to purchase a gift credit card to register for the night. We need something on file to charge for any damage to the room."

"Don't you usually require a bank credit card?"

"Yes, but his card was denied and he said he didn't have another one, so I had him do the next best thing. I allowed him to pay for his room with cash, but I still needed a credit card on file in case of any extra charges."

"And his response is why you remember him?"

"Yes."

Jack walked to his table and came back with a picture of Howard Hanson. "Is this the man you remember as Howard Hanson?"

"Yes. That's him."

Jack turned to Red and smiled. "Your witness."

Red stood and said, "Ms. Hogan, did Mr. Hanson ever tell you he had anything to do with a fire that happened that night?"

"No."

"So to your knowledge, all you can tell us is that he was in Wharton that night, correct?"

"Yes."

"Did you see him leave the motel at any point that night?"

"No, but I don't watch for that. Once someone is registered, I pretty well ignore them unless they have a problem or come into the motel office for something. I'm too busy to worry about who's going anywhere. Cars are coming in and pulling out all the time."

"But again, all you are able to tell us is that he was registered that night in your motel."

"Yes."

"Nothing further," Red said.

"The witness is excused," Judge Reilly said.

As she passed Jack, he gave her a wink to let her know she did fine. She smiled and left the courtroom.

Jack leaned over and whispered to Paul, "Go along with what I'm about to say." Paul looked back, his expression questioning.

"Your next witness, Mr. Turner," Judge Reilly said.

"The defense requests a short recess, Your Honor."

"Already?"

Jack nodded toward Paul. "Biology."

The judge banged his gavel. "We'll take a ten-minute recess. Bailiff, please remove the jury to the jury room." Addressing the jurors, he said, "I remind you again that you are not to discuss the case at all until you are asked to deliberate."

Jack leaned back down to Paul and said, "Go to the bathroom. Sit in a stall for five minutes, even if you don't have to go. I didn't want your father seeing Ms. Hogan in the hallway in case he recognized her, so I had Tom keep him in the coffee shop. I need to text him to get your father up to the courtroom."

"Okay," Paul said and headed to the bathroom.

37

After Jack texted Tom to bring Howard up to the courtroom, he asked Kelly to go wait for them outside the courtroom and let him know when they arrived. He had told Tom to stick by Howard's side until he was inside the courtroom itself. He didn't want to take a chance that Howard might get cold feet and leave the building.

Paul returned a minute before Kelly did. "He's here," Kelly said to Jack as she sat beside him.

"Good," Jack said and studied the notes he had for what he wanted to ask Howard. His entire case depended on this. His hope was to catch Howard in enough lies that the jury would immediately suspect him of setting the fire, which Jack firmly believed he did.

Judge Reilly entered as court was called back into session.

Turning to Jack, he said, "Your next witness, counselor."

Jack rose and announced, "Defense calls Howard Hanson to the stand."

Howard was summoned and entered the courtroom. Jack was watching Red's face to see his reaction. When Red saw Howard, his face grew pale. He looked at Jack, who just smiled.

He hated that Bob had never looked much into Howard as a suspect. He could have at least requested his physical characteristics, which would have included his height and weight. Of course, Tom hadn't done that either. At the time, nobody knew that the perpetrator was a small person.

After being sworn in and stating his name for the record, Jack stepped up to the podium.

"Hello, Mr. Hanson. Thank you for being here."

"Least I could do. He's my boy. I didn't know where he was until your man found me."

Jack smiled at this volunteered information. If Howard had hired a lawyer, he would have been told to answer the questions and say nothing else. Howard apparently felt invincible.

"Yes," Jack said. "Are you enjoying your stay in Denton?"

"Oh, yeah. That hotel you put me up in is real nice."

Jack smiled. Howard was treating this as if they were good friends talking about mundane topics.

"Ever been to Denton before?"

"Yeah. Paul's mother and me came down before he was born and visited a friend of hers."

"Any other times?"

"Nope."

Jack felt like dancing around the room at this answer. He glanced at Red, who had his forehead propped in his hands and wasn't watching the carnage to his case against Paul. But he was certainly listening.

"So on the night of the fire, you weren't here in Denton?"

"Nope. I was back home where I used to live—in Opelika."

Jack looked at the jury. It was easy to see they fully understood where this line of questioning was leading.

"So you didn't rent a room for the night at the Beachside Motel in Wharton on the night of the fire?"

It was, at least to Howard's thinking, the first question that had to do with the actual crime. Before that, he'd apparently thought the friendly banter was still in effect. His expression changed immediately, and he squinted at Jack. His eyes darted toward the jury and back to Jack.

"What are you sayin'?"

"I'm just asking if you rented a room at the Beachside Motel on the night of the fire."

He looked at the judge and toward the prosecutor's table. Perhaps because Red still had his head in his palms, he realized that there were probably things they knew that he hadn't known they knew.

Still, he denied it. "No. I was never there."

"Never?"

"Never."

Howard's demeanor had changed. His body was tense and his tone almost threatening. He was an image of hostility.

Jack brought a photocopy of the page from Ms. Hogan's ledger forward. "This is a copy of a page from the sign-in ledger of the Beachside Motel for the day of the fire. Would you look at the highlighted name?"

Howard looked at the ledger. "So? There's lots of Howard Hansons in the world, you know."

"Before you came in to testify, the owner of the Beachside Motel was here. She identified you from a photo as the person who checked in that day."

"Well, she's lyin'!"

"Why would she do that?"

"Maybe you paid her to say that!"

"Or maybe she's telling the truth."

"There ain't no truth to it. I never checked into that place."

"Mr. Hanson, how tall are you?"

"What's that got to do with anything?!" he nearly shouted.

"Just answer the question," Judge Reilly instructed. He knew Jack well enough to know he would never have bribed a witness. It was growing obvious that nearly everyone in the courtroom now knew who had set the fire.

"I'm five-three. You happy?"

"You have a small build for an adult."

"So?!"

"The person who started the fire that night had a small build."

"So do a lot of people! That don't mean nothin'!"

"Let's move to something else for the moment," Jack said. He wanted to keep Howard guessing about what questions may come. "You said you didn't know where your son was until my investigator found you."

"Yeah. So?"

"Why weren't you informed of that?"

"Because my wife left me and took Paul with her. She didn't even tell me she was going, so she certainly didn't tell me where she planned to go. I didn't know where she'd gone until you told me she moved here."

"Why do you think she wouldn't tell you she was leaving you?"

"I don't know. She was like that."

"She frequently ran off without telling you about it ahead of time?"

"No. She was just—I don't know—secretive about stuff sometimes."

"Isn't it true that you could become violent with her and Paul?"

"No."

"Studies show that's often the reason a woman leaves a man when she's not having an affair with someone else."

Red finally seemed to wake up. "Objection," he said. "Counsel isn't an expert on that and no such studies have been introduced into evidence."

"Withdrawn," Jack said before the judge could sustain the objection. He'd done what he needed to do on that point. Most people would easily accept that statement as fact whether or not proof was offered from a study, especially the women on the jury, some of whom may have been in an abusive relationship in their lives.

"Mr. Hanson, didn't you set that fire that night in a fit of jealous rage?"

"No."

"Did it anger you that she took off with your son without a word?"

"Yes, but I didn't kill her for it."

"Were you surprised your son survived the fire?"

"I didn't know about it, so how could it surprise me?"

Jack looked at the jury. The looks on their faces said everything. They didn't believe a word Howard had said throughout his testimony.

Paul was as good as free.

"Mr. Hanson, you used to do some work for a Mr. Jacob Dabney in Opelika, is that correct?"

"Yes." Howard's eyes narrowed.

"And Mr. Dabney did not pay you for some work one time, is that also correct?"

"Yes."

"Not long after that, Mr. Dabney's two rental houses were set on fire. Were you aware of that?"

"No," Howard said, but his blush contradicted his answer.

"You didn't have anything to do with those fires, did you?"

"No!" Howard nearly shouted. "I'm no firebug!"

His sudden anger caused some members of the jury to lean back in their seats, as if he might lunge for someone.

"Nothing further," Jack said. Then turning to Red, he said almost gleefully, "Your witness."

Red stayed seated for a moment before rising.

"Mr. Hanson, have you ever met a man of small stature such as yourself who could be mistaken for you in the dark?"

Howard sat up in his seat and said, "Of course."

"Did you ever know of a person who registered at a motel but someone else was mistaken for that person?"

"I certainly have. Identities are like that. People

make mistakes all the time."

Red considered another question. He'd been told by Bob Ebert that nobody knew where Howard Hanson was, and months ago, Jack had said he hadn't been able to find him. Until the testimony of the motel's owner, he hadn't considered that Howard Hanson could be the killer.

Now, Red had to be honest with himself. This case was dead. He would have to look into charges against Howard Hanson.

"No further questions," he said. Stopping at the defense table, he asked Jack, "Where is he staying?"

"The Marriott."

"Okay."

Defeated, Red sat at his table and texted Bob Ebert to bring Howard Hanson in. At the very least, questioning him was the prudent thing to do.

"Call your next witness, counselor," the judge said to Jack.

Jack knew his case was more or less won already, but he knew that Paul's testimony of how his father treated him would seal it.

"The defense calls Paul Hanson to the stand."

Paul rose and climbed into the witness chair. The resemblance to his father was noticeable, another plus for their case. He sat looking out at the courtroom before looking directly at each juror, something Jack had told him to do.

Jack went to the podium and said, "Paul, what was life like with your father?"

"Bad."

"How bad? What would he do?"

"He'd hit me a lot."

"Anything else?"

Paul struggled with his answer. It was obvious it wasn't because he was lying but because it was difficult to talk about. "He'd burn me with cigarettes for the fun of it."

"How do you know it was just for the fun of it?"

"Because he'd laugh when he did it."

"Did he cause scars?"

"Yes, but not like these."

"Didn't people notice the scars he caused with the cigarette burns?"

"No. He'd burn me where they would be hidden by clothes, like on my legs or my—" he paused. "My butt."

"You'll have to go through life with these fresher scars now, won't you?"

"Yes."

"Do you get picked on because of them?"

"Yes."

"Do you believe your father started the fire?"

"Yes."

"Why didn't you say something sooner about that possibility?"

"Because I didn't think he knew where we were. If he didn't know, how could he have done it?"

"You know now he did know where you were?"

"Yes."

"Were you planning to run away before the fire?"

"Yes."

"Why?"

"I was just unhappy. My mom never let me do anything."

"Why not?"

"I don't know. She wouldn't explain why when I asked."

"How did your mother feel about the possibility of your father finding where you were?"

"It scared her. She told me if my dad ever showed up at the house, I should run and let her handle it. That she didn't want me there."

"Why do you think she told you that?"

"Objection," Red said, standing. "Calls for conclusion." Jack could tell that Red's heart was no longer in it. He was mostly going through the motions to keep the trial fair.

"Your Honor," Jack said, "a son knows his mother, and since she can't speak for herself, he should be allowed to testify to what he knew of her feelings about being found by Howard Hanson."

The judge considered this and said, "Overruled. Witness may answer."

"She was afraid if he showed up, he might kill us."

"Did she tell you that?"

"Yes."

"So she was afraid of your father?"

"Yes."

"How about you? Were you afraid of him?"

"Yes."

"Were you afraid he might burn you with cigarettes again?"

"Yes, but mostly I was afraid he'd kill my mom and me."

"Did it surprise you that your mom thought he was capable of killing the two of you?"

"No, not really. I was just sad he was like that. All my friends had better dads than I had. To be honest, they had better moms too."

"Paul, how did the fire at your home in Opelika occur?"

"My dad started it. He was making meth and using my bedroom as a lab. There was a fire, and he was able to put it out himself."

"Where did you sleep if your room was being used for a meth lab?"

"In the living room on the couch. My clothes were in another closet and chest of drawers."

"Did you start any fires in your lifetime?"

"No."

"Why did you buy the charcoal lighter fluid?"

"I was planning to run away and needed something to help me start a campfire."

"That's the only reason?"

"Yes."

"Thank you, Paul." Turning to Red, he said, "Your witness."

Jack wasn't that surprised when Red said, "No questions, Your Honor." Paul had said little about the night of the fire, and the jury wouldn't appreciate it if Red fought against what Paul had said about his life with his father.

"Your next witness, counselor?" Judge Reilly asked.

"The defense rests, Your Honor."

38

At lunch, Jack praised Paul for the job he did on the stand. For his part, Paul had a few questions about what had happened in court that morning.

"Why didn't the prosecutor ask me any questions?"

"For several reasons. First, if he attacked your story about the abuse you suffered at the hands of your father, the jury wouldn't like it. Second, your testimony didn't address the night of the fire at all. The closest thing you said was that you had intended to run away, and making that look like a lie to the jury would be nearly impossible. Only browbeating you would serve to even raise any doubts you were telling the truth, and again, that would make the jury dislike him."

"Is it that important for the jury to like the attorneys?"

"It's important enough," Kelly said. "If nothing else, you don't want to give a jury a reason to go against you in their deliberations, even if it has nothing to do with the case, such as whether or not they like one of the attorneys."

Jack added, "Sometimes, you can do something that can make one or two jurors dislike you, but if he'd attacked your testimony, all of them would have gone into deliberations agreeing he was not a likeable person."

"Oh. Why didn't he ask me about when I ran away?"

"I think he figured by then it wouldn't matter. Besides, it would make it look like you wouldn't have killed your mother if you were prone to running away."

"Oh. What happens next?" Paul asked.

"The closing arguments begin after we return. First the prosecution, then us."

"What happens there?"

"We each summarize our cases. Red knows his chances of getting a conviction dropped considerably with the testimony of Ms. Hogan and your father. I wouldn't be surprised if he's taking the steps to at least have your father brought in for questioning, even if you're found guilty. Red may be a lot of things, but he's not someone who will happily watch someone who is innocent of a crime remain in jail. Depending on what can be discovered while investigating your father, he could arrest him and try him for the crime after making sure you're set free."

"Even if I'm found guilty?"

"Yes. If you are acquitted—and there's a good chance you will be—he will go after your father with everything he has. I'll never forget the look on his face when he saw your dad enter the courtroom. The blood drained from his face."

"Why didn't they look into my dad more?"

"All the other evidence pointed to you. Once Mark came forward and said it looked like a kid entering your house with the gas can, that sealed it. The prints, the fact nobody else was seen lurking in the area that night, the fact you had bought the charcoal lighter fluid just before the fire was started using that as an accelerant—all of that, coupled with Mark's testimony, looked like a slam dunk for the prosecution."

"But why wouldn't his prints be on the cans?"

"He probably wore gloves."

"How did he know about the charcoal lighter fluid? It's not like we always had some."

"He probably planned on using gasoline as the accelerant and found the can of charcoal lighter fluid, which is safer to use for such a purpose."

"So you think my dad did it?"

"I'm certain of it, but they'll need proof beyond a reasonable doubt to convict him."

"Doesn't the fact he lied on the stand about being in town that night do that?"

"Juries can be strange sometimes. Some juries take more convincing than others. But, yes, that will go a long way towards convicting him. After all, if he wasn't here to start the fire, why was he here? It's not as if he contacted you or your mother while in town."

"I see what you mean," Paul said and swallowed the last bite of his lunch.

When they arrived at the courthouse, Tom was waiting outside. Howard was not with him.

"Bob Ebert picked Howard up soon after he finished testifying," Tom said. "He was trying to start his car when Bob arrived at the Marriott."

"Why couldn't he start his car?" Kelly asked.

"Kinda hard to do when the fuses to stuff like the

fuel pump have been removed and left in the glove compartment," Tom said, grinning.

"Isn't that illegal?" Paul asked.

"Well, I didn't steal them since they are still in the car, and removing them might be a misdemeanor, but I doubt anyone will do anything about it."

"But isn't it vandalism?"

"Vandalism is damage that costs money to repair, like damaging the paint or smashing something that needed to be replaced. The three fuses I removed can be replaced in less than a minute, and they were technically still in the car."

"Oh."

Jack added, "But don't be doing that to anyone as a practical joke. Tom had good reason to do that, but doing it for fun isn't nice."

Minutes later, they were in the courtroom and the trial was again called to order. Judge Reilly turned to Red and said, "Your closing argument, Mr. Miller?"

Red rose from his seat and walked over to the jury. "Ladies and gentlemen, I want to thank you again for your time. Most murder trials last far longer than this, but even a day of your time is appreciated by everyone in this room.

"I wish to point out that while the defense has raised some questions, they have not provided proof that the defendant did not commit this crime. True, it's not up to them to prove anything, but it is still true that the defendant purchased the lighter fluid used as an accelerant right before the fire. His prints, and his prints only, are on that can of charcoal lighter fluid. His prints are on the gas can that was set just outside his mother's bedroom.

"A psychologist has testified that people the defendant's age are prone to misjudging such things as how quickly a fire can spread. If the defendant truly was planning to run away, it's possible that he didn't want his mother coming to find him. If he decided not to run away, perhaps he intended to die in the fire along with his mother. Nobody knows but the defendant.

"While it might be true that the defendant's father did a horrible job as a father, it's entirely possible he was in town for his own reasons. Perhaps they were reasons he did not want to admit to, such as being involved in a drug deal. Someone who would treat his son like that can easily be seen as someone who would become involved in such a scheme as selling drugs. The defendant himself testified that his father was involved in illegal drugs, so it's possible he didn't want to tell us about his stay in Wharton for that reason. There is certainly no proof that he set that fire."

It was a short summation, which Jack had expected. The evidence was scant, though damaging if taken in the way that Red had illustrated in his closing.

Jack stood and walked over to the jury. He thanked them himself before delving into his own summation.

"I have to be honest with you. The evidence the state has against the defendant is circumstantial at best. He bought a can of charcoal lighter fluid. I believe I bought one myself about a week ago. I'd hate to find myself defending myself from a murder charge because of it. And as the defendant told you, he planned to run away and needed the charcoal lighter fluid to help him build a campfire.

"That his prints were the only ones found on the two cans tells us nothing. The person who did this, and I have a strong suspicion as to who that was, would have likely used gloves. If it is the person who I suspect did this, he would have some knowledge of how to make sure he couldn't be considered a suspect after the fire was set. Leave no prints is a rule of criminals worldwide, especially if the crime is planned ahead of time.

You see, ladies and gentlemen, everything can be easily explained. That must leave a reasonable doubt in your minds that the defendant is guilty of this at the very least. In fact, I would think it would leave a rather large doubt in your minds.

We heard testimony and were offered proof that the defendant's father was in town the night in question. When asked if he had been here before, he failed to mention his being here at that time. He could have answered that he was here for a short vacation. After all, Wharton and Denton are frequently visited for that purpose. Instead, he lied on the stand. I can only come up with one reason he would lie about that, given it was the same night the fire was set.

"The defendant has testified as to how mean a person his father is. No, his father is not on trial here. At least not yet. However, I would implore you to keep this man in mind as you deliberate. He does, after all, fit the description that was given of the person who was seen entering the house that night with a gas can, despite his being an adult.

"Ladies and gentlemen, you hold the life of the defendant in your hands. I beg you not to convict in this case. The evidence is too shaky, and the distinct possibility that someone else committed this crime is too clear to send this nice young person to jail for the next several decades of his life. Thank you."

He sat and listened to the judge's instructions, which both he and Red had agreed to in deliberations in the judge's chambers recently. They were fair, boiling down to opposite ideas: If you believe the preponderance of the evidence suggests the defendant is guilty, you must convict. If you have a reasonable doubt that the evidence demonstrates the defendant is guilty, you must acquit.

The jury was out for just over three hours, and Jack saw this as a positive sign.

As they entered the courtroom, they did not look as though they had argued or fought over the verdict. Their decision appeared to have been an easy one to reach.

When they were seated, the bailiff took a sheet from the jury foreperson, a woman in her forties, and brought it to the judge. Judge Reilly looked at the paper without expression and said, "Madame Foreperson, I understand you have reached a verdict."

"Yes, Your Honor."

"On the count of arson in the first degree, how do you find?"

Paul felt like everything was being played out in

slow motion. The jury looked as though they were walking through sludge as seconds ticked by as if each one took a minute to pass.

The bailiff, too, seemed to move as if a video had been slowed to a crawl. The sounds of the words didn't slow, but the length of time it seemed to take for them to be spoken was almost painful.

Then the words were spoken.

"We find the defendant not guilty."

Paul felt as though he might lose his balance and be forced to sit. Jack pumped his fist in triumphant delight. The other verdict was a foregone conclusion.

"On the count of murder in the second degree, how do you find?" Judge Reilly asked.

"We find the defendant not guilty," the jury foreperson said. Paul let out a whoop of sheer joy.

When they were home that evening, Paul called Andy to tell him of the verdict and to see if he wanted to go for a hike the next day in Butler Park north of Denton. Paul had never been there, but he'd seen pictures of the forests and wanted to go. Andy asked permission and told Paul he would be glad to do that.

Following the phone call, Jack took Jenny and Paul out for dinner to celebrate. Jack asked if they could join Andy and Paul on their walk.

"Sure!" Paul said. "I'd love that."

When they arrived back home after the meal, Paul played with Darrow and went to bed earlier than usual as he felt the exhaustion from the stress of the trial take over.

When he was down for the night, Jack and Jenny sat up and shared some wine before heading to bed. It had been a few exhausting months for them as well as they dealt with the situation. Now, though, things were much less stressful for them.

As they drank their wine, they talked about the possibility of adopting Paul. It was a large step, but they felt good about it. Howard would probably not contest it, even if he never went to prison for arson and murder. Mostly, it would be up to Paul. They did not want to see Paul in the foster-care system until he turned eighteen, and because they loved him like a son, it made sense to make their relationship legally official.

39

The next day, Andy's mother dropped him off at the Turner home, chatted with Jack and Jenny, and drove off after congratulating everyone on the outcome of the trial. She trusted Jack's judgment, and knew that if Jack said Paul was not guilty, he was not guilty.

As they rode, they talked about anything but the trial. Paul wanted to forget about it, and visiting Butler Park for the first time would help him do that, at least for today. He didn't even care if his father was ever convicted of the crime. He only knew he hadn't been, and that was all that mattered to him.

An hour later, they were pulling into the entrance to the state park and parked near one of the trailheads.

Andy and Paul jumped out and started toward the trail, but Jenny stopped them.

"Boys! You can't go running off like that before you get some instructions."

The boys turned, impatience seeming to shimmer from every muscle in their bodies.

"First, stick to the trail. There are several trails here, and if you wander along a branch, it will eventually reconnect with the main trail you started on. Also, there are signs that will point you to the parking area. Pay attention to those."

"Yes, ma'am," the boys said in unison.

"And be back here in two hours. Paul, set the timer on your watch for ninety minutes to make sure you know when to start back to the car."

Andy said, "Aren't you coming with us?"

"We'll be walking, but I doubt we can keep up with you two boys. And of course, it goes without saying that you should not go anywhere with a stranger, no matter how nice they seem to be. Stick to the trails," Jenny said.

"Okay," Paul said. "Can we go now?"

"Yes. Have fun, and we'll see you back at this spot in two hours."

The boys ran down the path and quickly disappeared beyond the first turn.

They slowed down after about five minutes and talked about everything and nothing. Andy wanted to ask about the trial, but Paul told him maybe another time. He wasn't in the mood to discuss it because he wanted to enjoy the woods.

"What's it like having those scars?" Andy asked.

"You really want to know?"

"Yeah."

"It's awful. It's more than just having the scars. I feel like the ugliest person on Earth. I'll probably never have a girlfriend, and probably only a few friends. People don't want to be around me."

"I don't mind them," Andy said.

"You're the exception."

"Paul, the scars may be ugly, but you aren't. You're more than your body. My mom says our bodies are just like the shells that hermit crabs live in. They aren't us. They're just our covering.

"Well, that covering is pretty important to some people."

"Only the shallow ones."

Paul shrugged and changed the subject. His looks and the lack of any interest from girls was another thing he'd rather not talk about.

After twenty minutes, they saw something ahead that made them nearly gasp in awe.

The pathway ahead was awash in monarch butterflies. It seemed that thousands were flitting here and there. So many were floating on the air that it was difficult to see if they were landing or not.

"Where did they come from?" Paul asked.

"My dad said he's seen this before. Sometimes, a bunch of caterpillars will become cocoons on trees in one small area. When the butterflies hatch, they swarm the area, just like this," Andy said.

As they came closer, they could see that the branches of the trees and the thousands of leaves were covered with the butterflies.

That's when Andy looked at Paul and said, "Woah!"

"What is it?"

"You're, like, covered with butterflies."

Paul looked down and saw that Andy was right. It seemed that hundreds of butterflies had settled on his shirt and shorts. Now, some were alighting on his arms and legs.

"That is so cool, man!" Andy said. "You're like the butterfly whisperer or something."

"Why do you think they're on me and not so many are on you?"

"Maybe they think you're beautiful."

Paul smiled at this and felt a surprising sting of tears as emotion washed over him without warning.

He was covered in scars and many people would shun him for that throughout his life.

But the butterflies, one of the most beautiful creatures on Earth, thought he was beautiful. And who was he to argue?

EPILOGUE
Eight months later

Paul stood before the judge and considered how different this time was. Before, he had been charged with a terrible crime. People were trying very hard to send him to prison for many years, if not the rest of his life.

Now, though, he was being asked questions by a judge who was sitting at a desk, not up on the bench. The outcome of this appearance before a judge would make the rest of his life far better than it had ever been.

His life had changed for the better in many ways. Tom was giving him flying lessons every Saturday when the weather allowed, and Melody had actually asked if he wanted to take her to a school dance. He'd been so surprised that it was hard to say yes.

"Paul," the judge was saying, "is there any reason you do not wish to be adopted by Jack and Jenny Turner?"

"No, sir."

"You are aware that your relationship with your natural father will forever be severed. He will have no say in your upbringing. You understand this?"

"I welcome it."

Looking at Jack and Jenny, the judge said, "I have his natural father's paperwork wherein he surrenders all legal right as a parent. I understand he is in jail?"

"Yes, Your Honor. Murder and arson. Life without parole," Jack said.

"Then despite the fact you're a bit older than the typical people I see here wishing to adopt a child, I see no reason to deny this petition for adoption, especially considering the minor in question is a teenager," the judge said, and stood from behind the desk where he sat.

He shook hands with Jack and Jenny. They were in Pensacola for the adoption, so Jack didn't know the judge other than by reputation.

Turning to Paul, the judge reached out and shook Paul's hand. "Good luck, young man. I think you have a couple of fine people adopting you."

Paul smiled at his new parents. "I know," he said.

And that was as true a statement as he'd ever spoken.

Charles Tabb is a retired teacher and award-winning author whose work is enjoyed by readers worldwide. A pair of his novels, *Floating Twigs* and *Finding Twigs*, have been translated into Russian by AST Publishers, LTD, in Moscow. He is also the author of the *Detective Tony Pantera Series* about a flawed but caring detective with the Richmond police force and other books. Charles lives with his wife, her two horses and one donkey, and their two dogs and a cat near Richmond, Virginia. He is available for personal appearances on Zoom or in person. You can sign up to receive his monthly newsletter or contact Charles at charlestabb.com.

Made in the USA
Monee, IL
12 November 2024